LINDA JONES

Let Me Come In

LOVE SPELL BOOKS   ✦   NEW YORK CITY

LOVE SPELL®

September 1997

Published by

Dorchester Publishing Co., Inc.
276 Fifth Avenue
New York, NY 10001

Printed in the United States of America.

HER HONEY-BAKED LIPS

Ben placed a single finger beneath Celia's chin and lifted her face so she was forced to look at him. Goodness, he was perfect. Bright and shining and beautiful, from the dark blond wavy hair on his head to the mud on his expensive boots.

"Twice I've tried to kiss you, Celia Pigg, and both times we were interrupted."

"I know," she breathed.

"I'm going to kiss you now," he promised, "and I don't care if everyone you know comes to the door and watches. I'm not going to stop."

"Good." Could he even hear her soft answer as he settled his mouth over hers? She wasn't sure.

It was unlike any caress she had ever known or imagined. Ben moved his lips over hers, loved her, claimed her without any other touch. Only their mouths met, lips soft and warm and gently curious.

And Celia felt as if she were coming undone, unraveling from the inside out.

It was Ben who pulled away, slowly, and with an expression on his face that told Celia he was coming undone as well.

"No one's ever kissed me like that before," she whispered.

The stunned expression on his face faded slowly, and he smiled at her. "Good," he whispered, and then he kissed her again.

*Dedicated with love and appreciation to Shirley Faye and
Geraldine Floy, and their cabin in the woods.
And, of course, to "Sweet Pig."*

Let Me Come In

Chapter One

Piggville, Texas, 1884

The place looked familiar, even after all these years. Familiar enough that his stomach tightened and his heartbeat quickened as he walked away from the train station and toward the center of town.

What had once been the edge of town, the church on one end and the Pigg mansion on the other, was swallowed up by houses and shops and crisscrossing streets, but those two prominent landmarks had changed little. The church was white now, and its steeple towered above everything else. It was, and had always been, the heart of the town, a bright contrast to raw wood and dust and the bustle of everyday life. There was a serenity about the church, and that peacefulness, along with the bright white walls, isolated it from the crude surroundings.

The Pigg mansion was still painted that ugly pale brown, not beige and not tan but an unappealing in-between shade. They called it the straw house years ago, and probably now as well. Hamilton Pigg had been the first in town to use straw between the outer and inner walls of his home, insulation against the cold Texas wind.

There were more people out and about than he remembered, on the main street and in the shops that lined it. Once he'd known everyone he passed in this town, and they'd known him, but today the street and the boardwalk were crowded with strangers. They passed in and out of a number of shops, a café, a prosperous-looking bank. There were a number of freshly painted signs along the street, a sign of growth and prosperity.

Piggville had changed in fourteen years. But then, so had he.

Ben walked past the general store without glancing through the open double doors, even though he knew he was being stared at. Piggville was not so large that a well-dressed stranger would go unnoticed. He passed the saloon in the same way, without changing his pace, without looking to either side.

There ahead, past a barbershop and a small café, was the sign he'd been looking for: WALTER HUFFMAN, ESQ.

For the first time since stepping from the train, Ben smiled. It had taken years to pull this together, but the time was at hand.

Huff was waiting for him, pacing in the small office he'd rented a month earlier, chewing on that ever-present cigar.

"It's about time," Huff growled. He quickly looked Ben up and down, taking in the expensive suit and the new, polished boots. He didn't say a word, but shook his head in apparent wonder.

"The train was late." Ben propped his thigh against Huff's desk and grinned at his friend and ally. Poor Huff had never been completely sure of the plan, but he'd given his word. That had been twelve years ago, and they'd both been seventeen years old and full of indignity at the time, but a man's word didn't come with stipulations. Not in Texas. "Is everything in order?"

Huff chewed on his cigar with a vengeance, and narrowed dark eyes in Ben's direction. "Of course everything's in order. I've done my part."

"Did you find them?"

Huff didn't look happy. "I hired the best, but so far they've found nothing. All three of those women disappeared not long after you and your father left Piggville. Not that you can blame them. After what happened, I imagine they felt they had to leave."

"I imagine so," Ben said darkly.

He was disappointed. He'd hoped that Huff would be able to locate at least one of those women.

Ben helped himself to one of Huff's cigars while the attorney paced in his small office. "So," Ben said softly, "how are things here in Piggville?"

Huff took his chair, a leather monstrosity with wide arms that sat behind the desk. "As of yesterday, the mortgage on the Pigg house is yours."

Huff opened a drawer and withdrew a thick sheaf of papers. "By the end of the week, the new general store will be opened, directly across the street from the Pigg General Store. I don't yet have the mortgage on the strip of land the general store and the boardinghouse sit on, but it's in the works. Hamilton Pigg spread himself pretty thin in the last few years." Huff rifled through the papers until he found what he was looking for. "He took a mortgage on that property with a Dallas bank."

Ben wasn't interested in the papers that seemed to fascinate Huff. That was the lawyer's job. "What about the personal aspect of this engagement?"

"You make it sound like a damned war," Huff grumbled.

Ben didn't argue.

"The attorney, one John Watts, leaves today. If there are no complications, he will be out of town for a minimum of six weeks."

"That should be long enough," Ben whispered. "Who else will we have to be prepared for?"

Suddenly, Huff looked nervous. "As far as business goes, Watts is the one she'll turn to."

"And personally?"

"Cecilia Pigg is a quiet woman who keeps to herself." Huff looked out the window behind him. "She has her hands full, with the boardinghouse and the general store and those sisters of

12

hers. The twins won't be a concern. They're only thirteen."

"Who are you leaving out?" Ben asked, leaning across the desk.

Was that a sigh? Surely not. "Rosemary Cranston, Cecilia Pigg's closest friend." Huff continued to stare out the window. "No financial help there. She lives at home, and her father is a blacksmith. That's where Cecilia Pigg will turn for emotional support when things get ugly."

After all the years of waiting and planning, he was here. Ben smiled at his friend. "I don't want her to have anywhere to turn."

"I have everything well in hand." Huff's voice was distant, and he was looking everywhere but at Ben.

There was a long moment of silence, and then Ben burst into laughter. "So that's the way it is?"

Ben had never seen a lawyer blush, but Huff turned five shades of red. "I think you're making a terrible mistake."

"I don't agree."

Huff had never been one to keep his opinions to himself, and Ben should've known better than to expect the man to start now. When Huff had something to say, he couldn't rest until he got it out.

"Hamilton Pigg has been dead over a year." Huff straightened his stack of papers nervously. "I know you feel you're entitled, and I understand, I really do, Ben. But you don't have any quarrel with Cecilia Pigg and those little twins."

"They're Piggs, and I'm going to run them out

of town the way the old man ran my father out."

Huff was nervous. He shuffled his papers and looked down at the desk, at the floor, out the window. Walter Huffman, a man who was always so damned sure of himself, was obviously having doubts.

Ben knew Huff didn't understand his obsession with Hamilton Pigg. Sometimes he didn't understand it himself. He only knew he would have no peace until this injustice was avenged.

Huff shook his head. "You know, if I'd had Hamilton Pigg's money, I think I would have had my name legally changed."

Ben was in no mood for jokes. "You can make light of this if you want, but as far as I'm concerned Hamilton Pigg killed my father."

"I know."

"He didn't live a year after we left this place. The shame killed him."

Ben could still remember the night he and his father had left Piggville. No one would listen to Ezekiel Wolfe's pleas of innocence. They had laughed at him, spit at him, and Hamilton Pigg had been at the front of the mob. Ben had heard his father damn the man to hell a thousand times, usually in one of the drunken stupors that followed that night. As far as Ben knew, his father had never tasted whiskey before the night Pigg had run the two of them out of town.

"I won't rest until my father's honor is avenged."

"Don't you think that end might be better served by proving him innocent of the charges?"

14

Ben smiled crookedly at Huff's suggestion. "They didn't care about the truth fourteen years ago. What makes you think they care now? And besides, you can't locate even one of the women involved."

Huff leaned back in his chair, resigned at last. "You won't have an easy time of it. Cecilia Pigg is well respected in this community. She has an impeccable reputation."

"Not for long."

He remembered Cecilia Pigg, a little girl in braids who had been small for her age, and painfully shy. She'd taken a lot of teasing about her name, in school and in whispers at church, as she was walking down the street.

He wondered if she'd grown up to look anything like her father. Round and pink and fleshy, Hamilton Pigg had been a man whose body and face suited his name too well.

It didn't matter.

"Tell me, Huff, what's it going to take to sweep the well-respected Cecilia Pigg off her quiet, shy feet?"

"There she is," Huff said softly, nodding at the window. Ben turned just as a large woman dressed in black passed the window. She held her stubby nose in the air, and as she walked by she discreetly scratched a wide rump.

"Oh."

"Not her," Huff said impatiently. "Across the street, with Watts."

A wagon passed, and when the dust cleared Ben had a clear view of Cecilia Pigg. She stood

15

on the boardwalk with a thin gentleman who was carrying a traveling bag.

Ben gave the attorney Watts only a passing glance.

Cecilia Pigg bore little resemblance to the girl in braids he remembered. Her hair was still brown, but it was perhaps a shade darker than it had been fourteen years ago. There was nothing else to hint at the girl she had been.

She had an hourglass figure to rival the shapeliest saloon girl he had ever seen. That couldn't be disguised, not even by the prim, high-necked, long-sleeved gray dress she wore. Her hair had been shaped into a thick braid and twisted around the back of her head, and there was not a single dark strand out of place.

As he watched, she turned away from her attorney to face the street, and he had his first good look at her face.

She looked nothing like the old man.

"Well?" Huff said softly. "Still determined to run the Piggs out of Piggville?"

"Yes," Ben answered without hesitation, and without taking his eyes from Cecilia Pigg.

Huff shook his head. "Benjamin Wolfe." He sighed and returned the thick stack of papers to the drawer. "For the first time since I met you, I'm ashamed to call you my friend."

"You're not backing out now, are you?"

"No. I gave my word."

Ben watched Cecilia Pigg step gracefully into the street and take her lawyer's arm. Right now, Huff didn't have to be his friend. Right now, Ben needed an ally more than he needed a friend.

Pretty Miss Cecilia Pigg didn't have a chance.

"I'm happy for you, John, really I am," Celia said earnestly as she took his arm and they stepped into the street. "But what will I do if there's a problem while you're gone?"

John tried to soothe her, as he had for the past two days, but he couldn't disguise his excitement. "What problem could you possibly have?" he asked sensibly. "Certainly nothing will arise that can't wait till I return."

She wanted to ask John to stay, and she thought he probably would if she pleaded, but he wanted this opportunity so badly. The most prestigious law firm in Dallas had asked for his assistance on a scandalous murder case they were handling. John insisted that they must have heard of his work in the Gilley case, but Celia wasn't so sure. John was certainly a competent attorney, but no one had heard of poor George Gilley, she was sure, nor of the trial where he was accused and found innocent of killing his brother-in-law. No one outside of Piggville, in any case.

And the only reason poor George Gilley had been found innocent was because he'd been a good twenty miles away at the time of the murder. Anyone could have won that case.

She was afraid she'd hurt John's feelings if she voiced her doubts.

"Do me a favor while I'm gone," John said as they reached the train station.

"Of course."

"Don't loan out any more money." John stared sternly at her over the top of his spectacles. "Your cash flow is limited, especially after the loss on that last investment your father made before he passed. I don't care what sad story you're told; you must learn to say no."

Celia smiled. "Of course, John."

"Say it," he demanded. "Say no."

"It's just so hard when someone you've known all your life comes to the door and they're truly desperate. Hungry, John. Why, sometimes people come to me who literally don't have enough food to feed their families."

He was heartless. "No," he said again. "Or you may find yourself without enough food to feed Floy and Faye."

"No," Celia said without enthusiasm.

"Very good." John kissed her quickly on the cheek before he boarded the train. "You know where I'll be if you need me."

Celia stood on the platform and watched the train pull away from the station. She hadn't realized how much she depended on John until he'd told her he was leaving. Just a month or two, he said, but she wasn't so sure. If that law firm asked him to stay, he would. John loved his career more than anything or anyone.

She couldn't even turn to her best friend for comfort. Rosemary was so completely besotted by the newest man in town, the lawyer Walter Huffman, that she didn't have time for anyone else. If Celia did get a few moments with her friend, the subject of conversation was exclusively the marvelous Huff.

Celia really didn't want to hear how wonderfully Rosemary's romance was progressing. It depressed her horribly.

For two years before her father's death, there had been no time for romance. She'd cared for Hamilton Pigg when he would allow no one else near him, and he'd taught her all about his businesses. Between caring for her father and raising Faye and Floy and taking on the Pigg business concerns, there had been no time for courting.

After her father's death they'd come, one handsome and ambitious young man after another. They came from near and far to court Cecilia Pigg, and with her the Pigg fortune. Celia was disgusted with each and every one of them. While she was quite comfortable, there was no real fortune. She had often wondered what the ambitious gentlemen would have thought if she'd deposited herself at their feet and pleaded with them to take care of her and her sisters, as they were destitute.

She'd never had the nerve to try it.

John was the only man she trusted, and he'd never mentioned marriage. They did have a sound friendship, though, and Celia often thought that perhaps one day he would ask her, and she would happily accept. She couldn't imagine marrying a man she didn't trust.

Celia walked back toward the house alone, lost in her thoughts.

She wished there was no Pigg money at all. It

was such a great responsibility, one she was always aware of. Everyone in town felt free to come to her for a loan, and many of them had. She felt obligated to take care of these people, even when she was quite sure she'd never see repayment of the loan. If business was down at the general store, Jud and Ophelia Lucas still had to be paid. If the boardinghouse sat empty for a week, the widow Frances Hoyt still earned her salary. Then there were repairs, to her home and to the boardinghouse and the general store, and just when she thought the family finances were looking healthy, a loan payment came due.

She was sure her father's intentions had been good, but in the years before his death he had squandered much of his money on get-rich-quick schemes. Not one of those schemes had made so much as a dime.

If she had her way, she'd have a little farm, with a garden and maybe a few cows. A nest egg, a few dollars set aside in case there came a growing season where there was not enough rain or too much rain . . .

The noise startled her, and Celia was jerked from her daydream only to lift her head and see the team of horses bearing down on her. The driver pulled on the reins, but he was too close to stop.

Suddenly Celia was wrenched away from the horses. Her feet left the ground, and she literally flew through the air. The team passed so close she could feel their warm breath against her, and then she hit the ground and every bit of air left her. Her lungs were empty, and she couldn't breathe in because there was this . . . this man lying on top of her.

The wagon came to a stop, and the driver jumped from his seat. "I didn't see her, I swear. She just stepped right in front of me."

"I know." The man who was crushing her growled, and as he spoke he lifted his head. Celia found herself looking into the bluest eyes she'd ever seen. A lock of blond hair fell, a perfect wave, over his forehead. There was a very thin, very pale scar at the corner of his right eye, and goodness, he was heavy. "Ma'am," he said as he took his weight from her and sat beside her in the dirt. "You really should watch where you're going."

Celia sat up carefully. "I should." She was finally able to take a deep breath, but dust stirred all about her. She began to cough, and the man who had saved her from the team of horses whacked her on the back forcefully. He clapped a strong hand against her back again and again until she raised her hand and signaled for him to stop.

This was so embarrassing. She was sitting in the street, this strange man was seated close beside her with his hand on her back, and they were drawing a crowd.

As she stood, with the gentleman's assistance, Celia assured everyone that she was all right, and when she turned to thank the man who had pulled her from the street, it was too late. He was walking silently away.

"Wait." She pushed her way past the wagon driver and a concerned Frances Hoyt to follow the man. As he stepped onto the boardwalk she was able to grab his sleeve. A very expensive, very dusty sleeve. "Thank you, sir. I feel so very foolish. Are you hurt? Goodness, I don't even know your name." Celia silenced herself, realizing that she was rambling like Faye.

The man turned. There was a grin on his face, so Celia assumed he was unhurt.

She was sure she had never seen him before, since he didn't have the kind of face a woman was likely to forget. It was handsome, but not in a boyish way. His face was all lines and angles, strong jaw and tanned skin and that very tiny scar by the corner of his very blue right eye.

"Ben," he said in that wonderfully deep voice. "Pleasure to meet you, ma'am."

"Celia," she said with a smile of her own. No last names. He hadn't given his, so she didn't feel obligated to offer her own. He didn't know who she was, and even if he did, it was obvious from the fine suit he wore that he had money of his own, so if he expressed any interest in her at all . . .

"Thank you again," she said as Ben stared at her, saying absolutely nothing.

"Think nothing of it." He turned his back on her, and there was nothing she could do, but perhaps chase after him shamelessly.

It was tempting, but Celia was nothing if not strong in the face of temptation.

* * *

"Did you see that?" Floy asked breathlessly as she grasped her sister's sleeve. "I swear, Celia could have been killed."

By the time they'd made their way from the house to the center of town, the excitement was over, and Celia was speaking to the man who had whisked her from the horses' path. Thanking him, no doubt. Floy had been ready to rush to her eldest sister's arms and comfort her, but Faye had stopped her well short.

"He's new," Faye said in a thoughtful tone of voice that usually meant trouble.

"Who's new?" Floy turned her eyes to her twin. They were identical in appearance and when they dressed alike, as they usually did, and kept their mouths shut, only Celia could tell them apart. They dressed their blond curly hair in the same fashion, and they both had a passion for every shade of pink.

In personality they were quite different. Faye was fourteen minutes older and much bossier than Floy would ever think of being. She was also more devious, and that particular trait had gotten them into trouble countless times.

Floy didn't like the expression on Faye's face at the moment. The last time she'd seen this look, poor James Richardson had ended up cold, wet, and mostly naked. And when his mama had found him that way there was no amount of explaining that would make her not whup him.

Faye had declared six months ago that one day she was going to marry James Richardson, and Floy didn't doubt that would come to pass.

"Celia needs a beau," Faye said softly.

"I thought Mr. Watts was her—"

"He's a weasel," Faye interrupted sharply. "And he's so . . . so dull. Now that man"—Faye nodded to the hero who was now walking away from Celia—"he doesn't look weasely *or* dull, does he?"

"No." She shuddered as she watched him walk away from the scene without once looking back. "He actually looks a little wicked, Faye, and we don't know who he is or where he came from or *anything*," Floy remarked.

"We will," Faye insisted as she started to cross the street. With a sigh that spoke of surrender, Floy followed.

Chapter Two

"You know, if you'd simply remained there by the window and watched her get run down, this war of yours would be over now."

"Shut up, Huff," Ben growled.

It had been hours since he'd dragged the apparently addle-brained Cecilia Pigg from the path of that wagon, and his heart was still beating too fast. Yes, he hated her. Yes, he wanted revenge.

But not like that. It couldn't be all over in a heartbeat.

He'd left an obviously dazed Celia Pigg standing on the boardwalk, and he'd secured himself a room at the boardinghouse. Shortly after signing in, his baggage had been delivered from the depot, and he'd unpacked everything like a man who was settling in for the long haul. After unpacking, he'd enjoyed a hearty noon meal of stew and biscuits in the boardinghouse dining room, a meal that had been served by the apparent manager of the Pigg boardinghouse, a sour old woman named Frances Hoyt. He'd smiled charmingly and complimented her mediocre stew.

And all the while he'd envisioned Cecilia Pigg's flushed face gazing up at him from the ground, while dust settled in her dark hair. She had a lovely face, with enchanting dark brown eyes and high cheekbones and lush lips. And the body he'd trapped beneath his was a woman's body, rounded and soft, yielding and tender. A woman with a body like that ought not to be hiding it under matronly high-necked gowns and all those folds of heavy silk. What a waste.

Surely she took after her mother. He tried to remember what the woman had looked like, but there was no clear memory in his mind of Priscilla Pigg. Back then, Ben's days had been filled with school and his friends and his chores and his father. It had been a small, comfortable world, for a while, and Priscilla Pigg had not been a part of it. One truth was certain: Cecilia looked nothing like her father.

"It's not too late to give this up, Ben," Huff said sensibly. "I know how you feel, but—"

"You know how I feel?" Ben didn't turn to face his friend. "My father was a preacher, and a damn good one. He loved the people in this town, and he thought they loved him. He certainly thought they respected him." He'd been fifteen, but he could remember that Sunday as if it had been yesterday. He dreamed about it still, remembered it on nights when he was too tired to sleep. "Hamilton Pigg paraded a slut in front of the congregation, and the woman cried while she begged my father to marry her so their child wouldn't be a bastard."

"Your father was a young man. Maybe he—"

"Don't offer reasonable solutions, Huff. My father would never have touched that woman." A dirty woman in rags, a whore who would spread her legs for any man with a dollar. If it had been only Rizpah Tucker . . .

There had been two others. Elizabeth Holt had stood and shouted "Zeke, how could you?" Then she'd covered her horsey face with oddly long hands and sobbed loudly before running from the church. And then that last woman, Susan Woodbury, had stood up right there in church and called the preacher a no-good, sweet-talking son of a bitch.

Before the church was emptied, everyone in town had decided that Ezekiel Wolfe was a womanizer who was seducing the women of Piggville. That he was the devil himself, come to drag the town into the depths of hell. Within the hour, there were whispered rumors that some poor unidentified woman claimed the preacher had forced himself on her. Whispers of rape followed them throughout the long day and into the night. No one had listened to Ezekiel Wolfe, or to his son, and before that Sunday was over, they rode

27

out of town on a single horse, taking only the possessions they could carry.

Hamilton Pigg had been at the center of it all, throughout the day and into the long night. Give this up? The planning had kept Ben going for years, had spurred him on when he discovered that the ore from the first mine was not enough to do everything he wanted to do. He ate beans while his substantial wealth sat in the bank. He slept outside on the hard ground and dreamed of revenge, rather than staying in a hotel, because he knew he might one day need every dollar he had to ruin Hamilton Pigg.

"You know," Huff said thoughtfully, "Dad always said you'd make a good rancher. It's in your blood the way he always wished it was in mine. Why don't you take your money and buy your own spread? Forget the past."

"I can't."

It was true that he loved the life of a rancher. He'd given it up, left the Huffmans' ranch when Huff left for the university, because working on a ranch there simply was no way to build a fortune large enough fast enough. For that, he needed gold.

And he'd found it. A little bit of gold and a lot of silver. Lead, too, and in the last mine, copper.

"I owe your dad my life," Ben said. "If he hadn't taken me in after my father died, I probably would have come back here and tried to kill Hamilton Pigg with my bare hands and gotten myself hanged for my trouble."

"You know you're welcome there anytime. Last

time I saw Dad, all he did was complain that since Ben Wolfe had made his fortune he'd never come back to ranching, and he swears he never found a better hand than you."

Ben smiled. He did love the life. Maybe when this was all done . . .

"So," Huff said, business in his voice once again, "when do you begin?"

"Tomorrow." Ben turned away from the window to face his friend. "I begin tomorrow."

Celia tried to pay attention to the papers before her without showing any sign of panic. Bob Casson, a rancher who had dreams of expansion, stood before her desk with his hat in his hand. He shuffled his feet back and forth, cleared his throat every few seconds, and occasionally ran the back of his hand across his nose.

"It's just an extension," Celia said, as much to herself as to Bob.

"That's right, Miss Pigg. Six more months, and I'll be able to pay everything back."

She'd been expecting and depending on the repayment of the Casson loan. Payments of her own were due, most notably on the boarding-house and the general store property. The latest installment was overdue, but not by much.

Besides, it was clear Bob didn't have the money to pay her back, no matter how badly she needed the cash. She certainly didn't want his ranch.

"Six months," she said as she lifted her head to give him what she hoped was a no-nonsense and businesslike glare. "I can't extend the loan any more than that."

"Yes, ma'am." Bob Casson cleared his throat noisily. "And I surely do appreciate this." For the first time this morning, Bob smiled widely. He was as thin as a rail, and had been for as long as Celia had known him, even though he ate as much as any two men. At least it seemed that way at town social gatherings where food was a part of the celebration.

Bob was barely gone—the odors of sweat and dust still lingered in the air—when Margaret announced another caller. A Mr. Wolfe, she said with a persimmony pucker of her lips and a suspicious narrowing of her eyes. It was still quite early. Margaret was evidently in a foul mood, the twins were bustling on the second floor, and there hadn't even been time for a second cup of tea. It promised to be a very long day.

What could this Mr. Wolfe want? The name was not familiar, but he wouldn't be the first stranger to come to her for a job or a loan. The word that she was a soft touch had gotten out soon after her father's death.

She had to remember what John had said. *No*. She must learn to say *no*.

"If you daydream like this all the time, I guess I'll have to follow you around permanently to make certain you don't step into the street again without looking to see what might be coming."

Celia lifted her head to see the man who had rescued her standing in the doorway to her office. He had a small grin on his handsome face, and he was wearing yet another fine suit of clothes. Brown, this time, so that with the sunlight that poured through the window touching him he looked golden. It was fitting. His hair was like burnished gold, his skin warm and tanned . . . and suddenly Celia wished she were wearing something more attractive than a plain white blouse and butternut skirt.

"Yes," she said, rising slowly. "You're absolutely right."

If he needed a loan or a job she couldn't possibly refuse him. He had saved her life, after all. How could she say no?

Ben Wolfe entered her office, and Celia offered her hand across the desk for a businesslike shake. He took her hand, but didn't shake it at all. He kissed her knuckles lightly, released her fingers with obvious reluctance, and then he sat in the chair so that the desk separated them.

"What can I do for you, Mr. Wolfe?" Celia took her seat. The man on the other side of the desk looked comfortable, with his relaxed posture and small smile. Ben Wolfe was, she surmised, a man accustomed to being comfortable at all times. She envied him that.

"I hardly think we need to be formal, Celia. Please call me Ben. After yesterday's adventure I feel that's appropriate."

"Of course, Ben." She returned his smile, all the while wondering exactly what he wanted. "What brings you to Piggville?"

His smile widened, and she could almost imagine that his eyes actually sparkled. "You don't remember me, do you?"

Celia racked her brain. Remember him? Surely she would have remembered . . .

"I can see by the look on your face that you don't." He seemed not at all offended. "Of course, you were just a child fourteen years ago, when I was last in Piggville. Let's see, you would have been . . . eight?"

"Ten," she corrected, still searching her memory. It came to her in a flash, thanks to the name Wolfe. "Your father was a preacher."

She recalled as she said the words that his father had left under some sort of cloud. There had been a scandal, hadn't there? Her mother would have protected her from the details, but she remembered hearing whispers. "We called you Benjamin then," she said with a smile, avoiding the subject of his father and their departure. "You called me . . . you called me 'Little Pig' when I walked home from school, and you actually made oinking noises."

"I wasn't the only one."

"No," she said with a grin, "but you were the oldest and the loudest. My goodness." Celia relaxed and placed her folded arms on the desk before her. "What brings you back to Piggville?"

Ben leaned back and crossed a booted foot over one knee. "I'm thinking of settling here. My memories of this town are powerful, and when I decided to give up mining, this is the place that came to mind." He glanced around the office with an air of detached interest, which gave Celia a chance to stare unabashedly at the strong line of his jaw, at the powerful neck, at the hands that rested on the arms of his chair. Large, rough, and lovely hands that had seen their share of hard work. "I always loved this house. I remember thinking it was as fine as any castle."

He didn't want a loan, and he didn't want a job. What a relief. "You surprise me. Piggville is not exactly an exciting town."

As if she'd interrupted his thoughts with her remark, Ben stopped studying the office and turned his attention to her. He stared at her with relentless eyes. "Looks exciting from where I'm sitting."

She didn't know exactly how to answer a statement like that. To be honest, Celia knew at that moment that she didn't know how to handle a man like Ben Wolfe at all. He might be wearing an expensive and quite proper suit, but he was not at all like the businessmen she was accustomed to dealing with.

"So," he said, ignoring her lack of response, "would you be interested in selling the house?"

"Excuse me?" Celia leaned forward, certain she'd misunderstood.

"The house. This house. I'd like to buy it."

Disappointed that this was not purely a social call after all, Celia began to shuffle the papers before her. Of course this wasn't a social call. Why on earth would a man like Benjamin Wolfe be interested in a woman like her? "The house is not for sale, Mr. Wolfe. Is there anything else I can do for you?"

Her question was perfectly innocent, but Ben's answering smile flustered her a little. She knew then that Benjamin Wolfe might look like a gentleman, but he wasn't. He was a rogue, a rapscallion, a bounder.

"Actually," he growled, "there are several things you could do for me. Would you like me to tell you exactly what I have in mind?"

The word *no* came into her head, but didn't quite make it to her lips. "Yes."

He wasn't, at the moment, looking her in the eye. In fact, his gaze seemed to be riveted somewhat lower than her face. His tongue sneaked out briefly to brush across a lower lip, and then he raised his eyes to hers.

The look he gave her made her shiver, deep down where no one but she would notice. What exactly did Ben Wolfe want? "Introduce me to your friends, Celia," he said in a low voice that brought the shivers to the surface. "It's been too long since I've lived in Piggville, and it's grown so much. Why, I doubt anyone here will even remember me."

"Of course. A small party, perhaps."

"That would be nice."

Nice? Every unmarried woman in town would set her cap for Benjamin Wolfe, once they got a good look at him. They'd flirt and flutter and do whatever was necessary to claim his attention. Celia had never been very good at flirting or fluttering.

"I'm rather busy right now," she said with deceptive calm, "but perhaps in a few weeks."

"I'm staying at the boardinghouse for the moment, but of course that's a temporary arrangement. Since you don't seem interested in selling this place, I'll have to give some thought to building. Perhaps you could put me in touch with someone about obtaining a plot of land, preferably here in town."

Business. This was all business, she reminded herself. Her earlier wandering thoughts had been foolish, groundless, wishful thinking.

"Of course. Cory Anders at the bank, perhaps."

Faye burst into the room, a pink tornado, and Floy was directly behind her.

"Would you please tell Margaret that she's not my mother, she's the housekeeper, and she can't make me—" The tirade stopped suddenly when Faye saw Ben sitting there. "I didn't realize you had company, Celia." The tone of Faye's voice changed completely, from indignant to cloying, in a twinkling.

"Mr. Wolfe," Celia said calmly, "these are my sisters. Faye and Floy." The girls curtseyed in turn as their names were called, and Ben stood.

"It's a pleasure to meet you, girls," he rumbled. Floy bit her lower lip, and Faye smiled much too widely.

"It's him," Floy whispered, and Faye elbowed her sister discreetly.

"We saw you rescue our sister yesterday, Mr. Wolfe. It was quite impressive," Faye said boldly.

"It was nothing," Ben assured her.

"It was marvelous," Floy added, obviously un-

35

able to take her eyes off of the man who towered over her.

Celia wanted to moan and drop her head to the desk, but of course she didn't. If Ben Wolfe had this kind of effect on thirteen-year-old girls, heaven help the female population of Piggville.

"Faye, what's your problem with Margaret today?" Celia asked tiredly.

With a deep sigh, Faye took her eyes from Ben and faced the desk. "She said this dress is inappropriate for school, and then she demanded that I change."

"She's right." Celia gave Ben Wolfe a quick glance as he took his seat once again. "That's your very best Sunday dress."

"But it's James Richardson's birthday," Faye said softly.

Floy was wearing an identical dress, but Celia was certain the decision to dress for this special occasion and the resolve to resist Margaret had been Faye's.

"That's irrelevant," Celia said sternly. "A Sunday dress is not appropriate for school, no matter whose birthday it is."

Celia was prepared for a long argument. Sometimes it was simplest just to let Faye have her way, but if Margaret had no control over the twins, their care and discipline would fall exclusively to Celia. She didn't have time for this right now.

Faye started to pout, seemed to think better of it, and then she cocked her head thoughtfully. That could only mean trouble. "We can change quickly and not be late for school, if you'll invite Mr. Wolfe to dinner."

It was an offered compromise Celia didn't expect. "I'm sure Mr. Wolfe has plans. . . ."

"I don't, to be honest," Ben said softly. "And we wouldn't want to be anything less than completely honest with the children, now would we?"

That softly spoken *we* was much too intimate. Benjamin Wolfe had just arrived in town, and already he had insinuated himself into her life, with his daring rescue and his roaming eyes and his suggestive *we*. Yes, he was definitely making himself at home here, and she didn't know whether to resent that fact or accept it.

"If you don't hurry up, we won't have time to change, and we'll be tardy again, and Mr. Culpepper gets so cross when we're tardy, and—"

"All right," Celia looked at Ben and not at Faye and Floy. "Six o'clock, Mr. Wolfe?"

He simply smiled.

They practically had to run so as not to be late. Floy clasped her history book and tried to keep up with the triumphant Faye.

"Can you believe it?" Faye said breathlessly. "He was just sitting there, right in our house, like he was waiting for us to come in and ask him for dinner. What a splendid coincidence."

Floy had been just as surprised as Faye to find Mr. Wolfe sitting in Celia's office, but being a romantic, she was inclined to credit destiny rather than coincidence.

"Blackmail him for dinner, you mean," Floy corrected her twin softly.

"It wasn't blackmail, exactly, it was . . . coercion." Faye smiled widely. "That's what it was. Coercion."

The schoolhouse was ahead, and they were almost late. Once again they'd be the last to arrive.

Faye straightened the collar of her pink gingham. It wasn't as fancy as the church dress she'd really wanted to wear, but it was becoming and James Richardson would be suitably impressed.

"Now what?" Floy asked as they stepped to the schoolhouse doorway.

With her hand on the doorknob, Faye turned to face Floy. Floy had thought Mr. Wolfe looked wicked, but it was nothing to compare with the diabolical expression on her twin's face. No matter how much they physically resembled one another, Floy knew she'd never looked like *that*.

"I haven't decided," Faye whispered. "But I do believe Celia's going to need more coercion."

"Misses Pigg," Mr. Culpepper clipped as Faye opened the door, "would you please take your places?"

The seat next to James Richardson was vacant, and Faye placed herself there quickly, leaving Floy to sit with the whining and fidgety Estelle Pritchard.

Chapter Three

"Do you have a moment to hear me out now?" Margaret called crisply, and Celia turned slowly on the stairs to look down at the woman who was housekeeper and so much more. All afternoon Margaret had tried to grab Celia for a private moment, but it seemed the day had turned out as promised. One disaster after another, from Bob Casson's nonpayment to Benjamin Wolfe's unsettling visit to Frances Hoyt's strident demand that the entire third floor of the boardinghouse be remodeled.

"Can it wait? Mr. Wolfe will be here in less than an hour, and I simply must—"

"No, it can't wait, and in fact it concerns your Mr. Wolfe."

Margaret was a no-nonsense woman, a thin and energetic whipcord of energy. Though a few years older than Celia's mother would have been had she lived, Margaret had the vigor of a much younger woman—and her feelings were always there for the world to see. Love, hate, the occasional fear. And Margaret didn't like Ben Wolfe. Celia had seen it as Margaret led Ben to the door after their short meeting, and she saw it now, in a wrinkling of the older woman's nose when she mentioned his name.

"When he shows up for supper I'll tell him you've taken ill," Margaret suggested forcefully. "A fever, perhaps. And for goodness' sakes, if he shows his face here again, you send him on his way."

"Margaret Harriman," Celia said, and a smile crossed her face even though she was exhausted. "How ungracious of you."

Margaret snorted and crossed her arms defiantly. "You're too young to remember what happened when Benjamin and his no-good father left town, but I remember quite well." Margaret lowered her voice to a conspiratorial whisper. "Ezekiel Wolfe was a charlatan and a womanizer, a sweet-talker who had only one use for a woman. Why, there was even talk that those who refused him were forced—"

"Margaret," Celia chastised, "it's not like you to gossip. And besides, you can't judge a man by the acts of another."

"Like father, like son," Margaret said ominously. "He even has the same look about him as the Reverend Wolfe had, all dapper and . . . and swaggering about like he owns the world."

Without Margaret, the past year wouldn't have been difficult—it would have been impossible. Celia knew that no matter how tired she was, how little credence she gave Margaret's suspicions, she couldn't dismiss them without a second thought. Poor Margaret's feelings would be hurt terribly.

"Come on upstairs," Celia said, turning and resuming the ascent. "You can tell me all about it while I freshen up. Is Sarah preparing dinner tonight?"

"Yes, thank goodness."

Sarah Elliot helped Margaret out with the cooking and the laundry on occasion. It was just as well that Sarah was cooking, since it was apparent Margaret might well poison Ben's portion, given the chance.

Once she was in her bedroom, Celia relaxed. This was her favorite room in the house, the one place where she could relax and at least attempt to forget about the finances her father had left her in charge of, the businesses and the loans.

Decorated in shades of blue and yards of white lace, it was a room for dreaming.

"What should I wear tonight?" Celia asked casually as Margaret closed the door behind her. Her wardrobe consisted almost entirely of gray and brown and black, but there was the occasional frivolous purchase tucked away with the rest. "The blue, perhaps? Maybe the mauve."

"I suggest the black," Margaret said ungraciously. "If you intend to entertain the devil and invite death and destruction into this household, you should dress accordingly."

Celia closed her eyes and took a deep breath. Why did Margaret, the most reasonable woman she knew, have to take leave of her senses now? "Benjamin Wolfe is hardly the devil, and I don't see how we're inviting death and destruction by simply having the man to dinner. Besides, this is strictly business. He'll have questions about properties for sale, I suppose, and the economic growth of the region since he was last here. Leave the past in the past. Obviously Ben has, or he wouldn't be here."

Margaret paced in front of the closed door, that austere expression on her face not softening a bit. She was, in fact, obviously distressed. "I don't believe he's forgotten, and that's what makes me wary, Celia."

Celia crossed the room and took Margaret's hand in her own. "I'll be very careful, and if Ben shows any signs of being the rogue his father was, I'll toss him out on his ear and I'll let you help."

Margaret was not comforted by that offer. Celia sighed. The way Ben had looked at her just that morning suggested that perhaps Margaret was right. Perhaps he was a ladies' man like his father. And still, he'd made no improper advances, and he'd seemed at moments quite distant. If he was looking for a flirtation, there were far prettier girls in town.

She didn't share Margaret's extreme fears of

death and destruction, but she would be on her guard.

Celia sighed as she led Margaret to the edge of the bed and made her sit. "Now, I'll freshen up and change clothes, and you can tell me all about Ezekiel Wolfe." She went to her wardrobe and threw it open. "The blue or the mauve?"

"The blue," Margaret said sullenly.

"The mauve it is."

Dinner alone with Celia Pigg would have been best, but this was the next best thing. The twins chattered happily about school and James Richardson and new dresses, while Celia played the part of the down-to-earth sensible older sister. Watching her, Ben knew that underneath that prim dress and severe hairstyle, Celia Pigg wasn't nearly as pragmatic as she tried to appear. He'd seen her step in front of that wagon with a dreamy-eyed expression on her pretty face, and every now and then, when she glanced up and caught him staring at her, she looked like a woman who wanted nothing but to be properly kissed.

It was all very homey and comfortable, as though he already belonged.

As if she knew he was thinking salacious thoughts, Celia lifted her eyes to him almost warily. God help him, he wanted to do much more than kiss her.

"Celia's very clever," one of the twins said brightly. Faye, he thought, the more talkative of the two.

He took his eyes from the clever Celia and grinned at Faye. "Is she, now?"

"Yes." Faye set her fork purposely aside and gave him her full attention. The twins were pretty girls, blond and blue eyed and lithe. It was too early to tell if they would have their sister's hourglass figure, but they were graceful and pale, as ladies should be.

He should feel guilty for doing his best to run them out of their home, but he didn't. Huff had discovered a trust fund, a sizable amount that the twins couldn't touch until they were twenty-five. Only Celia would be left with nothing.

"She's very clever, for a woman," Faye continued.

"Faye," Celia said sharply, in a lowered voice.

"Well, it's true." Faye nodded at her older sister.

"Mr. Wolfe doesn't want to hear . . ."

Faye ignored the admonition and returned her full attention to Ben. "As you can see, she's modest, also. She can protest all she wants, but there's no denying that she's got a good head on her shoulders. She oversees the daily operations of the boardinghouse and the general store, as well as our late father's investments."

Ben lifted his eyebrows. "Really?"

"Faye!" Celia hissed.

Faye ignored her sister and continued. "Why, most women would be overwhelmed with such responsibilities, but not Celia."

It was a glowing description, but Ben was more concerned at the moment with the change that had come over Celia. She was tense, her shoulders tight, her eyes suddenly very tired.

"I think perhaps Celia would prefer not to discuss business at the supper table," he said lazily.

"Thank you," she said with a curt nod of her head in his direction.

"She's very pretty, too, don't you think?" Floy asked quietly.

A hush fell over the table, and Celia blushed a becoming pink before she went completely white. Beneath the table Faye kicked her twin, and Floy yelped, breaking the silence.

"I'm sorry, Mr. Wolfe," Celia said, refusing to look at him directly. "My sisters are—"

"Yes," Ben interrupted. "I think Celia is very pretty."

He would have laughed out loud at this particular turn of events, but laughter would be inappropriate at the moment. The twins were going to play matchmaker, and that could only speed matters along.

And besides, it was the truth. Celia was gorgeous. Not like her little sisters, who were bright and beautiful in a very ordinary fashion. Celia's beauty was subdued, enchanting, quite—quite indefinable.

Faye stood quickly, tossing her napkin to the table beside the plate of her half-finished supper. "Come along, Floy. If we don't study for that history exam tomorrow, we'll do poorly. I just know it."

"History exam?" Floy asked, and Faye answered with a glare. Moments later, the twins were scurrying from the dining room. Their footsteps echoed through the room as they ran up the stairs. Giggling.

Poor Celia had gone pale once again, and she refused to look directly at him. She'd played with her food all evening, pushing it around with a fork and eating very little. She pushed at an untouched pork chop before setting her fork aside once and for all.

"I'm so sorry," she said softly.

"Don't be."

"It's just that, well, they're so lively, and sometimes they do get carried away, as children often do, and I never know just what they're going to—"

"Celia," he interrupted softly.

"Yes?"

"You're babbling."

She looked into her lap, as if her napkin were of some interest. "Sorry."

"Celia."

"Yes?"

"Look at me."

She lifted her head slowly, but she did look at him. She was, at the moment, embarrassed. Tired. Uncertain. He could almost forget exactly why he was here.

Almost. "Do I make you nervous?"

The eyes that stared back at him were dark, warm, endless. A man could fall into eyes like that and get lost. She shook her head, but the single word that finally came from her mouth was a contradiction.

"Yes."

At least she was honest. How many truly honest women had he met in his lifetime? He didn't remember his mother at all, and the only full-time female on the Huffman ranch had been an old cook and housekeeper who spoke only Spanish. Saloon girls lied for a living, smiled at a man and told him exactly what he wanted to hear. A few of the miners he'd met had been married, and two of the wives had actually flirted with him while their husbands' backs were turned. One had openly propositioned him. He'd declined, and a week later that same woman had run off with a skittish tenderfoot headed east. Her husband had been quite surprised that his sweet wife would leave him without a word.

But clever, pretty Celia told him the truth. He would have known, anyway. Her face told everything.

"How about a walk?" he suggested, rising and offering his hand over the table.

"A walk," she repeated.

"You can show me all that's changed in Piggville." He rounded the table until he stood beside Celia. "Besides you," he whispered.

It had seemed a safe enough suggestion, and when Ben had mentioned a walk, all Celia had thought of was escaping from the dining room that was growing smaller and warmer and smaller. . . .

But once they were on the street, Ben took her hand and placed it on his arm, and then he pulled her near as he began to walk toward the center of town.

"I'd better keep you close," he said softly, "in case there are any runaway wagons on the streets of Piggville tonight."

He had the most comforting voice, low but not too deep. Easy, but not too smooth. She would be content, at the end of a long day like today, to listen to that soothing voice for hours.

It was not quite dark, and there were still several people on the street. Most of the activity was centered around the saloon, but there was a group of gentlemen, Cory Anders and one of his tellers and a number of others, standing in a knot near the closed bank, and at the end of the street a group of boys played ball, shouting and kicking up dust.

As they came to the center of town and stepped onto the boardwalk, Celia became aware of the stares. The gentlemen turned as one, and there were faces in windows that peered out curiously. She shouldn't be surprised. To some, Ben Wolfe was a stranger she'd taken up with much too quickly. To others, he was the son of Ezekiel Wolfe and a threat not to be taken lightly.

It wasn't fair that a man should be judged by the acts of his father. It would be an injustice to dismiss Ben for such a reason, and Celia decided that she would show the residents of this town just exactly what hospitality and impartiality were.

The problem was, she was feeling anything but impartial where Benjamin Wolfe was concerned.

She'd never been bothered with this silly and disconcerting physical attraction before, but suddenly everything Rosemary had been saying about her wonderful Huff made perfect sense.

Ben seemed in no hurry as they strolled down the boardwalk. He asked a few questions about the establishments they passed, the doctor's office and the small café, the new dress shop, but he didn't say a word about the general store or the boardinghouse where he was staying. Of course, he knew they were hers. Her father had never been a shy man, and both businesses bore his name, in large painted letters.

The saloon was, she thought thankfully, on the opposite side of the street, and Ben didn't even look in that direction.

There seemed to be some activity in the vacant building next to the saloon. She could have sworn she saw a man just beyond the window, but as she began to mention it Ben pulled her slightly closer and she forgot the very words that were on the tip of her tongue.

They walked, silent much of the time, and Ben pointed out some of the improvements that had been made since he was last in Piggville. Celia barely heard a word. She was much too focused on the large hand that covered hers, on the way Ben Wolfe leaned casually toward her, into her, making their simple stroll more familiar and wonderful than she could have imagined.

Too soon they had come full circle, and she was home. The sun had set long ago, but there was a bright moon, and Margaret had left a lamp burning in the front window.

It had been such a long and terrible day, and such a short and exciting night. She should be exhausted, but of course she wasn't.

"Here we are," Ben said as they stepped onto the front porch. Celia waited for him to release his hold on her arm, but he didn't.

"Yes."

"Dinner was wonderful," he whispered. "So was the walk. Thank you."

Somehow her back was against the wall beside the door and Ben was directly in front of her, taller than before. Broader. Half of his face was lost in shadows, while the other half was illuminated by the golden glow of the lamp in the window.

"You're welcome," she whispered.

He smiled, all bright and clear and wonderfully open, as if he didn't have a care in the world. How wonderful it would be to be unencumbered and easy and free.

He lifted a single finger to her throat, barely brushing her skin with lazy strokes. It was scandalous, of course, highly improper . . . and she liked it.

It occurred to her, as he continued to rock that lazy finger across her throat, that no one really touched her anymore. The twins were too energetic for anything more than a quick hug. John was likely to brush a cold kiss across her cheek if the occasion was correct, or to pat her hand if he felt she needed a moment's consoling, but it was nothing like this.

Her mother had been a hugger, and even her father, before his illness had made him take to his bed, had been given to big bear hugs at bedtime.

It suddenly seemed as though her body needed that contact as much as it needed food and water and air, and Celia's hands slipped up and around Ben's waist—lightly, uncertainly—and he came just a little closer. She could feel his body heat, smell the tang of sweat and the smoky odor of cigars that was uniquely male.

"Celia," Ben whispered huskily.

"Yes?"

"I'm going to kiss you now."

"Yes."

It was as if her lips ached for his, and he moved much too slowly as he dipped his head toward hers. Ben's lips parted slightly, and without thought she followed suit.

"There you are," Margaret called loudly, throwing the front door open. Ben took a single step back, and Celia licked her lips quickly. "I'd begun to think you'd gotten lost."

"In Piggville?" Ben asked, not making even the slightest attempt to hide his annoyance.

Margaret smiled, and it was not a pretty sight. "Come along, Cecilia," she said primly, "before you get a chill." She wrapped her fingers around Celia's wrist and pulled her gently but certainly toward the door.

"Good night, Mr. Wolfe," Celia called softly,

glancing over her shoulder as Margaret practically shoved her into the house. Ben was backing down the stairs to the street, and he didn't say a word.

She was ripe for the picking, and the realization made Ben incredibly angry.

He stalked toward the boardinghouse, reminding himself with every step that Celia was Hamilton Pigg's daughter, the keeper of his empire and even of his sins. Those three girls were Pigg's legacy, more than any house or business. More than any supposed fortune.

Celia had noticed movement in what would soon be the new general store as they'd walked down the street, but he'd been able to distract her with a simple move, drawing her just a hair closer. So simple, so predictable.

Ripe for the picking.

And why the hell hadn't Huff done anything about that witch of a housekeeper? The woman would be constantly underfoot, and from the few words she'd spoken, and the nasty glares she'd sent his way, Ben suspected he had an enemy in the old woman. This was exactly the kind of oversight he couldn't allow.

He went directly to Huff's rented room, a plain single room on the second floor like Ben's own and just down the hallway, but there was no answer to his knock. For a moment, he considered retiring for the night, letting Huff rest until morning, but that thought didn't last long.

Huff wasn't in his office either, a fact Ben was

convinced of only after knocking for a good five minutes and then peeking through the uncovered window just to be sure. The office was completely dark and quiet.

There was only one other place Huff might be, and Ben almost smiled as he headed for the nearest cross street and the modestly comfortable house where Rosemary Cranston lived with her parents.

His attorney was turning out to be dedicated, indeed, working so late and so diligently.

Ben was two houses away when he saw them, two rather indistinct shapes with their hands linked as they made their way through the small side yard. They vanished from sight behind the little whitewashed house next door to the Cranstons'. One of those shapes, the taller figure with a slight hitch in his step, definitely belonged to Huff.

Ben didn't stop, didn't give a thought to turning back and searching out his cold and lonely bed, but softened his step as he turned between the two houses.

There was no sign of Huff or the apparently entertaining Miss Cranston, and there was only one outbuilding. A small stable. It was almost laughable. Huff had rebelled and left his father's ranch for law school and a finer, more dignified life, and here he was looking for a tumble in the hay.

Ben's smile died slowly. A tumble in the hay sounded pretty damn good right now. Problem was, the only woman he saw when he pictured that particular pleasure in his mind was Celia Pigg, straw in her dark hair, lips parted and inviting, and that slightly dazed expression on her face—the one she'd worn before that witch of a housekeeper had snatched her out of his hands.

For all her efforts—the austere hairstyle and the old-maid clothes—Celia still looked like a woman who needed desperately to be kissed, who needed desperately to be introduced to the pure fun of a roll in the hay. And he wanted to be the one to introduce her to that pleasure.

He could almost believe that she'd been waiting here for him all these years, waiting for him to come along and show her just what she'd been missing.

Romancing Celia had been a part of the plan all along. Actually wanting her was another matter altogether.

He was beginning to wish she looked like her father.

Ben could no longer find any joy in ruining Huff's fun, so he turned away from the stable and left the Cranstons' property as silently as he'd arrived.

Chapter Four

"The housekeeper?" Huff leaned casually onto his desk, his inane smile irritating Ben more than it should.

"She's going to be a problem."

It had taken Ben hours to get to sleep last night. He'd tossed and turned, images of his father's face and then Celia's intruding just when he thought he might actually get some sleep.

When sleep had finally come, it had been filled with disturbing dreams. His father, as he'd once been. Celia, as he imagined her to be. Then he'd found himself rising at the crack of dawn, with the same images in his mind.

It was close to noon now, though it felt much later. Ben was tired, and he was cranky, and he wanted something to happen.

"It's not like you to be impatient, Ben." Huff

took a cigar from the top drawer of his desk, leaned back, and took his time getting the damned thing lit. Ben paced the small office while Huff puffed on his cigar and contemplated the next step. "You spent years planning this, and now, when everything's falling together just as you wish, you're getting anxious about an over-protective housekeeper. It doesn't make a lot of sense."

"She doesn't like me."

"Are you sure—" Huff began.

"She's a problem," Ben snapped. "Trust me on this."

A cloud of smoke hung over Huff's head, a hazy and ever-present fog. "All right," he said softly. "Money. That's what it will take. Once things start going very wrong for Celia, then surely the housekeeper will take advantage of a tempting financial opportunity. She won't have a choice in the matter."

"What kind of opportunity?"

Through a cloud of blue smoke, Huff smiled at Ben. "Leave it to me. I'll need to do some research before I proceed."

Ben was tired, but he couldn't stand still. He paced. If only he'd been able to sleep last night. Too many times he'd closed his eyes only to see Celia on a pile of straw—in her prim dress one time, naked the next.

"This is taking too damn long."

Huff laughed out loud at that perfectly serious statement. "Too long? You've been here two days, and already you've saved Celia Pigg's life, had dinner at her house, walked her around town at dusk, and to hear you tell it the twins have already declared you a couple."

His smile faded, and Huff leaned on the desk, cigar clutched tightly in one hand. He waved that cigar at Ben. "The new general store will be open in two days. That's where the bulk of Celia's ready cash comes from, and even that's not enough to pay off the mortgage on her house. The paperwork's done. You can call in the loan at any time. Hell, Ben, what did you expect? That you'd ride into town and I'd be standing in the street with the heads of the remaining Piggs on a silver platter?"

Huff's good mood was gone, had dissolved like the smoke that wafted above his head.

In truth, Ben was disturbed not because things were moving too slowly, but because he derived so little pleasure from the pending destruction of the Pigg household. He wanted justice for his father. And justice would be Hamilton Pigg suffering right now, not Celia.

From a distance, he'd convinced himself that it would be enough, that it would be almost the same to run what was left of Hamilton Pigg's family out of town, to destroy them the way Pigg had destroyed Ezekiel Wolfe.

No matter how much he needed to see this finished, it wasn't the same. Pigg was dead, Celia was innocent, and still, he couldn't let it go.

It couldn't get much worse.

Celia stood on the boardwalk and watched the

townspeople, smiles on their faces, entering and exiting the new general store. What a crowd there was! No one left without a parcel of some kind.

The sign over the open double doors, a fancy, painted monstrosity, read ZEKE'S in tall red letters.

Since she'd been standing on the boardwalk, a good twenty minutes she was certain, not a single soul had entered Pigg's General Store.

When she turned her head back to Zeke's, two very familiar heads came dancing out onto the boardwalk. Faye was grasping a long peppermint stick, and Floy had a handful of licorice. Celia was considering chasing after her sisters when they turned in her direction.

They were apparently oblivious to her presence until they had almost reached her and it was too late to turn back.

"Free candy," Faye said by way of an explanation, wagging her peppermint stick for emphasis. Floy said nothing. She, at least, had the good grace to look contrite. "And you should see their prices! I swear, Celia, the way people are buying their merchandise up, they won't have anything left by closing time."

Celia doubted that seriously. The only reason someone would move in on the sly like this, open their doors without a word of warning, give away candy, and offer outrageously low prices, was to run Pigg's General Store out of business. She doubted anyone who would go to all this trouble would make a mistake like understocking.

"Who's running it?" Celia asked tiredly. "Anyone you recognized?"

Floy shook her head silently, but Faye was quick to answer. "There's a stranger behind the counter. I guess he's Zeke, but I can't be sure. He was much too busy to stop and chat."

Celia turned her eyes to the general store her father had opened years ago. Ophelia Lucas, one-half of the older couple who ran the store for her, was standing in the doorway watching the excitement across the way. She held a broom but wasn't bothering to sweep the floor just inside the store. With no customers there was no need.

"Good afternoon, ladies."

She would have recognized that voice anywhere. It had been three days since Benjamin Wolfe had dined at her house and walked her through town, and she hadn't seen him in all that time. She'd thought about him, though, and waited for him to appear at her door while she was working.

"What's all the commotion about?"

Celia spun around to face him, more than grateful to turn her back on yet another disaster.

Faye was happy to fill him in on all the details, including the free candy, but Ben seemed only mildly interested in the goings-on at Zeke's. He smiled politely, but his attention didn't stay on Faye for long. He turned those intense blue eyes on Celia, and she had the incredible urge to fall against his chest and let him hold her. She needed a hug. Badly.

Once Faye had told Ben he'd better hurry if he

wanted any of the free candy, the twins hurried off to deliver a similar message to James Richardson.

Ben turned his attention to the excitement surrounding Zeke's, narrowing his eyes thoughtfully. Celia had no desire to look in that direction again if she could help it, so she looked at Ben instead.

"Competition?" he asked without taking his eyes from the new store.

"I'm afraid so." Celia sighed.

He looked down at her and grinned, an even and bright smile softening his face and making him appear as if he didn't have a care in the world and never had.

There was nothing she wouldn't give to be so carefree. She'd been mother to the twins for the better part of ten years, and since their father's death, she'd shouldered the financial responsibilities as well. The general store supported Jud and Ophelia Lucas and still made a decent profit, but that was changing at this very moment. The boardinghouse was barely a profit maker, but it did provide a small salary for the widow Frances Hoyt. Of course, there was always Margaret to think of. Margaret had no family, no home but the one Celia provided.

And the responsibility for all those lives and both those businesses fell squarely on her shoulders.

"It's the way of the world, you know," Ben said with a lowering of his comforting voice. "Competition. Change. Upheaval."

"Upheaval," she repeated softly, and with more than a touch of despair in her voice.

Ben took her arm and led her away from the sight of the bustling new store. "Yes, upheaval. Every now and then our lives get turned upside down, changed irrevocably." He leaned down so that his mouth was near her ear. "Don't tell me you expected your life to stay the same forever?"

"Well, yes, I suppose that's exactly what I expected," she admitted.

It was true. When she thought of her own future, she saw herself in her blue and lace room, in the house she'd been born in, seeing to loans and mortgages and running the businesses her father had left her. Businesses she had never wanted. She dreamed of her farm, but she never expected to see it.

Ben stopped in the middle of the boardwalk and spun her around so that they stood face-to-face. He was so tall, her first instinct was to take a step back so she didn't have to look up so sharply to see his face. He stopped her from doing so with a gentle hand at her back.

"I think you need a little upheaval in your life," he whispered.

No. The word came to her lips, but couldn't get past them. "I do?"

"Most definitely."

For a long and wonderful moment, Celia forgot about loans and mortgages and free candy. If this was the sort of upheaval Ben was speaking of—the way her heart beat fast and the way her stomach turned over, the way her knees went weak—then perhaps he was right.

"Would it be terribly scandalous if I kissed you right here and now?" Ben asked. "In the middle of the day, in the middle of town?"

"Yes," Celia whispered. "Terribly scandalous."

Ben grinned down at her, and it seemed he lowered his head just slightly. "No one's watching," he assured her. "They're all in the new general store grasping for free candy or a five-cent bag of sugar."

"That's true," Celia conceded, and then she faltered. "Five-cent sugar? Faye didn't say anything about—"

Ben placed a single finger over her lips to silence her, and with that simple touch he stole her words, her very thoughts. All she could think of was the feel of his rough finger against her mouth, the comfort she felt when he surrounded her this way.

Margaret was not around to stop them, not this time, and perhaps that was just as well. His hand was light at her back, and now she was certain that he was slowly lowering his head, bringing his lips closer to hers with every passing heartbeat. A waving lock of hair, that wondrous burnished gold, fell across his temple, and her fingers itched to touch it.

But she could barely move with Ben's arms around her.

"Celia, good heavens! Did you see what's happening?"

Celia snapped her head around to see Rosemary hurrying toward her with a grim expression on her face. Ben cursed under his breath, something foul and almost but not quite indecipherable.

Rosemary had gathered her pale brown hair into a simple ponytail with a white ribbon, and that ponytail danced as she hurried down the boardwalk. "Someone's opened a new general store, and they're practically giving their merchandise away. How can they do that? Can they do that? What are you going to do?"

Celia didn't want to think about any of those questions at the moment, much less answer them. "There's nothing I *can* do, Rosemary."

Rosemary gave Ben a quick glance, and then did a double take.

"Rosemary Cranston, this is Benjamin Wolfe," Celia said properly.

Immediately after the untimely interruption, Ben had been in a foul mood, but he smiled widely at Rosemary as he took her hand. "It's a pleasure, Miss Cranston," he said graciously, and with what appeared to be a touch of good humor.

At the moment, Celia could find nothing in the situation to be smiling about.

Rosemary went on and on about the new general store, and Celia half listened. If only her energetic and pretty and endearingly open friend had shown up just two minutes later. At this rate, she'd never know what it was like to kiss Ben Wolfe.

* * *

"Patience," Ben said to himself as he walked toward the boardinghouse and his room. Another meeting with Huff, a rather quick and quiet meeting after his moment with Celia that afternoon, had done nothing to bolster his confidence. Huff had dismissed him with a pat on the back and an insistence that all he needed was a little patience.

He normally had it in abundance, but at the moment he was very *im*patient to have this done and over with. He was also, he had to admit, anxious to get on with the personal aspect of this scheme.

Celia was so . . . so . . . Was it possible there had been some mistake, and she wasn't Hamilton Pigg's daughter at all? There was nothing of the vicious, overblown, conniving old man he remembered in Pigg's oldest daughter.

She had taken over for the old man, his businesses, his family, but she didn't look like a hardened entrepreneur. She looked for all the world like a woman who needed someone to take care of her. To hold her and kiss her and . . .

"Mr. Wolfe!"

Ben closed his eyes. He couldn't even *think* about kissing Celia without being interrupted. Since he recognized the voice, he had no choice but to turn around with a smile on his face.

"Ladies," he said, nodding his head in Floy and Faye's direction. Floy stood behind her sister, just a step or two, and Faye clutched in her arms a hairy and seemingly content ball of hair. The ball of hair lifted a head and fixed big dark eyes on Ben.

"You have a puppy, I see," he said, reaching out to scratch the mutt's head between two floppy ears.

"Well, yes and no," Faye said, an unlikely hint of indecision in her normally strong voice. "You see, James gave him to me. His dog had puppies, and his mother said he had to give them away when they were old enough, and I said I would take one, but Margaret hates dogs just because she was bitten once, years ago, and so Celia says I have to get rid of him, and he's so cute, and if I give him to Mr. Lucas he'll kick him around like he does that old three-legged dog of his, and I can't have that, and I thought maybe you would like a puppy?"

Ben's smile faded. "I'd love one, but I'm afraid Mrs. Hoyt won't allow—"

"Oh, yes, she will. Celia said it was all right, and it is her boardinghouse, after all, so there's nothing Mrs. Hoyt can do, even if she doesn't like dogs any more than Margaret does." Faye gave him a huge grin, and Floy smiled sweetly.

If he said no, if he admitted that he hated dogs, Faye would have her feelings hurt. No. He already knew Faye well enough to know that she wouldn't pout with injured sensibilities. She would get angry, furious even, if he refused her gift. And he needed the twins on his side.

Besides, it would give him someone to talk to at night, while Huff was busy with Rosemary

Cranston and Celia was locked up in that big house of hers all alone.

He didn't have to say another word. Faye carefully placed the puppy in his arms.

"What will you name him?" Ben looked over Faye's shoulder to a wide-eyed Floy to answer her question.

"I don't know," he said. "Do you have any ideas?"

"Lemon Drop," Floy said. "Since he's such a pretty yellow."

"No," Faye said with a grimace. "I thought maybe Fluffy would be a nice name."

Ben continued to smile. "Well, I'll have to give it some thought." *Ugly Mutt,* he thought as he scratched the puppy's head. Maybe *Rat Face,* or just plain old *Millstone.*

"Let us know what you decide to name him," Faye called brightly as she spun around.

"I will."

"We'd ask you for dinner," Floy said as Faye almost ran her down, "but Margaret won't—" Faye elbowed her sister soundly.

"Another time," Ben said.

When the twins had disappeared, after arguing softly all the way down the boardwalk, Ben turned toward the boardinghouse. The puppy was cradled in his arms, snuggled there quite comfortably and naturally.

"What do you say, Mutt, steak for dinner?" Mrs. Hoyt's steak was always tough as leather and just as tasty, but it was either that or sausage.

Once Margaret was out of the picture, he'd

have supper at the Pigg house every night . . . until he kicked the sisters out, of course.

The puppy lifted his head to stare up at Ben with wide, brown, desolate eyes.

"You don't like me any more than Celia's witch of a housekeeper, I see," Ben said pragmatically. "Well, it doesn't matter. I don't like you either."

The cute little puppy, Lemon Drop or Fluffy or Ugly Mutt, answered by choosing that particular moment to piddle all over Ben's favorite shirt.

Celia was the only woman Floy knew or had heard tell of who liked thunderstorms. For as long as she could remember, on stormy nights Celia placed her favorite rocking chair near the window and turned her face and her attention to the violent skies.

Tonight was truly stormy, with howling winds and heavy rain and occasional lightning that lit the sky and the town beyond the window. Thunder rumbled, nearby but not too close. The violence in the night skies fascinated Celia rather than disturbing her, and it had been this way for as long as Floy could remember.

Of course, Faye didn't like storms at all, and she'd already made her way to bed using a headache *and* a stomachache as an excuse.

Floy knew her outwardly fearless twin was not fearless at all.

"I think we should invite Mr. Wolfe to Sunday dinner," Floy said softly.

Celia turned her head away from the window and smiled. "I don't know. . . ."

"Margaret always makes a big dinner on Sunday, enough to feed half of Piggville. We wouldn't even have to tell her. We could just bring him home from church and set another place at the table."

Celia liked Ben Wolfe. Floy just knew in her heart that was true. And she did need a beau. She was too pretty and too sweet to be alone all the time.

"He's hardly a stray we can bring home like James did that old yellow dog of his." Celia smiled, but it was a sad smile. There was nothing more terrible, in Floy's opinion, than a sad smile. It was all wrong.

"Well, in a way he is a stray," Floy insisted softly. "A newcomer all alone in town. And he did save your life, for which I for one am grateful." She tried to imply that Celia was being ungrateful if she didn't agree. Celia was never rude. "And anyway, a man shouldn't have to eat Sunday dinner alone, especially when we'll have more than enough food for just the four of us."

Celia looked as though she wanted to relent. She wrinkled her nose and bit her bottom lip and cocked her head to one side, and when a flash of lightning lit the night, she didn't even turn to watch. She did like Mr. Wolfe, of that Floy was certain.

And surely he liked her, too. What man wouldn't like a woman who was sweet and pretty as Celia? They didn't have all the time in the world. Mr. Wolfe might get bored with Piggville and move on. Another girl might catch his eye.

John Watts would return one day, and he would surely complicate everything.

"I won't eat much," Floy added as she waited for an answer.

"I'll tell you what," Celia finally said. "If Mr. Wolfe comes to church tomorrow, and if the opportunity presents itself, we'll invite him to dinner. I'm sure there will be plenty for everyone."

Floy smiled brightly. That answer was quite good enough. If nothing else, Faye would think of something. Ben Wolfe would be at church, and opportunity would most certainly present itself.

Chapter Five

Celia made the short walk to church alone, since the twins had fled the house a good half hour earlier planning to meet a friend before the service began, and Margaret had begged off with a headache. It had been an unusual morning. The girls had risen just past dawn, with abundant energy normally not evident so early in the day. And Margaret never missed church services. Never.

Of course, she'd been cross since Benjamin Wolfe had come back to town. If anything had given her a headache, it was likely her own foul mood.

The road was a muddy mess, but Celia didn't care. Last night's storm had cleared the air. Everything smelled fresher, cleaner, and if the price for that freshness was a little mud, well, it was certainly worth it. With care, she would miss

70

the worst of the mud, and just in case she did happen to step in a bit of muck, she was wearing her oldest pair of decent lace-up boots.

The dress she wore, however, was one of her very best. It was a becoming shade of rose, quite unlike her everyday clothing, and was adorned with just a touch of fine lace. It wasn't frivolous, she assured herself, it was simply a bit more attractive than the gray or the brown she normally wore.

She wasn't quite ready to admit that she'd plucked the gown from her wardrobe because of the very real possibility that Ben Wolfe would be at church today. Why, that would be blasphemous, wouldn't it?

Margaret, on the other hand, had scoffed aloud when Celia had come down the stairs in the elegant rose dress, making it perfectly clear that she understood Celia's motives and was distressed.

There was already a crowd outside the small, white church, neighbors visiting, those who came in from nearby ranches talking to friends they saw only on Sunday, but Celia didn't see her sisters anywhere. She didn't see Ben Wolfe, either, even though she searched for his fair hair with painstaking diligence.

The minister, Curtis Rivers, greeted his parishioners at the door. His shock of thick white hair was unmistakable, as was his thin frame. He was seventy-five if he was a day, and he had been going steadily deaf for the past five years. His sight was not much better than his hearing, and in the past couple of years he had begun to forget the names of people he'd known since he'd arrived in Piggville.

Everyone loved him.

Reverend Rivers had baptized Floy and Faye and had spent endless hours at the bedside of Celia's mother, and years later her father, as they lay dying. He'd presided over the marriage of roughly half the residents of Piggville, baptized hundreds of babies besides the twins, and if he occasionally forgot names and faces in his old age, well, that was all right.

"Reverend Rivers," Celia said in a clear voice as he took her hand.

"Priscilla," he said with a wide grin. "Good to see you again."

There was a lump in Celia's throat, but she continued to smile. On occasion, someone still commented on how much she looked like her mother. "It's Cecilia, Reverend."

"Of course," he said, nodding as if he understood, and Celia stepped into the church. It was already near to full with churchgoers who talked quietly as they waited for the service to begin. As she had since childhood, Celia sat in a pew near the back. From here she would easily see Floy and Faye when they arrived.

There was a good crowd on this Sunday morning. Rosemary was seated near the front with her parents and Walter Huffman. Not long after Celia sat down, James Richardson came in with his parents and two younger brothers, and after a proper greeting they sat directly in front of her.

Ophelia Lucas wasn't far behind the Richardsons, and as usual she was alone. Jud rarely made it to Sunday services.

Doc Edwards entered the rapidly filling church, apparently sober, and squeezed his bulk into an aisle seat near the front. Celia's eyes were on him, so she didn't see Margaret until she stopped in the aisle. With a disgusted sigh, Margaret stepped carefully past Celia to sit in the middle of the pew.

"What about your headache? I thought you felt much too poorly to come to church this morning," Celia said under her breath.

"I do," Margaret whispered hoarsely. "Headache or no, I don't like the idea of leaving you all alone while that man is in town."

"I rather think it's safe to attend church without a chaperon."

Margaret's answer was an unladylike grunt beneath her breath. "Where are the girls?"

It was a good question. They certainly should have been here by now. "I don't know. But if they don't show up soon I'll . . ."

It started with a single gasp, and then a dozen heads turned to the open doors. One older woman harrumphed loudly, and another covered her mouth with a gloved hand. More heads turned. Some showed no emotion at all, others grew wide eyed and pale, and there was a small, collective gasp that silenced the rest of the congregation.

Celia turned to look at the doorway. What a picture they made, the three of them with the sun at their backs. Ben stood in the center, his wavy hair combed back, his eyes narrowed. He was always dressed nicely, but there was something about the black frock coat and white vest that suited him. It was elegant and proper, and at the same time gave him a sinister air.

Floy and Faye stood on either side, angelic in their best Sunday pink muslin.

By the time Ben and the twins stepped into the church, all eyes were on the three of them. It took a moment for the whispers to begin, but they did begin. And grow.

Faye smiled at James as she slipped between the pews, past Celia and Margaret, and moved down so she sat directly behind him. It was only then that Celia noticed how Laura Richardson had gone as white as Ben's vest. Ben motioned for Floy to follow her twin, and then he took the seat on the aisle, next to Celia.

He pretended to be oblivious to the stir he caused, turning a small smile to Celia and nodding cordially.

When Reverend Rivers entered the church, closing the doors solidly behind him, the whispers stopped. The stares didn't.

Margaret leaned forward and in front of Celia to whisper to Ben. "Well, Mr. Wolfe, you've made quite a spectacle of yourself."

"Margaret," Celia hissed, "don't be ridiculous. Benjamin didn't do anything wrong."

Ben smiled, apparently unmoved by Margaret's accusation.

"The Reverend Wolfe was given to black frock

coats and white vests," Margaret explained, whispering into Celia's ear. "And he wore his hair slicked back like that. Quite a dandy, he was, for one who claimed to be a man of God."

"Dearly beloved," Reverend Rivers began, and then there was a long pause. Ben's attention was centered on the old man who presided over the church his father had once been minister of. "We are gathered here today in the sight of God to witness the marriage . . ."

It was Doc Edwards who hurried to the pulpit and told Reverend Rivers, in a loud whisper directly into his ear, that this was not a wedding, it was a Sunday sermon. The reverend seemed not at all embarrassed or confused, but moved directly to an impassioned prayer.

This was the old man who had taken over for his father. Ben listened to the reverend ramble on. More than once the old man lost his train of thought, stumbled, and headed off in a new direction.

This was the preacher who had replaced Ezekiel Wolfe. Even fourteen years ago Rivers would have been an old man and no threat to the women of Piggville. Perhaps that was why he'd been chosen.

Ben could still remember his father's sermons. Full of fire and brimstone, Ezekiel Wolfe had been able to grab and hold a congregation like no one else. He had been a passionate, fierce preacher who could have his flock in tears one Sunday, frightened or laughing out loud the next.

It was charisma, yes, but it was also a deep love for the life he'd chosen, a conviction in his faith that had never failed until the night Hamilton Pigg had destroyed everything. In his years of travel before coming to Piggville, in the year and a half he was the preacher in this very church, Ezekiel Wolfe had never rambled incoherently as the Reverend Rivers did.

It was all Ben could do not to bare his teeth to the curious and sometimes frightened stares that turned his way during the sermon. Did they know he'd come to town for revenge? There was no reason for anyone to be afraid of him, unless they felt guilty.

Of course, Celia was the only one in town who personally had anything to fear, and she had no idea why.

He watched her out of the corner of his eye. Her attention was properly on the rambling sermon. Her chin was lifted, her eyes were steady, her lips were firmly set. A strand of dark hair had come loose and touched her pale neck. As always, it had been plaited into a thick braid and twisted up at the back of her head. So prim, so proper, and all he thought about when he saw that one small wayward lock, was unbraiding the rest of it.

Without warning, the sermon ended and the Reverend Rivers broke into a chorus of "Amazing Grace." One by one the congregation joined him, until the small church was filled with the oddly comforting sound of a favorite hymn being sung enthusiastically and just slightly off-key.

And then, with the service apparently over, most of the churchgoers stood, and several members of the congregation turned their full attention to him.

"We invited Mr. Wolfe to dinner," Floy said timidly as they all came to their feet. "You did say last night that would be all right, remember, Celia?"

"I remember," Celia said, and there was more than a touch of a sigh in her voice.

"If it's not convenient"—Ben turned his back on a woman in the aisle who absolutely glared at him—"I'm sure I can get a passable meal at the boardinghouse."

For the first time all morning, Celia turned her eyes squarely to him. Heaven help him, after all these years of planning, when she looked at him like this he forgot about revenge and family honor and everything that had brought him to this place. "Don't be silly. We'll be happy to have you to dinner."

They walked out into the sunshine, Celia on his left, the twins behind them, Margaret doing her best to come between them and not quite being able to find a subtle way to do so. It was enough to make a man smile.

"What are you doing here?"

The question was delivered in a voice that was condescending and hateful, and Ben was surprised to find that the woman who asked it was a rather pleasant-looking middle-aged woman wearing a conservative gray dress. There was a small crowd behind her, a crowd made up of the people who had stared the hardest all morning long.

Before he could answer, Celia took a step forward and spoke in his defense.

"Kay Anne Ascot, what kind of a question is that?" This was not the soft and dreamy Celia he had become accustomed to, but the businesswoman she had to be. She commanded the crowd easily. "I've never known you to be so rude. Why, we should all be welcoming Ben back to Piggville, not staring at him like he was some sort of . . . of . . ."

"Ghost," a low voice from the background contributed.

Kay Anne Ascot looked contrite. "Of course, you're right. It's just that he looks so much like his father, and it gave me quite a start, it did, to see him walk into the church like he never left. I was just surprised, that's all."

Several heads nodded in agreement, but a belligerent voice—most likely the same one that had supplied the word "ghost"—shouted out, "We don't need no Wolfes in this town!"

There was a rumble through the crowd, as they found validity in that statement as well.

"I'm ashamed of the lot of you," Celia said sternly, as if she were speaking to naughty children. This was no doubt the voice and demeanor she used with the twins when they misbehaved. "You're reasonable adults who should know by now that you can't judge a person by the actions of his kin."

Margaret scoffed, but everyone ignored her.

"Why, if that were true, I would have been run out of town a long time ago."

Ben tore his eyes from the crowd to look down at the woman at his side.

"My father, whom I did love very much in spite of his faults, was not always an easy man to love. He was ruthless when it came to business, and he could be a judgmental man. He was never known for his compassion."

Someone actually laughed at that, but Celia continued without pause.

"Not one of you has ever held the fact that Hamilton Pigg was my father against me. You've given me a chance to be myself, to earn or lose your respect on my own merits."

Off to the side, Huff caught Ben's eye. He was staring blatantly at Celia, his arms folded over his chest, his expression exceedingly bland. For some reason, Ben felt censure in that black stare.

"It's only fair that we give Benjamin Wolfe the same opportunity."

With a nod of her head, Celia was finished, and the crowd broke up and moved away, their fire extinguished by her dressing-down.

"That was wonderful," Floy said quietly. Margaret harrumphed. Faye just smiled, walking off with James Richardson and his family. After a moment, Floy joined her twin.

"Dinner in an hour," Margaret called after the girls, and they turned to her and smiled.

"We'll go by your room and get the puppy before dinner," Faye called as she waved energetically.

"Great," Ben mumbled.

As they stepped away from the church, Margaret finally managed to insert herself between Celia and Ben. She stepped in with force and agility and gave Ben a sour smile. The sooner Huff came up with a plan to get the woman out of Piggville, the better.

Last night's rain had turned the road that separated one side of the town's main street and the other into a quagmire of mud and puddles that everyone studiously avoided. The churchgoers stuck to the boardwalk that ran nearly the length of the town, crowding together, sidestepping impatient children who hurried past.

"Let's cross here," Ben said with a smile that broke out without warning.

"There's a high spot at the other end of the boardwalk." Celia looked with displeasure at the muddy road. "We can cross there."

Without warning, Ben stepped behind the interfering Margaret, scooped Celia off her feet, and stepped into the street with her in his arms.

"What are you doing?" she asked, just a trifle indignantly.

"That dress you're wearing is much too pretty to drag through the mud."

Behind them, Margaret grumbled under her breath. If Ben had the witch figured right, there was no way she would step into the muck he waded through. She'd be stuck on the other side of the street.

"You're ruining your boots," Celia muttered half-heartedly.

"I've got another pair."

"Everyone will see. . . ."

"They'll think I'm quite chivalrous."

"They'll think you're quite senseless."

"I like chivalrous better."

Celia was still trying to argue with him when they reached the other side of the street and he stepped onto the boardwalk. He didn't want to set her on her feet and let her go, but he did just that as soon as his footing on the boardwalk was solid.

She was blushing. A pretty pink flush had come to her cheeks, and she lowered her eyes as she smoothed her skirt.

And he felt something he had never felt before. At first he didn't recognize it, the paralyzing, suffocating, what-have-I-done sensation that came and went quickly.

Guilt.

Dinner at the Pigg house was usually quiet and dignified, and over very quickly. But then, they usually didn't have Ben Wolfe at the table.

His new puppy was settled in his lap. Floy and Faye had decided that they couldn't simply leave the poor little thing alone in Ben's room, or tie it up outside, despite Margaret's objections.

Of course, Margaret objected far more vehemently to Ben's presence than to that of a dog in the dining room.

Ben fed the puppy pieces of chicken he pulled off the bone, scowling and muttering each time he offered a morsel to the obedient dog.

Floy and Faye were both so anxious to impress Ben that they chattered brightly about school and their friends. Even Floy, who was usually content to allow her more demonstrative sister to do the talking, shared happenings from the week that Celia hadn't heard. A good grade on an exam, a boy who'd given her a handful of daisies.

Children needed a man in their lives. Someone strong and solid and protective and giving. Celia hadn't been a child for a very long time, but she needed a man in her life for all the same reasons. And more.

Usually Margaret joined them for meals, but since Ben and the puppy were present, she protested by eating, and sulking, in the kitchen.

When Floy and Faye excused themselves and ran upstairs to change clothes, Ben and Celia stepped into the parlor. In this pleasant room, Celia felt a little out of her element. She'd spent so many hours in what had been her father's office and was now hers, that a purely social situation made her tense.

"What are you going to call the dog?" she asked as she sat on the edge of the sofa. It seemed a safe enough question.

"I was thinking of Ugly Mutt. What do you think?"

He sounded and looked quite serious, but Celia laughed. "You can't name that cute little puppy Ugly Mutt."

"Why not?" He ignored the empty chair that faced the sofa, and sat beside Celia.

"You just can't."

He was so close she could feel his body heat. They'd been this close before, and every time set her heart to racing. She looked down at the puppy in his lap, and Ben leaned just a little bit closer.

"Then you name him for me, Celia. Anything you want, even . . . Fluffy or Lemon Drop." He actually cringed as he offered those names.

She reached down and scratched the dog's back lightly. He hunkered down, content enough to close his eyes while his head rested on Ben's thigh.

"Lucky," she whispered.

"Why Lucky?"

Because he's yours. She couldn't possibly offer that explanation. "Well, if you made a fortune mining, then you have a bit of luck yourself, wouldn't you say?"

"Perhaps."

"And he's found a good home, and I'm sure you'll take excellent care of him."

She'd been staring at the puppy in question as she gave her reasons for the offered name, but Ben placed a single finger beneath her chin and lifted her face she was forced to look at him. Goodness, he was perfect. Bright and shining and beautiful, from the dark blond wavy hair on his head to the mud on his expensive boots.

"Twice I've tried to kiss you, Celia Pigg, and both times we were interrupted."

"I know," she said breathlessly.

"I'm going to kiss you now," he promised, "and I don't care if everyone you know comes to the door and watches. I'm not going to stop."

"Good." Could he even hear her soft answer as he settled his mouth over hers? She wasn't sure.

It was unlike any caress she had ever known or imagined. Ben moved his lips over hers, loved her, claimed her without any other touch. Only their mouths met, lips soft and warm and gently curious.

And Celia felt as if she were coming undone, unraveling from the inside out.

It was Ben who pulled away, slowly, and with an expression on his face that told Celia he was coming undone as well.

"No one's ever kissed me like that before," she whispered.

The stunned expression on his face faded slowly, and he smiled at her. "Good," he whispered, and then he kissed her again.

"What do I do now?" Ben asked softly. In the privacy of his rented room, he paced. "When she stood there and told half the town that they should give me a chance, that you shouldn't judge a person by what his father had done in the past . . . I felt awful."

He stopped pacing and dropped into the single chair by the window. After leaving Celia, he'd actually considered going straight to Huff and calling off the whole thing. Doubt. It was, he was sure, a side effect of the guilt he was unaccustomed to.

If Celia found out—about Zeke's general store, about the mortgage on her home and her other properties—she'd turn on him as surely as had that Kay Anne Ascot.

"I've planned this for years. Since the night my father died, since the moment I realized that getting run out of this town made him lose his will to live, this is all I've thought about." He looked to the bed and the resting occupant. "Should I forget it all now, just because Celia Pigg is a pretty woman? Just because she's a first-class kisser?"

There was no answer to his questions, of course.

"I have completely lost my mind, sitting here long past bedtime talking to a damn dog."

The mutt squirmed, as if he knew he'd been insulted.

"Lucky." Ben muttered under his breath. "There was a moment, half a minute, maybe, when I thought she named you Lucky because you were sitting on my lap, and that's where she wanted to be." The hairball yawned, bored already with the one-sided conversation. "Pretty stupid, wouldn't you say?"

Pretty stupid. Was he really going to forget everything that had happened to his father just because Hamilton Pigg was dead? Just because a pretty woman looked at him with those deep, dark eyes a man could get lost in?

Ben slipped the gold watch that had been his father's from his vest pocket. The metal was cold to his fingers, cold and solid. This was all he had left of Ezekiel Wolfe, a gold watch he'd kept when everything else was gone, a timepiece he'd been grasping on his deathbed.

In the semidark, with no one but Lucky for company, Ben's doubts faded away. Of course Celia Pigg was a nice person. She'd never known a moment's trouble in her charmed life. Never been hungry, never had people she thought were her friends turn on her like a pack of dogs. It was easy to be sweet and caring and magnanimous when you knew nothing else.

He'd come to town ready for a fight, armed for war, willing and able to meet any challenge.

This was still war. Celia's methods were different. Her weapons were soft. Cunning. Perhaps even deadly.

But he couldn't allow her to make him forget.

Chapter Six

Celia stared at the column of numbers before her until they began to blur. With Zeke's taking all her customers, the Pigg General Store was losing money, and the boardinghouse was only slightly profitable. This was distressing, and she couldn't even sound all this out with Margaret, at the moment, since she was spending the day helping Ophelia Lucas.

Another payment was due on the property those businesses sat upon, and there was barely enough in her account to meet that obligation. Where had the money from this particular loan gone? If she remembered correctly, her father had invested with two so-called geologists who claimed to have found a mountain that was riddled with gold and gems beyond his wildest dreams. His investment would be repaid, they said, a hundredfold. Perhaps more.

Of course, they had never seen the money again—or the geologists.

He hadn't always been so gullible, or so greedy, but in his last years Hamilton Pigg had changed. The change had come gradually, in the years following his wife's death, and he'd made what could only be called foolish decisions.

At least the twins' trust funds were secure. It seemed that Hamilton Pigg had maintained the good sense to leave them untouched.

There were many times, especially of late, when Celia wished her father had left her a small sum of cash instead of the house and the businesses and the responsibilities that went with them. He'd thought he was doing right by her, leaving her so much, but sometimes it was *too* much.

But it was all hers, like it or not.

"Hello."

Her head shot up at the sound of Ben's voice. He stood there in the doorway in a tan suit and a new pair of boots, a smile on his face that faded as he watched her.

"What's wrong?" He stepped into the room, filled it without even trying.

"Nothing," she said out of habit. Ben stared down at her, and it was obvious that he didn't believe her. He knew her too well already. "Everything."

She found herself telling it all, unburdening herself as she could with no one else. And he listened. He didn't dismiss her as John always did, with a pat on the hand and an assurance that all would be well, and he didn't get that bored and blank expression on his face as Margaret often did when Celia discussed business.

The next thing she knew, Ben was holding her hand. He stood beside her chair and cradled her hand in his own, and it was such a comfort. There was no cool and condescending pat of his hand on hers, but a warm and comforting attachment that joined them together.

"I never wanted this," she said softly, expressing her doubts for the first time since her father's death. "The businesses, the responsibility. All I ever really wanted was a little farm somewhere, with chickens and maybe a couple of cows."

It sounded silly, childish even to her ears. This was the first time she'd said the words aloud. She'd never told anyone about her dream. There was no point. This was her life, and she was stuck with it.

"Sounds very nice," Ben said softly. "Very simple." He rocked his thumb against the palm of her hand.

"I know. It's . . . absurd. Illogical and quite selfish, really. Most women would dearly love to be in my position. I have my own home, the responsibility for the family business . . . I don't have to depend on the whims of a man, and I've never feared for my own comfort and safety." She sighed. It was selfish of her to feel that the world was coming to an end because of a little setback.

Ben tugged on her hand so that she rose from

her chair. Without a thought he gathered her against his chest and held her there with a strong and steady hand against the back of her head. "I'd like to make you forget all about your troubles, Celia," he whispered. Goodness, she had come to love the sound of his voice, so deep and smooth and soothing. "I'd like to make all your dreams come true."

His hands steadied her, physically and emotionally. It was wonderful, comfortable and exciting at the same time. And safe. Here, now, she was secure, and she could so easily forget the damning numbers on her desk and lose herself in Ben's strong arms.

"They're silly little dreams, I know."

"There's no such thing," Ben said softly, "as a silly dream."

Celia lifted her head to glance up at Ben's calm face. As always, he looked as if all was right with the world and every worry that plagued her—all her anxiety—was for nothing.

Perhaps that was true.

"Do you know what I dream about?" he asked. "I dream about kissing you again."

He was smiling as he lowered his head to kiss her, and golden sunlight from the window touched his hair and his face. Margaret called Ben Wolfe a devil, and Celia herself had thought him a bounder, but at this moment he was an angel, a beautiful and heavenly being who had come to her when she needed him most.

Her eyes drifted closed as his lips met hers. The kiss was perfectly wonderful, warm and marvelous and . . . and heavenly. Ben moved his mouth against hers, the enchanting movements unhurried and firm and all-consuming. As the heartbeats passed, Celia became aware of his chest pressing against hers, of the hands at her back, of the thigh that was butted against her hip. Of the very closeness of him. Ben didn't simply hold her; he was all around her.

When he used his tongue, she thought she would die. She'd never known that anything could be so good, so fierce and terrible and marvelous all at the same time. This deep kiss touched her all over, chilled her to her very bones.

Ben's hands crept up her back, caressed her neck, and found the pins that held her hair up. One by one he removed the pins and tossed them to the floor. Celia heard them hit as they bounced off the desk or landed on the hardwood floor.

Once all the pins had been disposed of, Ben ran his fingers through the thick braid until it came apart. As he ran his fingers through her hair, her hands slipped to his neck and the dark gold curls there. She couldn't hold him hard enough, fast enough to suit her.

He pulled his mouth away slowly, breaking contact by degrees.

"I feel like I'm coming undone," Celia whispered as she opened her eyes.

"Do you now?" Ben said softly. His eyes were hooded, his face no longer complacent. There was a harshness there that was new, an urgency, perhaps.

"I do."

He almost smiled as he lowered his head to her throat to kiss her there. "And now?" he asked, his breath warm against her neck.

"Yes."

With a subtle shift, Ben turned so that Celia's backside was against the edge of the desk. She was trapped there, the hard edge behind her, Ben's body pressed tightly to hers. This time when he kissed her he lifted her, rubbing her entire body against his before he sat her on the edge of the desk and settled himself between her thighs.

"Ben," Celia whispered against his lips, "this isn't right. It's not . . . it's not . . ." He silenced her with a forceful kiss.

"Not proper?" he finished for her as he slipped his mouth away.

"It's not."

"Neither is this."

He flicked open the top two buttons of her blouse, and then lowered his mouth to the exposed base of her throat.

Celia knew she should tell him to stop, but she couldn't. This felt too good, too right. She could feel her heartbeat, the thrum of blood through her veins, a throbbing between her slightly spread legs, there where he stood. Her body had been sleeping all these years, and Ben Wolfe was waking it up.

A hand slipped up her side; a thumb brushing against her ribs crept gradually higher until it reached her breast. His hand was large and comforting and warm through the thin cotton, and instead of pulling away—as she knew she should—Celia leaned into his hand.

He kissed her hard as his fingers danced over her breast, and before she knew what had happened, a few more buttons had come unfastened. Ben's mouth left hers to trail down her throat to the newly exposed skin, to the swell of her breasts.

Fingers slipped inside her blouse and found a hardened nipple, and she arched uncontrollably as Ben covered her breast with his bare hand. It was shocking and wonderful, as furious and undeniable as a Texas thunderstorm.

He leaned over her, pressed her back and back until she was practically lying on the desk. Ben never released her, not for a second. He kissed her, and his hand fell against her knee, softly, and then crept up to her thigh to rest there.

Ben was everywhere. Kissing her lips, fondling her breast and her thigh, standing there between her legs and hovering above her. Celia knew she should tell him to stop, but she was caught in this amazing whirlpool of sensation and she didn't want it to stop.

"Celia," Ben rasped, pulling his mouth from hers. She saw, for a moment, a flicker of indecision in his blue eyes. With a hand at the back of his head she pulled his lips to hers to take away all the doubts.

He groaned. The hand at her thigh traveled higher, and with a simple move of his hips Ben was actually against her, layers of fabric—her skirt and Ben's trousers—between them. She moaned, because it was wonderful and because she wanted more.

"Mercy!"

The shouted word from the doorway killed every astonishing sensation as surely as a bucket of icy water would have. Ben jumped back, and Celia jerked into a sitting position. When she glanced over her shoulder, she died a little. Kay Anne Ascot, Frances Hoyt, and Rosemary's mother, Bay Cranston, were huddled together with almost identical shocked expressions on their faces.

Celia slipped off the desk with as much dignity as she could muster. Ben had backed away, but not very far. Celia bumped into him as she stepped away from the desk and straightened her tangled skirt. Quickly, but not nearly quickly enough, she fastened a couple of the too-small buttons of her blouse, and she smoothed her hair as she turned around.

No one had moved. The expressions hadn't changed at all. She doubted if any one of the three women who stood in the doorway had so much as taken a breath since Frances Hoyt had shouted "Mercy!"

It was Bay Cranston who, though pale and shaken, gathered her composure and stepped forward. "Didn't you say one o'clock, Mr. Wolfe?"

With mounting dread, Celia turned her eyes to Ben. He was composed—not at all embarrassed or angry. Moving without urgency, he reached into his vest pocket and retrieved a gold watch.

With a flick of his thumb, he tossed back the cover to reveal the face. "It's five after, Mrs. Cranston."

"I knocked for several minutes," she began, before turning red and backing away.

Frances Hoyt lifted her chin haughtily. "Mr. Wolfe said you had some changes for the boardinghouse in mind. I suggest we discuss them at a later time."

With that, Mrs. Hoyt spun away and disappeared. The front door slammed forcefully, and everyone flinched. Everyone but Ben.

Kay Anne Ascot glanced quickly from Celia to Ben and back again. "I tried to warn you," she said softly. "You can't say I didn't. I don't suppose you really wanted to discuss an addition to the church in your father's name."

Celia shook her head, and Kay Anne left—a little more quietly than Frances Hoyt.

"Oh, Celia," Bay Cranston said, shaking her head slowly. Then she backed out of the room, leaving Celia alone with Ben again.

Every pleasant sensation, every warmhearted notion she'd ever had about Ben Wolfe, was gone, wiped away quickly and completely.

Despite the urge to run from the office in shame and in tears, Celia faced Ben Wolfe without a tear or a tremble. "Well, it seems I was wrong to give you the benefit of the doubt." There was a lump in her throat, a disturbing weight in her chest. For a few wonderful moments she'd felt a part of something warm and wonderful . . . and it had all been a joke, a bit of fun for Benjamin Wolfe. "Everyone else was right. You're a no-good womanizer, a liar, and a cheat just like your father."

He seemed unmoved by her accusations. There was no flash of anger in his eyes, no telling color in his cheeks. His eyebrows went up just slightly, and that was his only physical reaction to her words. "My father was never accused of cheating."

"You did this on purpose!" Celia stomped her foot, a childish and completely ineffective move on her part. She'd been so certain that Ben was affected by some of the same emotions and sensations that fascinated her. "Why would you do such a thing? Why . . . why go out of your way to humiliate me like this?"

Ben tried to leave. He brushed past her without a word, and Celia reached out to grab his sleeve.

"I deserve an answer."

He spun around and looked down at her. All his usual nonchalance was gone. This was a hard man, a determined man. "Tell me, Celia," he whispered. "How does it feel to be disgraced in front of people you thought were your friends? Where are they now? They turned their backs on you so fast, I'm surprised they didn't knock each other down getting out of this house."

"This is all for your father, isn't it?" She could hardly believe it was true. That he would come back to Piggville after all these years, just to take his revenge. On her. "I didn't have anything to do with—"

Ben turned his back on her and headed for the

door. Celia followed him into the hallway, her anger growing with every step.

"I want you out of town," she said as he opened the front door wide. "Today."

His back stiffened, but when he turned to look at her there was a smile on his face. "You're running me out of town?"

"You're staying in my boardinghouse, and I demand that you leave immediately."

Ben relaxed, leaned against the doorjamb, and crossed his arms over his chest as his grin widened. "You demand?"

Celia straightened her spine. It was difficult to look dignified when her hair fell in complete disarray around her shoulders, and the top three buttons of her blouse were still unfastened. Her lips were probably as well-kissed red as Ben's were, and the heat in her face told her she was blushing. Dignified. It wasn't easy, but she did her best. "I demand."

Ben reached into his vest pocket and withdrew a neatly folded sheet of paper. "In that case, I must demand that you vacate this house immediately."

"Don't be ridiculous."

"I tell you what," Ben said brightly. "I'll give you until Friday noon to pay off the mortgage." He waved the folded paper in her direction. "You can see my lawyer, Walter Huffman, to make the arrangements."

She'd never fainted in her life, but suddenly Celia was light-headed and weak. There wasn't enough money to pay off the mortgage, not by Friday.

Ben's smile faded, and he stood up straight. "I'm calling in the loan, as is my legal right. If you can't pay and I suspect you can't, I want you out of here Friday by one o'clock."

"You can't just . . . just run us out of our home like this." Surely he wouldn't. Surely there was some goodness in his heart.

"I can't?"

"You won't," she said softly. Some of what she'd seen in him, some of the warmth and kindness that had drawn her to Ben Wolfe from the beginning, had to be real. It wasn't all an act. It wasn't.

"Watch me," he whispered, and then he backed away, closing the door behind him.

Word was already out. Blatant stares followed Ben down the street; whispered accusations followed.

He smiled. It didn't matter what these people thought of him, whether they liked him or not. He didn't have any good name to lose, not in this town. When this was over—when the Piggs had nothing, and the town was hurting—he would move on. It wasn't as if he had any real desire to stay here.

His smile faded as he neared Huff's office. Celia had opened herself to him so easily, so naturally, kissing him with an innocent enthusiasm and arching against his hand and his body until he lost his senses. He hadn't intended to go so far, hadn't intended to be caught with one hand inside Celia's blouse and the other under her skirt.

It didn't take much to ruin a lady's reputation in a small Texas town like Piggville. Alone with a man, in a compromising position, would have been enough. That had been his intention, when he'd asked the ladies—separately, of course—to meet Celia at one o'clock. A passionate kiss, a well-placed hand, her hair loose . . . But she'd responded to him too well, and he'd almost forgotten that time was moving on. Damn it, she had a body that was made for seduction. Lush, rounded, purely female. A touch or two, and he'd almost allowed himself to forget why he was here. Hell, five more minutes, and he would have been inside her.

Wouldn't that have been a sight for the fine ladies of Piggville.

Huff was sitting at his desk when Ben entered the office, nose in a sheaf of papers, cigar smoke rising above his head.

"I told her to be out by Friday," Ben said without preamble. "If you think we need an eviction notice to keep it on the up-and-up, see to it."

Huff lifted tired eyes. "You did it?"

"I did."

"All of it?"

Ben smiled, but it was an effort. "No one will be thinking of Celia Pigg as a sweet, innocent little maiden any longer."

Huff sighed in obvious despair. "It wasn't necessary. I told you that a thousand—"

"Humiliation is part of the package," Ben said

harshly. "She'll try to contact Watts now, I suppose."

"That's taken care of," Huff snapped. "Martin will intercept any telegrams or letters that arrive at the office for their visiting attorney."

"And if he tries to contact her?"

"Martin will handle everything." Huff's voice was a bark as surely as Lucky's was. "He's a greedy bastard."

Ben reached for one of Huff's cigars as he leaned against the desk. "Is he a *reliable* greedy bastard?"

"Absolutely."

The light from the window was blocked by a passerby, but instead of flitting across Huff's polished wood floor, the shadow stayed. Ben glanced to the window, and as he caught the eye of a curious citizen, the man jumped sharply back and moved on.

"How are you coming with the mortgage on the boardinghouse and general store property?"

"Next week, if all goes well," Huff said solemnly, "it'll be yours."

Huff leaned back in his chair and took a long draw on his cigar. "Hamilton Pigg was not as rich as you seemed to think. During the last ten years, since his wife died, he's been robbing Peter to pay Paul. Moving money, taking loans he really shouldn't have. Gambling, but with his businesses instead of cards or dice."

Huff swiveled thoughtfully in his chair.

"Is this conversation going anywhere?" Ben snapped.

"As your lawyer, I'm advising you to call a halt to this contemptible war of yours." He puffed on that damn cigar with relish. "The general store has been hurt, maybe even fatally. It wasn't exactly generating a fortune before you arrived. The boardinghouse barely supports itself. As far as I can tell it's as full now as it's ever been. Celia Pigg has no head for business, and she's been making one bad loan after another. Hell, Ben, leave her alone, and she'll be broke in five years anyway."

"Not good enough," Ben answered quickly.

Huff sighed and shook his head, and turned his full attention to the papers on his desk.

Ben looked out the window to the busy street and the passing townspeople. Some stared toward Huff's office; some passed unaware. Soon enough, everyone would know what was going on.

He knew, deep down, that he should take his lawyer's—his friend's—advice. Hamilton Pigg was dead. Celia was far from the pampered rich girl he'd expected to find. If Huff was right, there would be nothing left of the so-called Pigg fortune in five years. Celia would be forced to marry, maybe that ass John Watts, maybe some farmer who would give her the life she really wanted.

He should, and he could, but he wouldn't. He'd actually considered walking away, when Celia had looked up at him and asked "Why." He'd actually walked to the front door of the Pigg house with every intention of taking the next train. This was not what he'd intended, not what he'd dreamed about all these years. One wide-eyed look from Celia Pigg and he'd been ready to forget the vow he'd made to his father, ready to forget it all. . . .

And then she'd made the mistake of ordering him to leave town, and he'd changed his mind.

Chapter Seven

For once in her life Faye was silent, as she had been all evening. It was downright unnatural.

Floy glanced at her twin, and then at Celia's closed office door. Rosemary Cranston was in there, and had been for several minutes. Goodness, the people had come and gone all day, and through it all Celia looked positively ill. When she'd called them, Margaret and Faye and Floy, into the parlor to tell them that they were most likely going to move to the boardinghouse on Friday, and that Mr. Wolfe would be moving into the house, Faye had laughed. She'd thought it was a joke.

But Floy had known all along that it was no joke. Celia had been absolutely white, and every time she said "Mr. Wolfe," her nose twitched slightly. Her hands, grasping a cup of tea, had

103

trembled visibly, and once Floy had been certain there were tears in Celia's eyes.

Celia never cried. She was the smart one, the practical one, the glue that held this family together. If she fell apart, there would be nothing left.

"I wish I hadn't given him that puppy," Faye said sullenly.

"He doesn't deserve a puppy," Floy agreed.

This was all her fault, Floy was certain. Faye was impulsive, and she'd been taken with the idea of playing matchmaker from the first time she'd laid eyes on Mr. Wolfe, but she did *sometimes* listen to Floy, and if ever there was a time for reason . . .

"I hate him," Faye whispered.

Floy hated Benjamin Wolfe, too, but she felt more disappointment than anger. When she'd first seen him she thought he looked wicked, but once she got to know him he had seemed so *nice,* and she'd been so certain that he liked Celia. That he liked her and Faye.

In a way, he must have liked Celia a little. The way he looked at her and smiled at her, that couldn't be faked, could it? And they'd already heard the disgraceful stories, though Celia had assured them that most of what they heard was gossip and exaggeration.

Most.

The stories had been told in whispers, and all the twins had been able to catch were snatches of hushed conversations. They'd heard something about Celia's desk, and another snippet about scandalous kissing.

Perhaps when Celia was feeling better she could explain why a man would kiss a woman one minute, and toss her out of her home the next.

"I told Huff that he had to choose," Rosemary said indignantly. "He can have that . . . that animal for a client, or he can have me."

Celia looked up from her desk. Rosemary was the only friend who had offered support instead of accusations. The only one who didn't look at her as if she were sullied. Poor Rosemary. Her eyes were filling with tears, and she sniffled again as she turned to Celia.

"He said he had a legal obligation to that . . . that brute, and that it had nothing to do with us."

Rosemary looked as miserable as Celia felt, pale faced and bleary eyed, that full bottom lip red from being chewed so much. And while it was true that misery loved company, Celia couldn't bear to see her friend so upset. "He's right, you know," she said softly. "A lawyer does, on occasion, have to represent those who are undesirable."

Poor Rosemary bit one side of her lower lip. She leaned her head to one side and played with the tip of her ponytail, as she always did when she was distraught. "So you won't be mad if I forgive Huff? After a suitable waiting period, of course."

"Not at all," Celia said softly, though in her

heart she wasn't sure. She didn't ever want to see or hear anything that reminded her of Benjamin Wolfe, not ever again. And Huff, his name or his presence, would surely remind her. Still, there was an immediate rush of relief and healthy color on Rosemary's face, and Celia felt a moment's chagrin at her uncertainty. "You really like him, don't you?"

"Oh, Celia." Rosemary dropped tiredly into the wing-back chair by the window. The drapes were pulled tightly shut, as they had been since Celia had seen the first curious face there, just a few hours ago. "It's more than that. I think I love him."

There was a strange and powerful tightening in Celia's chest. A pain. Anger, jealousy, heartbreak. She'd begun to think herself in love with Benjamin Wolfe, but it had been nothing more than an overwhelming physical attraction, not love at all.

"I'm not here to talk about Huff," Rosemary said sensibly. "What on earth happened here today? Mama wouldn't tell me exactly what she saw, but I've heard the most outlandish rumors. And I know something happened. Mama was absolutely livid."

Rumors. Celia knew how they had a tendency to grow and change. She needed to know; she didn't want to know. The simple truth was bad enough. "What did you hear?"

Rosemary hesitated. She screwed up her face, laced her fingers, and leaned forward. "I just can't—"

"Tell me," Celia insisted.

Rosemary turned a bright shade of pink, took a deep breath, and punched her clasped hands into her lap. "I heard that you and Benjamin Wolfe were . . . right on the desk . . . that you were completely naked . . . and he was—Oh, I can't say it!"

"I was not naked," Celia insisted indignantly.

"They say that you and Benjamin Wolfe were . . ." Rosemary bit her lower lip again.

"Your lip is going to fall off if you don't stop that," Celia snapped.

"I don't blame you, I really don't," Rosemary said passionately. "Why, a couple of times"—she lowered her voice and glanced at the closed door—"Huff and I have almost done it. It's easy to get carried away, to forget and just . . . Oh, but Celia, what if you're pregnant?"

She had thought that this day could get no worse, but Rosemary proved her wrong. "People are saying that Ben and I were"—her face grew hot, and she knew she was blushing terribly—"intimate? On this desk? And we were caught?"

Wide eyed, Rosemary nodded. "Isn't it true?"

Celia dropped her head into her hands. "This is terrible."

She realized now that she'd been spiraling toward that transgression. The sensations, the haze that blocked out everything else, the careless impulsiveness. Would it have happened if they hadn't been interrupted? Most likely.

Was that what Ben had planned all along? Most likely.

"We were just . . . kissing," she lamented, unable to face this new turn of events. "And he touched me." She couldn't tell anyone but Rosemary this, and she needed to tell someone. "And he let my hair down, and unbuttoned my blouse. But nothing else happened. Nothing, I swear."

Rosemary looked relieved, and a little disappointed, too.

"What am I going to do?" Celia whispered.

"Did you wire John?"

Celia nodded her head. "I did."

"Surely he'll be here as soon as possible. By the end of the week, at the latest."

"I hope so."

With a start, Rosemary clapped a hand over her mouth. "What is he going to say when he hears?" she said through slightly spread fingers.

"About the mortgage? If he gets here soon enough, maybe he can help me raise the cash to—"

"Not about the house, Celia," Rosemary interrupted. "About you and Benjamin Wolfe."

Rosemary looked terrified, but Celia barely gave the concern a second thought. "I'll simply tell him the truth."

"And he'll believe you?"

"Of course he'll believe me." Celia felt an uncomfortable passing concern. John would believe her, wouldn't he? But of course, even the simple truth was scandalous.

"Well, what are you going to do about the house?" Rosemary asked, leaning back in her chair. "Did you talk to Mr. Anders at the bank?"

That question brought back another wave of unpleasant memories. "Cory said there's no way he can make me another loan, not with the outstanding loans I've already got and the problems with the store." She wondered, not for the first time, if his refusal was based purely on sound business reasoning.

Cory Anders was a well-respected man, but Celia went out of her way to avoid the man. Cory didn't look at her; he ogled her. With a simple shifting of his eyes, he managed to make her feel unclean. On the rare occasions she'd found herself alone with the banker, he'd found every opportunity to lay his small, clammy hands on her—patting her arm or her shoulder, occasionally taking her hand—and there was something oddly repulsive about those simple gestures.

Cory hadn't been at all receptive to her request for a loan. It had been humiliating, to beg for assistance, to subject herself to his barely disguised leer and sweaty, comforting hands, but she had endured. Cory hadn't looked her square in the eye, not once. As she'd explained the situation as calmly as possible, his gaze had dropped often to lock somewhere beneath her chin. Unlike Ben's warming stare, those probing eyes had turned Celia cold, had in fact left her feeling queasy. But she remained calm. She endured.

And after all that, Cory had flatly refused, in what could only be called smug satisfaction.

"What are you going to do now?"

"If I can't raise the money, then on Friday

morning Margaret and the girls will move into the boardinghouse. There are two connected rooms on the third floor." The rooms hadn't been used in a while, and they needed a thorough cleaning, but they would suffice. "They'll be quite comfortable there until I decide how to proceed."

Rosemary narrowed her eyes suspiciously. "And what about you?"

Celia placed her elbows on the desk and leaned forward. For the first time since Ben had walked away, she felt as if all her depleted strength was coming back. "If Benjamin Wolfe wants me out of this house, by God he's going to have to break down the door and drag me out."

Ben sat in the almost empty dining room of the boardinghouse, his back to the wall, an unappetizing plate before him. Cold creamed potatoes had been slopped into the center of the dented tin plate, and a burnt steak—possibly the smallest he'd ever seen—had been tossed atop the coagulating white mound.

Huff sat at the other end of the long plank table, and to Ben's eyes the meal on his plate appeared to be slightly more edible. Very slightly. Mrs. Hoyt had delivered both meals with her nose in the air, a tragic and put-upon sigh, and a bit of wrist action as she tossed the plates to the table.

"Look what you've done," Huff said quietly, pushing at his seared steak warily with a dull knife. "We'll likely starve before you finish this feud of yours."

To prove Huff wrong, Ben cut into the steak on his plate and popped a small, blackened piece into his mouth. "I've had worse," he lied as he chewed.

Huff pushed his plate away and leaned back in his chair. "I'm not very hungry, anyway. I had a big lunch. Rosemary brought it over for me, before all this hoopla started. Fried chicken, fresh baked bread, a big bowl of snap beans, these little teeny potatoes, boiled up and sprinkled with all kinds of seasoning . . ." Huff was lost in his own world, dreamy eyed as he held his thumb and forefinger together and envisioned the potatoes.

"Shut up," Ben grumbled as he lifted a forkful of cold potatoes. He hadn't eaten since breakfast.

"Fried pies," Huff continued. "Apple *and* peach, since she wasn't certain of my preference." He sighed. "And now she won't even speak to me."

Ben glanced up warily. Huff sounded strangely morose, almost maudlin. "I thought you had everything 'in hand,' " he said softly. "Rosemary Cranston is supposed to side with you in this."

"Well, she didn't," Huff snapped. "And damn it, I'm glad she didn't."

The steak was edible, but tasteless and tough as an old boot. Ben ate it anyway, primarily just to prove that he could. "You're glad," he mumbled after he swallowed a particularly gristly piece.

"What kind of a woman would turn her back on her best friend when a conscienceless bastard comes into town for the express purpose of ruining the poor girl?" Huff pulled a cigar from his vest pocket, fondled it briefly, and then returned it to its proper place. Mrs. Hoyt was always chasing Huff and his "stinking ceegars," as she called them, out of the dining room. Perhaps he was afraid that tonight the old bat would come after him with something more lethal than her sharp tongue.

"A conscienceless bastard like me?" Ben asked lightly.

Huff scowled—at his plate, at Ben, out the window. "A conscienceless bastard like us," he said reluctantly.

Ben had choked down all of the horrid meal he could stand. He pushed the plate away, leaned back in his chair, and grinned at his old friend. "Now, who's got who in hand? I can't believe that you're going to let some skirt make you question a strategy we've planned for years."

"*You've* planned for years," Huff clarified. "Don't make me a bigger part of this than I already am. And Rosemary's not just a skirt."

It wasn't easy, but Ben continued to smile. "Walter Huffman, Esquire, a man for whom ranching wasn't good enough, a man who claimed the city and a finer life called to him. A man who's apparently fallen for a small-town girl who would be lost and miserable in the big city."

"You don't know that," Huff said quickly. "She might be perfectly happy. . . ." His words trailed off into nothing. "What am I doing to myself? It doesn't matter. Rosemary blames me for this, you know. She'll likely never speak to me again.

Did you have to use her mother? Of all the women in town, Ben, why Bay Cranston?"

Ben grabbed what was left of his steak. "The mutt will be hungry," he grumbled as he left the dining room.

He couldn't stand to sit there for another minute and listen to Huff whine like a girl. This was his ally, the one person in Piggville he should be able to look at without seeing accusations and condemnation.

Hell, Rosemary Cranston was just a woman. Dallas was full of women prettier and more sophisticated than the enchanting Miss Cranston.

Celia Pigg was just a woman.

Ben threw the door to his room open, then slammed it shut. Most of the room was lost in darkness, shapes and shadows, but he could make his way to the end table and the lamp there by the hint of moonlight that shone through his curtained window.

Before he reached the table he was attacked. Something hit him low, with a growl and a vengeance, and there was a thorny sting just below his knee.

"What the hell?" He kicked at the invisible opponent, trying to loose it from his leg, and with a filthy curse reverberating in the room, Ben threw the remnants of his steak to the floor.

His eyes adjusted to the light, and he saw the little furball that was attached to his right leg.

"Let me go, you ugly mutt," Ben ordered.

Lucky held on.

With the puppy attached to his leg, Ben lit the

lamp on the bedside table and then sat on the edge of the bed. In the newly lit room, Lucky lifted his eyes to Ben and released his hold to drop gracefully to the floor.

"Don't pretend you didn't know it was me." Ben massaged his leg. There didn't appear to be any blood, but it hurt like hell. "You can see perfectly well in the dark, and you're a dog, for goodness' sake. You should be able to smell me by now."

The mutt could sure as hell smell the steak. Lucky turned away from the bed, sniffed his way to the burned meat, and began to nibble at the edges.

"Finish that up," Ben said as he fell back onto the bed, "and I'll take you for a walk. Again," he grumbled.

He threw his arm over his eyes, took a deep breath, and thought about how well his plan was proceeding. It didn't matter that the entire town hated him. He'd known that would happen, and he was well prepared to watch his back at all times.

Huff . . . now that was an unexpected development. Huff was his lawyer and his friend, and Ben had expected, through all the planning and waiting, to have his unconditional support.

Realistically, Huff didn't have to agree with everything. He just had to do his job.

Celia . . . well, of course she hated him. The plan wouldn't work any other way.

She was the enemy, and there was no way to carry this off without her learning who was behind her downfall. Purposely caught in a compromising position, ordered from her home, she knew well and good what was going on. Hell, he *wanted* her to know.

Celia was supposed to hate him; she was supposed to fight back. You couldn't have a war without both sides knowing exactly what, and who, they were up against. It wasn't that he regretted that particular part of the plan; it was just that before Celia had discovered that he was the enemy, she'd tasted and felt so damn good. . . .

There was a now-familiar stinging sensation at his calf, the feel of sharp little teeth penetrating twill and stabbing his flesh. He sat up, grabbed Lucky by the scruff of the neck, and gently forced the mutt to release his hold.

"Hellfire," he said as he carried Lucky toward the door. "Even my own dog hates me."

Chapter Eight

It had been a long week.

Ben stood in the street and looked with mounting satisfaction at his new home. The sun was shining, a light spring breeze danced gently across his face, and all was quiet, not only in the former Pigg home, but up and down the street.

Floy and Faye and that witch of a housekeeper had moved into the boardinghouse just that morning, carrying with them all they could manage. There were several trunks that no doubt contained household goods and clothing, as well as a few light pieces of furniture. A rocking chair, a stool, a small and intricately carved table, they hauled it all—with the grudging assistance of Jud Lucas from the Pigg General Store—to the third floor.

They'd ignored his brief presence, a passing on

the stairs. All except for one of the twins. She screwed up her pretty little face and stuck out her tongue. Like the cad he was, he'd returned the gesture.

During the move he hadn't seen Celia at all. Hadn't seen her, in fact, since he'd delivered his ultimatum four days ago.

Ben slipped the gold watch from his vest pocket. It was one o'clock, exactly. People began to congregate silently—a hushed crowd on the boardwalk, in the middle of the street—and everyone kept their distance.

Dropping the watch into his pocket, Ben strolled to the porch. It was time.

There wasn't any need to knock. This was his house, after all. He placed his hand on the doorknob, twisted firmly, and pushed. Nothing happened. Had he really expected this to be easy? Of course not. He smiled grimly at Celia's solution to her problem.

She'd locked him out.

"Celia," he said softly, knowing that she would be on the other side of the door and not upstairs or in the rear of the house. She'd been waiting and watching and she was right there. "Come on, Celia, let me in."

"I won't." Her voice was muffled by the door, but unyielding just the same.

"This is my house, sweetheart," he said sensibly. "Unlock the door."

"This is not your house, and it will never be your house, no matter what kinds of papers you have," she snapped. "You tricked me, and I don't

117

intend to simply walk away and let you have my home."

People were watching, waiting, and his initial amusement with her weak attempt at rebellion faded quickly. He stared at the door as if he could see through it, as if she could feel the heat of his gaze through the barrier that separated them. "Celia," he said through gritted teeth, "unlock the damn door."

This time he was answered with complete silence.

Ben spun around to find that those curious citizens of Piggville who had come from all corners of the town had congregated in the middle of the street to watch and listen. It was no longer just a few brave and meddlesome onlookers; it was damn near the entire town. There to one side was his only ally.

"Huff," he said, taking only a single step away from the front door, "bring me a sledgehammer."

"You're not serious," Huff answered, and it was then that Ben saw Rosemary Cranston, just behind Huff and with a stilling hand on his sleeve. "Wait her out. She can't stay in there forever—"

"No," Ben interrupted.

"You could break out a window," an unknown man suggested. He was rewarded with a punch on the arm from a woman, most likely his wife.

Ben didn't want to wait, and he didn't want to break out a window. This was his house, and he was going in through the front door.

"Sheriff, you can't allow this to happen," Margaret Harriman said. Ben hadn't seen her until that moment. She was all but hidden behind two very tall men who looked like brothers, but that voice—that crackling, bitter voice—was unmistakable. The twins were nowhere to be seen, but he felt certain they were watching from a window or a doorway or a cranny somewhere.

The sheriff stepped reluctantly forward. He was an older man, wearing spectacles and a bowler hat, and he didn't even wear a gun. It wasn't necessary in a quiet town like Piggville. Only the star on his vest identified him as the town's keeper of the law. He looked, Ben decided, more like a schoolteacher than a sheriff. "Mr. Wolfe," he began hesitantly.

"Show him the papers," Ben said before the peculiar lawman could go further, and Huff stepped forward with the proper documents in his hand.

When the sheriff was satisfied, Huff stepped back to his place in the crowd with Rosemary Cranston at his side. Ben stared for a moment at the locked door.

"Celia," he said reasonably, "don't make this any more difficult than it has to be. Let me come in."

"I won't," she said loudly.

"If you don't unlock this door, I'll break it down. Don't think I won't."

"Never." The single word that came from the opposite side of the door infuriated him.

"A sledgehammer," he muttered. It was a reasonable and effective solution. "Huff." Ben

119

turned to his oldest friend, but Huff was shaking his head slightly.

"I don't believe 'fetch and carry' is included in my obligations to you as a client." Rosemary Cranston gripped his arm even tighter, and Ben turned away.

He could get his own sledgehammer. Walk down to the well-stocked general store—*his* general store—and be back here in a matter of minutes.

But he didn't move from his place on the porch. The crowd was silent, and they waited.

He stepped back, raised his leg, and kicked at the locked door. His boot connected solidly, and there was a cracking sound that told him he'd done considerable damage. One more good kick and the door would swing in.

One more good kick, and that was exactly what happened. The door flew open, Celia squealed, and the crowd gasped as one. Celia stood in the entryway, her skirt in her hands as if she were poised to flee. Her face was unnaturally pale, her eyes incredibly wide.

Ben stepped over the threshold, and Celia took a tentative step back and away from him. When he was inside his new house, he turned to the waiting crowd, scowled with appropriate animosity, and slammed the broken door shut.

She'd couldn't believe he'd actually broken the door in, and in front of all those people. For a moment, Celia was unable to move. Ben stood there, in front of the closed door with a splintered lock, and stared at her with a weary and yet savage expression on his face.

She turned and ran.

Without thinking, she dashed up the stairs to her bedroom, the room that had always been her sanctuary in this house, slamming the door behind her and locking it quickly. Any moment, she expected Benjamin Wolfe to stop her, to catch up with her, kick in yet another door and literally carry her out of her home.

But when she heard his footsteps on the stairs, they were slow and heavy.

"You can't throw me out of my own house. I'm not leaving," she said, yelling at the locked door when she heard Ben's footsteps in the hallway.

"Fine," he said. His normally soothing voice was tinged with determination, and was irate enough to suit the expression he'd worn moments earlier as he'd broken in the front door. He sounded oddly tired, too. "Stay put, if it makes you happy."

"If you would drop dead this instant, that would make me happy," Celia retorted.

"Wouldn't be much fun for me, now, would it?"

He was so smug. The same carefree attitude that had once attracted her was suddenly infuriating. "You are a low and worthless man, the scum of the earth, a . . . a rapscallion."

"I may be all that and more, Celia, sweetheart, but at least I'm not a Pigg." There was a touch of humor in his voice.

"How juvenile," she countered calmly.

"How true."

She waited for Ben to step away from the door, but she didn't hear him so much as move. She'd never hated anyone in her entire life. Her mother had taught her to be forgiving of others' faults, to dismiss their shortcomings and turn the other cheek.

But she hated Benjamin Wolfe.

"I will not allow you to throw me out of my home like this," she said stridently. "There are legal proceedings I can pursue; I just haven't been able to get in touch with my attorney." In truth, she wasn't sure there was anything John could do. "If you think I'm going to walk out of here and give you my house, well, you're quite mistaken."

There was a moment of silence, and then a deep sigh. "Do you want me to bust down this door, drag you down the stairs, and toss you out of the door and onto the street? If that's what this is about, Celia, you've got a long wait coming. Trust me, sweetheart, you can stay here as long as you want, and no one will say a word . . . that they haven't already said, that is. Actually, I don't think anyone in Piggville will be surprised to learn that we're living together."

It was too much. Celia unlocked the door and threw it open. She couldn't argue effectively with a man she couldn't see, and she wouldn't hide in her room like a little girl. She wasn't a child—and hadn't been one for a very long time.

"How dare you?" she asked as she stepped into the hall and poked Ben in the chest. "If you were any kind of a gentleman, you would have taken care of those outrageous rumors by now."

"Evidently I'm not a—" Ben began.

"Hush," she said with another poke to his chest. "I'm not finished." She stared at his broad chest, unable at this point to look him in the eye. Goodness, she had forgotten how big he was. What had made her think she could stand up to him? "And you don't have to tell me that you're not a gentleman. I'm quite aware of that fact."

"I guess you are," he growled.

She was going to have to leave this house. She couldn't fight Ben—not physically and not legally. Her home, the house she'd been born and raised in, was his. She'd never in her life felt so helpless.

"I think you are a snake," she said softly. "A sidewinder. A scoundrel and a rake. You're as horrible as your father was, and worse."

It was the insult to his father that seemed to move him. Ben grabbed the hand that continued to jab at his heartless chest, and jerked it down. Celia was pulled forward, and almost against his nonexistent heart.

"My father was a good man, and this town— Hamilton Pigg in particular—killed him. They killed his soul first, took away everything he loved and believed in, and less than a year later he was dead." He spoke in a grating, low voice to the top of her head, his mouth too close, his hand at her wrist too tight. "As he lay dying, I swore I'd see justice done."

She wanted out—out of Ben's grasp, out of this house. If she'd been thinking straight, she would have moved into the boardinghouse that morning with Margaret and the twins. Perhaps there would have been some dignity in that decision. There was certainly none in her present situation.

"My father never would have run an innocent man out of town." It was becoming harder and harder to breathe, and the hallway was suddenly stiflingly hot.

"He did it," Ben assured her.

"You're wrong."

A strong finger beneath her chin forced her to look up into that face that had once seemed angelic, to lips she had kissed with such abandon.

"Make this easy on both of us," Ben rasped. "Get out of town."

"I won't," she assured him in a whisper. "I won't allow you to run me out of town."

His eyes were narrowed so that she couldn't tell exactly what he was thinking. He didn't seem to be angry any longer, but he still looked terribly tired. "Run, Celia," he said softly.

She didn't know exactly what he meant. Run out of town? Run from him, now, this instant? She couldn't. His grip at her wrist was tight, unyielding. And he was lowering his lips slowly, as if he actually meant to . . .

"I won't allow you to kiss me," she said without moving away. It was dreadfully mortifying, it was immoral, but there was still something within her that wanted Benjamin Wolfe's touch. She remembered his kisses with such warmth and wonder, even now.

"You won't," Ben whispered.

Celia licked her lips. She tried to understand why he'd gone to so much trouble just to sweep this house out from under her. Even though he was wrong about what had happened all those years ago, he was only defending his father. She tried to understand. She wanted to understand.

"It's not too late," she whispered.

"Not too late for what?"

"It's not too late for you to let it go." There was a moment of puzzlement on Ben's face, a wrinkling of the fine lines at the corners of his eyes, the beginnings of a frown, perhaps. "Forget what happened to your father. It was a long time ago, Ben. It has nothing to do with . . ." She almost said *us*, and then she remembered there was no *us*.

"Go back to the boardinghouse," she continued. "And give me a little time to pay off the mortgage. I can, you know. I simply need more time."

Ben didn't answer her, just stared down through narrowed eyes.

"Let it go," she whispered again, and she lifted her lips to his.

He did kiss her, briefly, almost reluctantly, a brush of his mouth against hers. "Tell me, Celia," he said huskily, and the anger was back. She could feel it—in the hand at her wrist and in the tightness in his chest—and she could see it in his eyes. "What are you willing to do to keep your house? Are you willing to whore yourself for four walls and a roof?"

With a shocked gasp Celia backed away, but Ben refused to release his grip at her wrist. "Release me," she said shakily.

Instead of doing as she asked, he gripped her chin and forced her to look up at his face again. "Get out of town," he ordered harshly, "and this is over."

"And if I don't?" she asked breathlessly.

"Then it's just begun."

He meant it, every word. It wasn't a threat; it was a dark promise.

"Celia, are you all right?" It was Rosemary's voice, anxious and bright.

"Get back here," Huff ordered. He was evidently right behind her, in the entryway downstairs. "I told you, this is Ben's house now, and you can't simply—"

"Oh, shut up, Huff," she said shortly.

"Rosemary!" he hissed.

Ben smiled, a cynical and sad smirk. "Trouble in paradise," he whispered.

"Celia?" Rosemary called again. Her footsteps echoed in the rooms below, hers and Huff's, and still neither Celia nor Ben moved.

"Let it go," Celia whispered, trying one more time.

"Get out of town," Ben answered just as softly.

Celia sighed. He wasn't going to give, not an inch. "I can't."

"Neither can I," Ben answered.

Celia pulled gently against the hand that gripped her wrist so tightly. "Then I guess this is it," she said, and all at once Ben released her.

Suddenly she was free, and she almost fell backward.

"I guess so," he said softly.

Celia descended the stairs sideways, all but backing down them with her eyes fastened on Ben. He was still dreadfully handsome, but he was also cruel and hard and determined to win. When she was halfway down and could no longer see him, she called out to Rosemary and turned to run down the stairs. She heard one more word from Ben as she hurried down to a waiting Rosemary.

War.

It was God's idea of a joke. Ben sank to the top step as the damaged front door closed behind Rosemary Cranston and Celia.

And what a joke it was. After all these years of planning, after all the sleepless nights and the sworn oaths to his long-dead father—he wanted Hamilton Pigg's daughter more than he'd ever wanted another woman. More than he'd known it was possible to want a woman.

But giving up now—simply because he had an incredible lust for Cecilia Pigg—would be an insult to the memory of his father and to everything he'd made himself in Ezekiel Wolfe's name.

"Nice job," Huff said bitterly, coming to stand at the foot of the stairs and lean against the banister. "Anyone in Piggville who didn't already hate your guts now wants to string you up. The sheriff practically had to arrest Margaret Harriman and half a dozen other people to keep them out of here after you busted the door in. Were bodyguards ever a part of your brilliant plan?"

"No."

"They should have been."

Huff reached into an inside pocket and withdrew a sheaf of folded papers. "The mortgage on the strip of property the boardinghouse and the general store sit on." He tossed the papers up the stairs, where they landed with a soft thud a few steps away from Ben. "It's yours. What are you going to do with it?"

Ben stared at the innocent-looking documents, but he didn't move to pick them up.

"She can't pay," Huff continued, his voice low and sardonic. "There's no Pigg fortune. You've humiliated Celia beyond my wildest expectations, just like you wanted. At the very best, she and the twins can eke a comfortable living from the boardinghouse and the general store, but only if you stop this now. Isn't that good enough for you?"

"No," Ben said quickly. "I promised my father, as he was dying, that I'd run every last Pigg out of this town. I swore on his last breath. . . ."

"You were just a kid," Huff said, and his bitterness had faded somewhat. "From what you've told me of the Reverend Ezekiel Wolfe, he was not a vindictive man. He wouldn't hold you to a promise like that. You've made your point, Ben; you've done enough."

It didn't feel like enough. It didn't feel like justice for all the suffering his father had endured.

Would it be enough when Celia and the twins rode out of Piggville with nothing?

Hell, he didn't know anymore.

"By the way," Huff added as he turned away from the staircase. "I had a letter from Martin."

"Your greedy associate at the law firm in Dallas."

Huff nodded and grunted as he withdrew a cigar. "Yes. It seems our friend John Watts is quite taken with the big city, and with a lovely lady friend of Martin's, as well. Even if he had received Celia's telegram, he might not have returned."

He should be happy that a part of his plan was going so well. He didn't want Celia to have anyone . . . he didn't want Celia to have anyone but him.

With an angry swipe, he reached down and picked up the mortgage papers on the boarding-house and general store.

Chapter Nine

"I won't go," Margaret said stubbornly as she read the telegram in her hand yet another time. "You girls need me here."

Celia placed a trembling hand on Margaret's arm. It was true, she did need Margaret. The housekeeper was her shoulder to cry on, her emotional support. How could she survive without Margaret?

But this news was so very important for Margaret's future, Celia knew she had no choice. "You can't turn your back on a gift like this. The truth of the matter is, I can't even guarantee that I'll be able to pay you next week, much less next year."

"I've never cared about my salary." Margaret sounded highly insulted, and she probably was. As long as Celia could remember, Margaret had always been more a part of the family than a housekeeper.

Celia glanced down at the telegram from Boston. "It's a considerable amount of money. Enough to live the rest of your life in relative comfort."

Margaret frowned thoughtfully, screwing up her face as she considered the situation. "We could use the money."

"It's yours—"

"It's ours," Margaret interrupted harshly. "And on that fact I'll accept no argument. Maybe we could use this money to give the general store a boost. All we need to do is find something people want, something that Zeke's doesn't carry. We can add a bakery; that's what we'll do."

"No." Celia shook her head. "I won't risk your inheritance."

"Our inheritance," Margaret insisted, even though there was not a drop of blood relation between the Harrimans and the Piggs. "From an uncle I saw once when I was two years old," she snapped. "This is very unexpected. I assumed Uncle George had passed years ago, and I never suspected that the ne'er-do-well had made something of himself. Goodness, he must've been ninety years old. If you won't allow me to use it for all of us, I won't go to Boston at all."

"If you don't claim the inheritance, it will go to a charity."

"I'm sure Uncle George chose a worthy cause."

Celia relented. She could never defeat Margaret in a war of wills, and in fact they could use the money. The boardinghouse generated very little income, and the general store was losing money, since their competition had taken over. Perhaps if her reputation hadn't been ruined, a few faithful friends other than Rosemary would have continued to shop there, but as it was, what cash she had was used to pay salaries, and even that reserve was all but depleted.

"The telegram advises you to plan to stay in Boston for as long as two months."

"I'm sure I'll be able to speed things along. I'll be home within a month, I promise."

A lot had happened in the past month. What was to come? Nothing good, that was for certain.

"When I get back we'll turn things around," Margaret said with enthusiasm. "We'll add a bakery to the general store and fix up the boardinghouse and see if we can't attract a few new residents. And when we're back on our feet we'll send that Benjamin Wolfe packing the way we sent his daddy packing."

"All right," Celia said. "When you're home we'll use the money however you want." She knew good and well that if something didn't happen soon the general store would be closed down by the time Margaret returned, but she didn't mention that fact. At least Margaret wouldn't be completely destitute when this war with Benjamin Wolfe was over.

They'd been living in the boardinghouse for three days, and in that time Celia had sent two more telegrams to John, each one more desperate than the last. She'd known all along that he would love Dallas, that he would love working in a big law firm and living in the city.

But she'd never suspected that he would desert her like this. And now, even though she was encouraging Margaret to go to Boston—even though she knew it was *necessary* that Margaret go to Boston—she felt as though she were being abandoned again.

"We'll be all right," she said soothingly. "These rooms are quite comfortable." It was a lie, of course, and Margaret surely knew it. The mattresses were thin, there were a number of bugs inhabiting their rooms, and Frances Hoyt was a terrible cook. The twins were miserable and angry.

And it was all Ben Wolfe's fault.

Celia helped Margaret pack, and gently talked her through the three uncertain moments when she changed her mind. At those times, Margaret was confident that she was needed here in Piggville more than the money her uncle had left her was needed.

In the afternoon, Celia walked with Margaret to the train station. The short excursion was terrible, as her own doubts assaulted her, but she continued to smile. Most of the people they passed, longtime friends and acquaintances, ignored her. There were a few—a very few—who smiled uncomfortably and nodded briefly before turning away. She spotted Cory Anders watching her progress from the bank's front window, and he didn't look uncomfortable at all. In fact, he looked incredibly snobbish and satisfied.

She didn't see Benjamin Wolfe anywhere, and that was good. At this moment, she could likely kill the man with her bare hands.

Heaven help her, when it came time for the passengers to board, Celia almost grabbed Margaret and held her there on the platform so she couldn't leave.

She did no such thing, of course, but smiled and assured Margaret that all would be well until she returned. Margaret actually tried to leave the train moments before it left the depot, changing her mind once again, and Celia smiled warmly as she shooed Margaret back.

And as Celia watched the train pull away, she felt so alone—so *lonely*—that she almost cried.

Ben looked over the pitiful selection of cigars. He couldn't complain. His instructions to Huff had been simple. Open a general store and run the Pigg general store out of business. If he'd specifically wanted a decent selection of cigars, he should have mentioned it.

Huff had a supply of the best in his office drawer, but the lawyer wasn't easy to get along with these days. He was crotchety and bitter and argumentative. Ben grabbed a few of the cigars. Perhaps they weren't premium, but at least they didn't come with a lecture.

As he passed the counter he nodded to the clerk. Toby Willett, the young man Huff had hired to put this place together and run it for the duration, was doing a fine job. The place was always busy.

He saw Celia as soon as he stepped from the store to the boardwalk. Foolish woman, she was standing in the middle of the street as if she were dazed, staring transfixed at a point above his head. After checking the street in both directions for wagons or horses, he glanced up, curious as to what held Celia's attention so fully.

All he saw was the sign Toby had painted. ZEKE'S, in tall letters.

Celia's gaze slowly dropped, and she stared at him with that same dazed expression. "Zeke's," she said softly, and she cocked her head. "This is . . . this is *your* business, isn't it? Named for your father."

Ben smiled, brightly he hoped, and stepped down into the street. There was a wagon approaching, and though it moved slowly he had no doubt that Celia was completely unaware of its advance. "Yes, as it so happens . . ." He reached out to take her arm and she jerked away, took a wide path around him, and stepped onto the boardwalk.

She didn't look good. Celia needed a day or two in the sun, a smile on her face, a bright calico dress instead of the drab gray silk she wore. She needed to laugh.

Ben shook the foolish thoughts from his head as Celia stepped away from him.

In the middle of the boardwalk, she stopped. "That's why you knew about the five-cent bag of sugar," she said as she came to accept that this was another part of his scheme. With a defiant and brave whirl she faced him. "I let you romance every drop of good sense right out of my head. The truth was there all along—the clues, the hints, the warnings from those who kept their heads—and I ignored it all. I suppose I got what I deserved."

He couldn't allow Celia to attack his emotions this way. He couldn't feel guilt, or regret, or sympathy . . . and he sure as hell couldn't look at her and want to undo everything he'd planned so carefully. He couldn't, he *wouldn't*, want to take care of her.

Celia didn't wait around for a response, and that was good. For the first time in his life, Ben was hopelessly tongue-tied.

"What are we going to do?" Floy hissed. Hidden just to the side of the boardinghouse, she and Faye watched Benjamin Wolfe cross the street.

"I haven't decided," Faye whispered.

There was a terribly diabolical look on her twin's face, a feral gleam in Faye's blue eyes.

Floy chewed at her bottom lip. She hated Benjamin Wolfe as much as Faye did. He'd taken away their home, so they had to move into that dreadful boardinghouse, and worse than that he'd made Celia miserable. It wasn't right, not at all.

But she worried about Faye, at times.

"We won't actually hurt him, will we?"

Faye shot her a cutting glance. "And why not?"

"I don't want to go to jail," Floy said sensibly. "It would upset Celia terribly, and she doesn't need any more worry."

"All right," Faye whispered, turning her eyes back to Benjamin Wolfe. "We'll try not to do him any actual physical harm, but we have to hurt him somehow."

"How?"

The subject of their conversation slipped into the office of that accomplice, Walter Huffman.

"We find out what's important to him, and we take it away," Faye said softly. "I just don't know what's important to a man like that."

"Money?" Floy offered.

"Perhaps."

"Those fancy clothes of his?"

Faye smiled. "He does dress nicely, doesn't he?"

They watched the closed door of the lawyer's office. "I don't know," Floy whispered. "I don't think Benjamin Wolfe cares about anything."

Faye flattened herself against the wall and closed her eyes tight. She was thinking hard. "Everyone has a weakness," she whispered. "Everyone cares about something."

Just a few days ago, Floy had been certain that Benjamin Wolfe cared about Celia, that maybe he even cared about all of them.

But then, she was just a naive kid, as Faye liked to remind her. Faye always thought she was smarter, and just expected Floy to play along.

Being the youngest—even by a mere fourteen minutes—had its disadvantages.

The final solution to all his problems would be arriving by rail in a matter of days. Celia was stubborn and willful, but there were some indignities even she wouldn't tolerate.

Ben closed the newly repaired door behind him, and stepped into the quiet house. *His* quiet house. Right now it was too quiet. His footsteps echoed as he walked through the rooms, every hollow ring reminding him that he didn't belong here.

Before he left town, he'd burn the damn place down.

As always, he found himself in Celia's office, in her leather chair. This was the one room in the house where he felt he belonged—perhaps because it looked and felt like a man's room—perhaps because he had spent time here with Celia.

A clock ticked. The wind rattled a loose windowsill. Outside, a creaking wagon passed by. The house was so quiet he could hear every turn of the wheel.

"Dammit," he muttered, and he sprang from the chair.

Well, he did his best to spring, but something tried to hold him back, so that the best he could manage was a slow motion up and forward.

He turned to look down at the leather chair. It glistened, and globs of an unnaturally thick substance caught the rays of light that slanted through the window. He reached out his hand, suspecting what he would find, and traced a finger slowly across the seat of the chair. He brought it to his lips without hesitation.

Honey. There was a coating of it on the seat of the leather chair, and on his backside as well. On his jacket and his trousers, on his hands as he brushed them against his sticky suit of clothes.

His first thought was *Celia*, but he dismissed that notion quickly. This was not her style. It was much too juvenile. . . .

He smiled. The twins.

Margaret had been gone two days, and in that time he'd seen the girls spying on him from a distance at least a dozen times. They were hard to miss, with all that blond hair and the prerequisite pink dresses. They whispered and stared and slipped around corners. This was their idea of revenge? Honey in his chair?

He could almost see them, sneaking in through a window, smearing the honey on this chair . . . and what else? His smile faded. He'd have to check every chair in the house, his bed, and what else?

The immediate concern was getting out of the sticky clothes.

He even checked the steps as he climbed to the second floor. Would they go so far as to set traps for him? Floy, no. Faye, probably.

He managed to reach his room—the one that had been Celia's—without incident. Nothing here had changed. It remained a woman's room, pale blues and white lace. An oil painting of a vase of roses against one wall. He kept telling himself that one day he would rip it all out, and turn this into a man's room. And then he reminded himself that he wouldn't be here much longer.

Ben stripped off the suit, the jacket and the

ruined trousers, and opened the wardrobe where his suits hung.

Or what remained of them. Half a dozen expensive suits, a necessary expense to carry out his charade, had been cut to ribbons. Jackets, trousers, starched shirts . . . even his silk ties. Ruined.

He could send Celia a bill for the ruined clothing. That thought made him smile. She didn't have the money, so it might speed things along. The sooner she got out of town, the better.

In the meantime, he could borrow a few things from Huff, and pick up some clothing at the general store. He'd missed the comfort of worn Levi's and cotton shirts, but he sure as hell wouldn't miss the ties and restrictive jackets.

He stepped back into the sticky trousers—since they were all he had left—and tossed the honey-stained jacket into the wardrobe with the remainder of his ruined clothes. He tossed the fancy boots aside, and grabbed his Justins from under the bed.

At least the twins knew how to fight back. Celia sure as hell didn't.

Perhaps it was time Celia met the real Benjamin Wolfe. With a smile on his face, he stepped into one boot. He felt the sickening squish, and closed his eyes. Not the Justins. He could live without the suits, but damn it, you didn't mess with a man's boots.

Celia was wiping down the table with a damp cloth, brushing away the crumbs that were left from dinner, when he came storming through the front door, across the main room, and into the dining room like he owned the place. How dare he?

The normally well-dressed Benjamin Wolfe was more than a little disheveled. His hair was lightly mussed, as if he'd combed back the wavy strands with his fingers, and he was wearing wrinkled trousers and a shirt that wasn't even buttoned to the neck. It fell open, exposing a light dusting of pale chest hair.

In a moment she noticed that one foot was bare, the other was covered with only a sock, and he was waving a pair of boots at her.

"Do you have any idea what these cost?"

Celia stopped what she was doing and stared pointedly at the boots. It was easier than looking at his face. "I don't have the vaguest idea. Should I?"

He didn't answer, but turned one of the boots upside down and waited while he continued to stare at her. A muscle high in his cheek twitched, just once. A strand of his usually perfect blond hair had fallen over his forehead, and he didn't seem to notice.

Finally, she saw what Ben had obviously been waiting for. At first she thought it was syrup, but it was golden when the light hit it, and thicker than molasses would be, so it had to be honey. The sweet mess rolled from within the polished boot and fell, first in a wide glob, and then in a thin stream, to the floor.

141

"You're making a mess on the floor," she chastised.

"You should see my house," he said in a low voice.

It galled her to hear him call it *his* house, even though it was, legally, the truth. "How you keep your house is none of my concern. Hire a housekeeper, if you're unable to handle the chores yourself." This time she did look him square in the eyes. She'd heard, through Margaret, that he'd tried and failed to find even one woman in Piggville who was willing to work for him.

"The twins did this," he accused, ignoring her suggestion. "They smeared honey on every seat in the house, cut up my suits, and did this to my boots." He shook a boot, the one that still emitted a thin stream of honey, in her direction.

"They wouldn't," Celia said firmly, though she felt a horrible, sickening churning in her stomach. Of course they would. "Why on earth would they—"

"Ask them," Ben seethed. "They've been watching from the second-floor landing since I walked through the door."

Evidently they had been listening, because right on cue the twins descended the staircase, casually, calmly, as if they didn't have a care in the world. That was when Celia knew her sisters were guilty.

"What's *he* doing here?" Faye asked haughtily. "And, my goodness, Mr. Wolfe, what's that all over the back of your trousers?"

Floy hung back, hiding behind her sister as she often did.

"Were you girls in Mr. Wolfe's house?" Celia asked calmly.

"Why, whyever would we go into Mr. Wolfe's house?" Faye asked innocently.

The girls stopped on the staircase, halfway down. Celia didn't know if they were afraid to get any closer to Ben, or if they simply enjoyed looking down while they spoke.

"Floy?" Celia said softly, knowing that Faye would never tell her what she wanted to know.

Faye continued to look confident until Floy opened her mouth. "Do we have to talk about this now?"

Faye spun on her twin. "Shut *up*," she hissed.

Floy looked pointedly at her feet.

"Floy?" Celia prodded gently.

"He deserved it," Floy said softly, and Faye groaned. "And worse, after what he did."

Inwardly, Celia groaned as despairingly as Faye. She would have to make reparations, and she had so little right now. There was nothing to spare. "You girls go to your room, and stay there until I come up, do you hear me?"

Without a response, they turned and ran to the third floor. Before they'd reached the second-floor landing, Faye was denouncing her twin sister loudly.

Ben seemed somewhat mollified by the admission of guilt. He'd righted his ruined boot, so that no more honey dripped to the floor, and there was something almost serene about the expression on his face.

"I'll pay you for the damage, of course," she said firmly. "I can't pay right away—"

"Forget it," he interrupted.

Forget it. Then why was he here? Had he rushed here in a burst of anger and then changed his mind? It seemed unlike Benjamin Wolfe. Once he made up his mind, she doubted he ever changed it.

"Well, you have my apology." She couldn't believe she was actually apologizing to the man who had ruined her reputation and her business and stolen her house out from under her, but it seemed the right thing to do, given the circumstances.

Without a word, Ben turned and walked toward the front door. He was oddly disheveled, for Benjamin Wolfe, with one foot bare and one in only a sock, and she could see the streaks of honey on his backside. His ruined boots swung, one in each hand, at his side.

She didn't mean to laugh, not really, and it was barely audible. He couldn't possibly have heard her.

But at the door he stopped. He stood there for a moment, motionless, perhaps thoughtful, before he turned to her and crossed the room again.

"I almost forgot," he said calmly, dropping the boots to the floor and reaching into his shirt pocket for a folded scrap of paper.

She didn't believe it. Benjamin Wolfe wouldn't forget anything.

"Your father mortgaged this property with a Dallas bank, and you've missed a couple of payments."

"Well, I . . ." Celia stammered.

"I bought the mortgage. If you can't pay, I'll just claim the property for myself." He tried to toss the paper at her, but it attached itself in two places to his sticky fingers. As he tried to dislodge it the sheets of paper fluttered like the wings of a wounded bird.

"You're kicking me out . . . again?"

He seemed not at all moved by her plight as he peeled the document from his hand. "Of course not," he said with a smile that revealed not a hint of good humor. Cold and calculating, it was the smile of a snake. "You and your sisters can stay here as long as you like. You can even work here, if it suits you."

Ben's suggestion shocked her out of her bewildered haze. "Are you suggesting that I work for you?" She'd rather starve, she'd rather live in the street . . . she'd rather leave town. Of course that was exactly what he wanted.

He shrugged his shoulders and turned away from her again, this time leaving the damning paper on the dining room table she'd just cleaned, and his ruined boots on the floor.

Chapter Ten

The noise that drifted to the third floor was a raucous, grating torture. Laughter, shouts, the crash of broken glass.

In a mere eight days, Ben Wolfe had managed to completely ruin a perfectly respectable business. He'd had this planned all along, she was certain, otherwise things wouldn't have fallen together so neatly, so easily.

With a groan, Celia pulled her pillow over her face, trying to drown out the sounds, as well as the moonlight that poured through her window, but she failed on both counts. The moon was full tonight, round and large and bright, and the noise . . . the hullabaloo refused to abate.

How could he? How could he turn her boardinghouse—*his* boardinghouse—into a saloon? Piggville already had a saloon, a run-down, cheerless place called the Smoke House. Celia had only glimpsed it through the doors, of course, but the Smoke House was a dirty little place with a few rickety chairs and a bar that consisted of a couple of barrels and a long plank. No self-respecting gentleman frequented the Smoke House.

This new saloon promised to be very different. There were gaming tables, a fancy polished bar, and mirrors, all arriving by rail within the past week. More proof that this was a diabolical plan and not a whim. At one end of the long room, where there had once been a comfortable arrangement of chairs and delicate tables, there was now a raised stage. At the moment, there was a woman attempting to sing, probably from that very stage.

The catcalls were drowning out her pathetic attempts at a screeching ballad.

Celia sat up and tossed her pillow across the room, where it bashed quietly and ineffectively against the door. It certainly wasn't doing any good over her ears. Then she sat up and threw her legs over the side of the bed. For two cents she'd go downstairs and give Benjamin Wolfe a piece of her mind.

Thunderous applause shook the once peaceful boarding house. There was the shattering of glass again, a sharp and repeated sound that assured Celia the patrons were throwing their glasses against the wall. The twins had school tomorrow, for goodness' sake. How were they supposed to get any rest with this racket going on?

In a matter of minutes, and without bothering to light the lamp, Celia was dressed in her plainest dress—a high-necked nut-brown monstrosity that even Margaret declared ugly—and she'd twisted her braid up and secured it with several pins. Plain. It suited Celia's purpose, for the moment. If there were an ax handy, she'd carry it downstairs with her and see what kind of damage she could do to all those new green-felt tables and that fancy bar.

She'd never been a supporter of the temperance movement, but at this particular moment she could easily change her mind.

The twins' room adjoined hers, and she opened the connecting door easily, just in case they were asleep. Sure enough, they were slumbering soundly in their narrow beds, innocent in sleep as they never were while awake.

This was for them. Everything she did, she did for Floy and Faye. She'd been a mother to them for most of their lives, both mother and father for the past year. There was probably some way to get into their trust, their inheritance, but she wouldn't do that. That money was their future, a promise that they would never have to do anything they didn't want to. They wouldn't be burdened with a loveless marriage or the daily grind of making their way.

If Benjamin Wolfe tried to take that from them, she would kill him.

Celia closed the door as softly as she'd opened it. The girls didn't stir.

In the hallway, she closed her eyes and took a

deep breath. Facing Ben had never been easy, but in the past week it had become almost impossible.

Oh, no. The supposed singer was at it again, caterwauling. It was, of course, much worse here in the hallway than it had been in her room. Louder, more immediate, more irritating.

Celia walked slowly and silently down to the second floor. She'd simply ask Ben what time he was going to close, and perhaps request that he try to keep the noise down. Surely she and the twins weren't the only ones in the building trying to sleep.

She descended the final set of stairs very slowly. She'd never seen this room so brightly lit, so filled with people. Men from town and outlying ranches, strangers and old acquaintances, all were gathered together in this smoky room. They played cards and dice, and gathered around the stage to watch a woman—a slender redhead Celia had never seen before—dance and sing.

No wonder they screamed like animals. The woman was half-naked.

She saw Ben right away, as he leaned against the bar and watched the entertainer with a half smile on his face. He was surrounded by men, but he was the one she saw. Her ability to spot him in a crowd was uncanny, a curse, a horrid and unwanted affliction.

Perhaps he suffered from the same curse, because his eyes turned to her before anyone else noticed her presence there on the stairs. His easy smile faded away.

As she watched him, Celia's strength came flooding back. With renewed determination, she made her way through the thick crowd to the bar. It was only when she reached Ben that she noticed the man behind the bar.

The bartender was old Jud Lucas, a man who had worked for her until just a few days ago, when Ben had closed the Pigg General Store for good. He blushed as she caught his eye, and quickly looked away. She shouldn't be surprised or dismayed to see him here. Jud needed a job, Ophelia needed someone to take care of her, and there was nothing she could do to help.

"Celia, sweetheart," Ben said as she approached. His smile was back, wide and artificial. There was no amusement in his eyes. "Can I buy you a drink?"

The crowd parted, making way for her to stalk straight to Ben. "No, you may not," she said primly.

He looked different tonight. His fine suits had been destroyed, and he was given now to denim and leather, like any ordinary cowboy. Benjamin Wolfe was anything but ordinary. In the denims it seemed his legs were incredibly long and fluid. Every move, every shift of his hips, made her mouth dry.

She ignored the inexplicable reaction. "When are you going to close?" she asked as she reached him. The crowd around Ben broke up and moved away, leaving them somewhat alone.

"Close?" he asked, a blank expression on his face.

"You know," Celia said sharply. "Send people home. Turn out the lights. Close the doors and tell your many patrons good night."

"Oh." Ben scratched his head, like a moron. "I haven't really given it any thought, and this is our first night open for business. Hell, things are going so well we might not close at all."

The music stopped, and Ben joined in the enthusiastic applause.

"Thank goodness that's over," Celia said as the redhead left the stage.

"You don't like Ginger's singing?" Ben asked, as if he couldn't believe such a thing.

"It's horrendous."

"Well, Ginger's not really a singer, by trade."

"I'm shocked," Celia said, her anger growing with every passing second.

Ben leaned down and placed his mouth close to her ear. "Maybe you'd like to take her place. Put on a pretty little outfit and get up on that stage and sing your heart out. Wouldn't you be something in one of Ginger's getups." His eyes strayed. "I told you I'd give you a job."

Celia resisted the urge to slap him, simply because she didn't want to make a scene. He'd love that, drawing her into a saloon brawl. "No, thank you."

Ben leaned back against the bar, casual, seemingly content. "That's too bad. I happen to know, Celia, sweetheart, that this is the only place in town where you're likely to get a job."

"Don't call me—"

"Celia, sweetheart?" He smiled down at her,

and stared at her through narrowed eyes. "Why not?"

"Because I'm not, nor have I ever been, nor do I ever intend to be, your sweetheart." She tried to remain calm.

"But we came so close." He reached out and brushed a finger against her chin.

With an angry jerk she pulled away from that indolent finger. She couldn't argue with him. No matter what she said, she got angrier and angrier, while nothing seemed to affect him. Without offering a response, Celia spun on her heel to return to her room. What ever made her think she could reason with a man like Benjamin Wolfe?

He stopped her with a quick hand that snaked out and grabbed her arm. Before she knew what was happening, she was looking up into his face again, and he'd pulled her almost entirely against him. He smelled of smoke and whiskey and warmth, and even though she hated Ben, she liked this closeness. It hadn't taken many moments like this before she'd become accustomed to having this man in her life. Of course, that had been before he'd shown his true self.

"If you need anything, I'll be in my old room," he whispered. "I believe it's directly beneath yours."

"What do you mean? You moved out of my . . . out of your house?" The thought of living under the same roof with Ben was too much to handle.

He nodded. "That house is just too big for one man, and I had come to like my room here.

Lucky seems to like it better, and now that I own the whole building he has the run of the place."

It was all temporary. All the anxiety and the heartache. She might be able to move back into her home after all. "What about the house? Do you think—"

Before she could inquire into making arrangements to move back into the house, he interrupted. "I'm turning it into the Piggville Gentlemen's Social Club."

"The . . . the what?" she asked softly.

"The Piggville Gentlemen's Social Club," he said again. "That's the real reason Ginger is here. Why, she came all the way from Denver to help me get this place going. The other girls will arrive at the end of the week."

"The other girls?"

It took her a moment, but when she realized exactly what kind of "club" Ben was turning her home into, everything in the world faded but for his face and the hand on her arm.

"You wouldn't," she breathed.

"I did," he whispered back.

It was a good thing he held her up, because otherwise she would have slumped to the floor. Her home, the house she'd been born and raised in, was going to be transformed—in the hands of Benjamin Wolfe—into a bordello.

She gathered her strength quickly and shook off his hand. "You are a vile, contemptible excuse for a man," she whispered. The only response was a faint flickering deep in his eyes, a hardening of his lips. "You derive such pleasure from

153

tearing my life apart. Benjamin Wolfe, you are a petty little man, and this is a petty little war." She took another step back. "Tomorrow morning my sisters and I will move out of your boarding-house."

"Stay as long as you want, Celia, sweet—"

"Don't," she whispered as she spun on her heel. "Please, don't."

People moved out of her way as she hurried to the stairs, but they seemed to take no real notice of her. She was invisible, insignificant . . . nothing.

Tears blurred her vision as she hurried up the stairs, as she rushed to the sanctuary of her tiny, miserable room. She almost panicked when she heard the voice behind her, the anxious voice softly calling her name . . . but as she recognized that voice as belonging to Cory Anders, and not Benjamin Wolfe, she stopped. There on the first step of the final flight of stairs, she waited.

"Are you all right?" Cory asked anxiously, and as he reached her he took her hand.

It was a ridiculous question, given the circumstances. At least here, in the dimly lit hallway, he wouldn't be able to see her red and tear-filled eyes.

"I'm as well as can be expected," she said, and her voice trembled only a touch. She tried gently to pull her hand away, but he held it tight.

He patted the top of the hand he held, stroked it. "Celia. I'm so sorry. My decision not to make you that loan was a hasty one, and in my haste I didn't take personal considerations into account."

Celia felt a spark of hope, a spark that made her tears dry and her heart beat fast. "Do you think you might be able to make me a loan now?"

It was a ridiculous question. She was in a far worse financial situation today than she had been when she'd first asked for the loan.

"Ahhh." Cory stood before Celia, and since she stood on the bottom step they were about the same height. "I can't possibly risk the bank's money . . ."

Her hopes died.

". . . but I might be able to make you a personal loan." As he finished the sentence, he took her other hand and leaned close. It was then that she smelled the whiskey. The sharp smell, more intense than the trace that had clung to Ben, stung her eyes and her nose. "You might not even have to pay it back."

"Cory Anders!" Celia hissed. "You're drunk." She tried to wrest her hands free, but he held on with his clammy hands. "Let me go this instant!"

"No," he muttered, and with a quick twist he held both her wrists in one hand. "I won't. I can't."

Celia jerked her hands down, but Cory held fast. With his free hand he touched her breast, softly and then with a cruel twist. She tried to draw away from him, back . . . into herself . . . but he wouldn't let her move.

"I've always wanted to do this," he said softly, and his whiskey breath washed over her face.

"Every time you came into the bank, in one of those homely dresses just like this one, all I could see were these." He touched her again, his hand moving from one breast to the other.

"Stop it." Celia pushed against Cory with all her strength, and it worked. He fell back and away from her. He blocked the only way down, but she had a clear path to the third floor.

She turned to run, but took only one step before he grabbed her skirt and she fell, face first, onto the steps. And then he was on top of her, pressing her chest into the hard, bare wood.

Celia screamed. It was a weak effort, since Cory had knocked the breath out of her when he'd forced her down, and she knew no one would hear her over the noise downstairs. Still, the cry startled Cory and he grabbed her hair, lifted her head slightly, and banged her head against a step.

"Quiet," he whispered hoarsely as he slammed her head down again.

The pain in her head was intense, and for a moment—for a horrible moment—Celia thought she would pass out. She didn't want to pass out, didn't want to be helpless with Cory on top of her like this. Still, everything threatened to fade away.

"You lifted your skirts for that damn Wolfe, and all I want to do is touch you. Calm down, Celia."

Calm down. The sound went first, fading away into nothing, and then the light faded until all was gray. Her head was numb, her arms, and then her legs, until she could hardly feel anything at all. There was a single throb of her battered skull, and Cory's anxious hands traveled up her sides . . . and then everything went black.

Ben watched the empty stairs, and the certainty that something was wrong grew until the hairs on the back of his neck stood up.

After Celia had rushed away, Ginger had claimed his attention for a moment. Usually it was an easy task for the beautiful woman, but Ben's thoughts kept drifting back to Celia and he finally sent Ginger on her way to entertain his customers.

Something wasn't right. It was a gut feeling, instinct, the kind of nagging certainty he couldn't ignore.

With his eyes on the stairs, Ben pushed away from the bar. It wouldn't hurt to walk up to the third floor, just to make sure that all was quiet and as it should be.

He was halfway up the stairs when he heard the whispering voice. "You lifted your skirts for that damn Wolfe, and all I want to do is touch you," and from there he ran.

Cory Anders, that slimy banker, was lying on top of a very still Celia, and he had his hands all over her.

Ben didn't think, didn't say a word, but lifted Anders by the back of his jacket, spun him around, and delivered a punch that would send most men reeling.

It knocked Anders out cold.

He dragged the unconscious man to the stairs, and tossed him down. The bastard bounced and rolled, knocking against the railing several times as he fell. When Anders's body landed in the saloon, all activity came to a stop.

"We're closed!" Ben shouted. "Everybody out!"

The patrons scrambled toward the doors, Anders groaned loudly, and Ben returned to Celia. If she was dead . . . if that bastard had killed her . . . He rolled her gently onto her back, and touched the trickle of blood that ran down from her temple and into her hair.

"Celia, sweet—Celia?" he called softly. He placed his fingers across her lips, sighed with relief when her warm breath touched his skin. If Anders wasn't already dead, he might not have to kill him after all. Oh, he'd beat the meanness out of the banker, and then he'd ruin him, bankrupt him and run him out of town and maybe beat him one last time just for fun.

Celia gasped, took a deep breath, and parted her lips.

"That's right," he said. "Now open your eyes."

She wouldn't, or couldn't.

"Ben?" she whispered shakily. "Is that you?"

He closed his eyes, in relief that washed over him as surely and strongly as any hate he'd ever felt for Hamilton Pigg. "Yes. It's me."

"My head hurts." She tried to lift a hand to her head, but couldn't quite manage it.

"I know," he whispered. "Come on." He slipped his arms under her, lifted her, and all at once she tensed.

158

"Cory . . ."

"Don't you worry about Cory Anders," Ben said soothingly. "I took care of him."

He carried Celia to his room, opened the door, and waited for the protest that was sure to come. She said nothing until he placed her in his bed.

"Ben?" she whispered.

"Yes?" he leaned over her, waited for the words to cross her lips. *Thank you*, perhaps, or a prim and proper *I shouldn't be here*. He was wrong.

"This is all your fault."

Ben dampened a cloth at the washbasin and sat on the side of the bed to clean the blood and the quickly swelling knot at Celia's temple. All his fault. He could argue with her, but he'd heard Cory's words. "You lifted your skirt for that damn Wolfe. . . ."

"You're right, of course," he whispered.

"Of course," she breathed.

Celia didn't say a word as he cleaned her wounds and then washed her face in cool water. He thought, for a moment, that she had passed out again. She was perfectly still, not responding at all to the cool cloth he passed across her face. But then she began to speak almost clearly.

"Do you think my clothes are homely?"

Ben looked at the brown dress she wore, a spinster's garment if ever he'd seen one. "Are we talking about this particular dress?"

"Not necessarily."

She was out of it, half-delirious, and probably wouldn't remember anything of this conversation in the morning. And if she did, he could always tell her she was mistaken.

"Some of the clothes you wear are downright hideous. Dark and heavy and . . . and made for old women." He wiped her forehead gently. "But it doesn't seem to make a damn bit of difference what you wear. You're still the most beautiful woman in town."

She forced one eye open. "Am I really?"

"Really."

Celia covered both eyes with her hands. "I must be hallucinating. You can't possibly be pleasant to me, or to anyone else, I imagine." She peeked between two slightly spread fingers. "Yes, this is definitely a hallucination."

"If you say so."

"I feel horrid, my head is spinning, and all I want to do is go to sleep."

"Then go to sleep," Ben whispered.

"I can't," she responded, and then she did.

Her breathing was even, her color was good, and her heartbeat was steady. She was going to be just fine. In all his years, Ben couldn't remember ever feeling relief so strongly that it washed over him tangibly. His heartbeat was affected, the air in his lungs, the strength in his legs.

When Celia had been sleeping for a few minutes, Ben slipped her shoes off. He hadn't realized, until he held them in his hands, what tiny feet she had, delicate and nicely arched. A few minutes later, he unfastened the top three buttons of her ugly dress. So she could breathe. Only so she could breathe.

It occurred to him a moment later that she surely didn't sleep with her hair pinned back like that.

He took out the pins, easily, slowly, one at a time, until her dark hair fell free across the pillow.

He didn't dare touch her again.

A good while later, he heard a familiar scratching at his door. He let Lucky in, and then closed the door very quietly behind the mangy mutt.

Ben sat in the only chair in the room, and after a while Lucky jumped into his lap. For once, he was glad for the company.

"What if he'd killed her?" he asked, scratching absently between Lucky's ears. "She's right. This is all my fault. Anders never would have dared. . . ."

On the bed, illuminated by moonlight that fell across her body, Celia stirred. At the sound of his voice? At the mention of Anders's name?

For a second or two—no more—Celia seemed to strain against her clothing, to fight some invisible monster. She'd fought enough real ones lately.

Including him.

And then she was still, peaceful and quiet once again. Ben watched over her and listened to the even rhythm of her breathing, and he ignored the urge—the craving—to crawl into his bed and hold her.

Chapter Eleven

It was the brightest moonlight she'd ever seen. Intense, sharp, intruding. In an instinctively protective move, Celia threw her arm over her eyes to shield them from the extraordinary moonlight.

In spite of that defense, the sleep she craved wouldn't return. Her head throbbed, at her temple and behind her closed eyelids, and the dark shelter of her arm didn't help at all. Lights danced behind her eyelids, in a rhythm that matched the ache in her head.

And what was that noise?

She peeled her arm away from her eyes, and discovered that it wasn't moonlight at all, but a full morning sun shining through the window, that hurt her eyes. And the noise, the noise was Benjamin Wolfe. Snoring.

He was sleeping in a chair, his body relaxed, his head lolling to one side. Lucky was curled up in his lap, awake, but content to lie there with his tail wagging and his head resting on Ben's thigh.

Everything that had happened the night before—the argument with Ben in the saloon, the confrontation on the stairs with Cory—came back. She remembered very clearly the moment Cory had banged her head into the step, but after that her memories were fuzzy.

She must have been completely addle-brained to allow Benjamin Wolfe to bring her here. And she did remember Ben carrying her into his room. Bathing her face. Placing the quilt around her shoulders. They were fuzzy, dreamlike memories, disturbingly warm and comforting, but she couldn't shake them.

Slowly and with as little noise as necessary, Celia rolled up and slipped her legs over the side. Despite her efforts to be silent, her dress rustled and the bed creaked. An alert Lucky lifted his head to watch her closely as she stood.

Ben didn't move.

Her shoes had been placed neatly side by side at the end of the bed, and she scooped them up as she headed for the door.

Ben didn't speak until her hand was on the doorknob.

"Good morning," he growled sleepily.

So much for a nice, quiet escape. Her heart sank as she glanced over her shoulder.

"How's your head?"

Lucky leaped to the floor, but Ben didn't stand.

He looked very comfortable in that chair that should have been very *un*comfortable.

"It's fine," she said softly.

"Fine?" Ben stretched out his long legs, and rolled his shoulders. With a yawn he raised his arms above his head, straining the fabric of his shirt as he worked the kinks out of his back.

"Well, it hurts quite a bit, actually," she said honestly. Then, rather than bolting from the room like a frightened child, she let her hand fall away from the knob and she turned to face Benjamin Wolfe. "I have no intention of thanking you, if that's what you're waiting for. It was your machinations that put me in this situation in the first place."

"I seem to recall we had this conversation last night," he said blandly.

She wasn't about to tell him that she didn't remember that particular fact. "I just want to make myself perfectly clear."

"You did."

"And why on earth did you bring me here? My room is right up the stairs."

"Have you ever actually tried to carry someone up a flight of stairs? It's not as easy as it looks."

He was infuriating her again. "At the very least you should have removed yourself to another room. This entire building is yours, as you so like to remind me. I feel certain you could have found yourself another—"

"I'm no doctor, but I do know that head wounds are peculiar." Ben unfolded his body from the chair and stood slowly. He was still fully dressed, except for the boots that had been placed at the side of his chair. He ran his fingers through tousled hair, stretched again, and turned toward Celia and the door. "It would have been downright irresponsible of me to leave you unattended."

"Irresponsible," she repeated. "Well, we wouldn't want Benjamin Wolfe to begin behaving irresponsibly at this date, now, would we?"

He smiled, sleepy and amused and apparently content. And Celia hated him as she'd never hated anyone.

She reached for the doorknob again.

"Celia, sweetheart," he said lazily, and she hesitated. "Has anyone ever told you that you look absolutely beautiful in the morning?"

She refused even to look at him this time, as she turned the knob.

"You'd better . . ." Ben added insistently just as Celia threw the door open.

". . . peek out and see if anyone's in the hallway," he finished in a less urgent tone of voice.

Just this once she should have listened to him, but of course now it was too late.

Floy and Faye were halfway down the staircase from the third floor, dressed for school and carrying their books. They stopped and stared.

Frances Hoyt was at the top of the staircase that led to the ground floor, a small traveling bag in her hand as she prepared to leave the boardinghouse for the last time. Ben had offered to let her stay, but she'd refused to work in a "den of iniquity." She took one look at Celia, harrumphed with her nose in the air, and began her descent.

Walter Huffman, two doors down, was just closing his door behind him, and he turned a censuring and startled face her way.

Standing in the doorway, she spun to face Ben. Her shoes were in her hand, her hair was a tangled mess, and she was leaving a man's room. It didn't take a mind reader to understand what they were all thinking. "You've done it again," she whispered. "This is just another one of your schemes."

Ben shook his head innocently. "Not this time."

Floy came running down the stairs, and Faye was right behind her. There was absolute terror on Floy's face as she rushed to Celia . . . then past her and straight to Ben.

"You hit my sister!" she screeched, and then she kicked Ben, square on the shin.

He yelped and stepped back. "I did not."

The normally quiet Floy was on a rampage, and she either didn't hear or didn't believe him. "And to think," she said as she raised her thick history book, "I used to *like* you. I thought you were *nice*." She punctuated her words by swinging her book at Ben's head. He managed to avoid the worst of it, cutting first to one side and then to another, and then he raised pleading eyes to Celia.

"Would you please tell her that I didn't hit you?"

Celia looked down at Faye, who by now was

standing quietly at her side. She was evidently as bemused by Floy's aggressiveness as Celia was.

Faye raised a tentative hand to the bump at Celia's temple. "Are you all right?"

For the first time that morning, Celia smiled. "I'm fine."

It was a simple enough matter to stop Floy. Celia placed a stilling hand on her arm—her swinging arm—and Floy stopped her attack.

"Mr. Wolfe didn't hit me," she said softly, and when Floy turned around Celia saw the tears in her sister's outraged eyes.

"But your head . . ."

"I fell," Celia said quickly, cutting her eyes to Ben and silently ordering him not to betray her. The girls didn't need anything more to worry about, not even a drunken Cory Anders. "And I hit my head on a step. I'm afraid I knocked myself out. Mr. Wolfe was kind enough to see to my injury." She smiled down at Floy. "That's all."

Floy cut a disbelieving glance at Ben. "Are you sure he didn't hurt you?"

"Listen, Faye—" Ben began.

"Floy," all three Pigg sisters corrected at once.

"Floy?" he repeated. "Nice, sweet, quiet Floy?" They had managed to surprise him, at last.

Floy lifted her chin into the air, and her pert nose followed. In that instant, Celia could see the woman Floy would be, beautiful and tenacious. Fiercely protective of those she loved. A prize for any man. Beside her more outgoing sister, Floy sometimes paled, but she would never be second to anyone.

"I don't have to be sweet when someone is abusing my sister," she said haughtily. "I won't apologize for hitting you, Mr. Wolfe. You deserved it, even if you didn't strike Celia."

"I would never hit a woman," Ben defended himself to Floy.

"Oh, never," Celia said brightly. "Mr. Wolfe has scruples."

He cut her a biting glance as she put her arm around Floy's shoulder.

"No school today, girls," she said as she turned away from Ben. "We've got too much work to do."

"What kind of work?" Faye asked from the doorway.

"Packing and moving. I want us to be out of this place well before dark."

Faye went pale, almost white. "We're leaving Piggville?"

"Of course not," Celia assured her.

"Then where are we going?" Floy whispered.

Celia didn't answer, but released Floy and sent her and Faye up the stairs to start packing. She turned to Ben when the twins were at the top of the stairs.

"Where are you going?" he asked in a low voice.

Celia smiled, through the heartache, through the pain, through the knowledge that her future was uncertain. "Someplace where you can't touch us."

* * *

It was another beautiful day, springtime in Texas. The sun was shining, there wasn't a cloud in the blue sky, and a cool, gentle breeze washed over Ben as he crossed the street. All was right with the world.

Or should have been. Celia was, at this very minute, preparing to move out of the boarding-house, and where could she go but out of town? The fine home that had once been hers was now his. The Pigg General Store was closed. The boardinghouse was now Lucky's Saloon, and there wasn't a decent family in town who would take Celia in. Not now.

So why did he feel so miserable?

Huff was sitting at his desk, and he didn't even bother to look up as Ben entered the office.

"Good morning," Ben said brightly. He got no response.

Reaching past Huff, Ben opened the drawer where the fine cigars were kept. Huff moved swiftly to shut the drawer, almost on Ben's fingers.

"Buy your own damn cigars," he said lowly. "It's not like you can't afford them."

Ben propped himself against the desk. "What's your problem this morning?"

"My problem?" Huff said brightly. "My problem is you. You've gone too far, Ben. You've lost all perspective. Celia Pigg is almost broke. The idea of recovering through a respectable marriage is out of the question, since you've gone to such lengths to sully her reputation, and still it seems you're not satisfied. What's next?"

Ben didn't allow his anger to show. "Cory Anders."

"The man you almost killed last night?" Huff asked, his eyebrows snapping up sharply.

"Too bad I didn't break his damn neck when I threw him down the stairs," Ben whispered, more to himself than to Huff.

"You'd be dead now if you had," Huff said matter-of-factly. "The way people feel about you in this town, there wouldn't have been a trial. They would've tossed a rope around your neck and strung you up without asking a single question."

Ben thought about telling Huff what had happened, but he remembered Celia's lie to the twins. She didn't want her sisters to know what had happened. Maybe she didn't want anyone to know.

"Cory Anders is a self-righteous horse's ass," Ben said easily. "I don't like him. I want you to find out where he's got his money, if he's carrying any debt. I want to know what his weaknesses are, who his friends are, and then I'm going to ruin him."

"Ben—"

"Don't try to talk me out of this," Ben interrupted.

Huff ran his fingers through once immaculately styled dark hair. "I can't. This isn't right. Is what Anders said last night true?" Huff lifted tired eyes to Ben. He didn't like this, but then, he hadn't been enthusiastic about the methods of retaliation for some time.

"What did he say?" Ben breathed.

"He said that the two of you got into a fight over Celia. That even though he's a peace-loving man and not given to violence, he was trying to protect her from you." Huff opened the drawer and withdrew two cigars. "He said she didn't seem to want to be protected from you. And after what I saw this morning, I have to assume that he was telling the truth."

Ben cursed softly as Huff passed him one of the cigars. Ruining Celia's reputation had been part of the plan all along, so why was he so irritated that Anders was perpetuating the lie? Huff seemed content to wait him out, as he lit his own cigar.

"That lying son of a bitch," he finally said clearly. "If I tell you something, will you swear not to tell anyone else? Not even Rosemary Cranston?"

"I'm your attorney," Huff said with indignation as he chewed on his cigar. "I don't have to swear."

Ben turned away from the desk.

"All right," Huff said quickly. "I swear."

Last night there hadn't been time to think. Everything had happened so fast, and when he'd tossed Anders down the stairs he hadn't even considered following him down, or explaining . . . he hadn't even had time to question his anger. That anger welled up inside him again, a sickening, gut-churning fury.

"He hurt her," Ben said softly. "He pushed her down, and banged up her head, and then he put his hands all over her. What was I supposed to do?"

Behind him, Huff sighed loudly.

"I suppose you've told yourself a hundred times that you'd be just as angry if it was any other woman. If Anders had accosted Mrs. Hoyt, or Ophelia Lucas, or your friend Margaret Harriman, or any other decent woman in Piggville, you would have thrown him down the stairs and then extracted your revenge by ruining him financially."

"Yep," Ben said.

"Believe it yet?"

"Nope."

Ben stood there for a long time. He hadn't allowed himself to think too much about his reaction. Hadn't tried to analyze his anger. It was simply there.

"She's moving out of the saloon," Ben said, after Huff began to shuffle his papers nervously.

"Where's she going?"

Ben puffed on the cigar, and then ran a hand over his stubbled jaw.

Someplace where I can't touch her.

"I don't know."

Where would she go? How would Celia try to fight him next? Hell, she'd never really fought. She'd run. She'd survived. But she'd never fought back.

"Cory Anders," Ben said coldly. "I'm going to take care of him. Do we do it your way or mine?"

"Mine," Huff said quickly. "That way maybe I can keep you alive and out of jail."

"Maybe?" Ben asked, only half joking.

"Ben?" Huff's voice stopped him before he

reached the door. "As your lawyer . . . as your friend . . . I'm asking you to stop this. It's gone too far."

Ben didn't answer. He just opened the door and stepped into a deceptively beautiful day.

"We're going to live here?" Faye asked harshly. "We can't possibly—"

"Hush," Floy said softly, and then she nodded toward Celia.

It had been a long time since she'd seen Celia look so contented, so happy. There was a nice breeze that met them full in the face as they stood side by side by side. Long strands of Celia's hair had fallen from the normally neat style, and the wind pushed the dark hair away from her face, like the wings of an angel.

"It's a pile of rubble," Faye said in a hiss. Celia seemed not to hear.

There were an awful lot of weeds, and the small house was a square pile of bricks with a few windows here and there. Rubble? Perhaps that was too harsh. Cottage? Much too kind. Shack? The perfect description, if you could call a brick house a shack. There wasn't really even a road to the old house, just the remnants of a path.

"You girls never knew Grandma and Grandpa Hart, but this was their house. This is where Mama grew up." Celia turned to them and smiled widely. At least she wasn't pale anymore. There was color in her cheeks, a healthy blush in spite of the discolored bump on her temple.

173

"I used to come here when I was a little girl," Celia said in a low and serene voice. "Mama kept the house even after Grandma and Grandpa died, and sometimes we'd . . . we'd escape. We'd bring a picnic, and after we ate we'd dig through old trunks of remembrances, and usually end up spending an entire afternoon right here."

The property was, Celia had said, just at the edge of Piggville. They weren't actually in town, not on the main street or a cross street, but they were within the city limits, and in five minutes they could be in the center of it all.

Floy had thought, at first, that they'd had to leave the boardinghouse because she hit Mr. Wolfe. Celia had assured her that was not so, and while she'd chastised Floy lightly for resorting to violence, she'd smiled faintly the whole while.

Celia declared that she simply refused to live in a saloon, and she refused just as adamantly to allow her sisters to live in a saloon. It wasn't, she'd said insistently, proper.

"I don't remember this nasty old house at all," Faye said crossly.

Celia's smile faded. "After you girls were born, Mama seemed to lose interest in this place. I don't think she ever brought the three of us here." There was a thoughtful expression on Celia's face, but then Celia often looked as though she were considering the problems of the world and trying to come up with solutions for them all. "Of course, it's difficult to make even a day trip with three children, and when you girls were three, that's when Mama started getting sick all the time, so she certainly couldn't pack us up for a day of adventures."

She stiffened her spine and clenched her fists. "It's not much, but it's mine." There was a passionate possessiveness in that statement that made Floy shudder, just a little. "There's no mortgage, and I've paid the property taxes over the years, so it's mine, free and clear."

Celia looked at Faye and smiled. "So while it might look like nothing but a pile of rubble, it's much more. It'll be a lot of work, but by the time we're finished it'll be home. And there's no way Benjamin Wolfe or anyone else can ever take it away from us."

Chapter Twelve

The inside of the old brick house was much worse than she had feared. In her mind, as she'd yet again packed the belongings she could carry and prepared to leave the saloon, she'd imagined it as it had been thirteen, fourteen years ago, when she and her mother had still visited here regularly. Small and comfy, cozy and warm . . . the same place it had always been, but perhaps with a thick layer of dust.

She hadn't counted on dry rot, or rodents and spiders, or the hole in the roof over the kitchen. Besides that one obvious gap there were several other, smaller openings that allowed shafts of sunlight to peek through. She hadn't yet dared to inspect the outhouse.

It was a simply arranged house. There was a main room at the front, the room her mother had always laughingly called the parlor. The two windows in the parlor faced the front of the house, and the sun shone through tattered and rotting lace curtains.

At the back of the house was the kitchen, which was primitive and filthy. It had been home to several critters over the years, she was sure. There were, here and there, small mounds of dried leaves and grass, bedding for a few of those critters, she assumed. She shuddered at the thought of tackling that mess.

The two bedrooms were on the south side, small, plain rooms with a single window in each. The girls' window faced the front of the house, while the window in Celia's room looked out on the vastness that lay beyond Piggville. Those windows were opened already, as well as the windows in the parlor, with the hopes that the fresh breeze would sweep the staleness from the air.

Celia started in the parlor with a broom, sweeping furiously over the cellar door. She tried to push the certainty that this was an impossible task from her mind.

The twins worked in the bedrooms, cleaning for a while and then squealing in disgust as they ran to join Celia for a moment. She smiled, and assured them that no spider or mouse or dirt would hurt them. They could step on the spiders, shoo the mice away, and clean up the dirt.

She smiled as she told them this, but inside she was sick.

There were still a couple hours of light left, and she intended to make use of those hours. For tonight, she decided, they would sleep in the parlor. It was the cleanest room in the house, after all. They could huddle together, and she would tell the twins stories of the grandparents they had never known, and the stories her mother had told her of growing up in this house.

They would have to work very hard to make this parlor livable, even for the night.

What remained in the cellar? she wondered as she swept past the square door set in the floor. Full of ancient trunks and shadowed corners, it had been a place of dark wonder for a little girl, scary and exhilarating at the same time. What waited in those dusty trunks? Treasure or monsters? Wonder or fright?

Celia heard the rumbling of the wagon long before she could see it. She leaned her broom against the wall and went to the closest window, and she was watching the path and waiting anxiously as the wagon came bouncing around the bend. Surely Ben wouldn't have tracked her down already. She held her breath until she saw Rosemary in the front seat, then groaned when she saw that lawyer Walter Huffman at her side, driving the old wagon.

Not aware that she was being watched, Rosemary frowned in apparent dismay as the wagon came to a stop in front of the dilapidated house.

Of course, by the time Celia opened the front door to greet her visitors, Rosemary was wearing a cheerful smile.

"I thought you might need some help making this place livable," Rosemary said as she jumped from the wagon's seat. "And I rounded up a few supplies you'll need, and some of the things you left at the boardinghouse."

It was then that Rosemary noticed how full the back of the wagon was. There was her rocking chair tied securely down, with several folded blankets and quilts on the seat. Trunks she recognized as her own. A small table. Two more brooms were propped in one corner, and there were a number of unmarked sacks.

Celia glanced at Huff as he jumped from the driver's seat. "Does Ben know you're here?"

Huff shook his head slowly, shot a quick glance toward Rosemary, and jumped into the back of the wagon to untie the rocking chair.

Rosemary put her hand around Celia's waist and turned her about so they faced the house. "Where do we start?" she asked cheerfully.

Celia noted again the falling bricks, the rotting roof, the weeds. And the inside of the house was as dismal and hopeless as the exterior. "Dynamite, I think," she said softly.

Rosemary laughed lightly.

Huff carried everything in. He placed the rocking chair and the table in the parlor, the trunks in the front bedroom, and he piled the sacks in the kitchen. There was flour, meal, potatoes, apples, a sack of sugar . . . all from Ben's general store.

"Let me pay you," Celia said as Rosemary grabbed one of the new brooms and went to work.

"It's a housewarming gift. Huff fetched the

rocking chair and the other pieces of furniture from the storage area at the boardinghouse, with Jud's help, and he brought all your clothes and things, too."

"But the food . . ."

"Huff bought it. It's the least he could do," Rosemary said haughtily. "Don't you dare pay him a penny."

Celia picked up her broom, and together they swept away dust and dirt and cobwebs.

"You should have been there," Rosemary said as she swept above her head, brushing away a huge spiderweb. "When we were in the general store buying your supplies, Kay Anne Ascot came in, and I gave her what-for."

"You didn't." Celia groaned. Rosemary was much too fond of saying exactly what was on her mind.

"I did," Rosemary said vehemently. "And it was nothing more than she deserved. Why, you made her husband that loan just six months ago, and he hasn't paid back so much as a penny."

"Things have been hard," Celia began.

"And you didn't even ask him to pay it back when things got hard for you," Rosemary snapped. "And they're not the only ones in town who owe you money, and now they're all acting so sanctimonious, like they never made a mistake, like they're all so superior." Rosemary whacked at a spider. "Kay Anne wasn't the only one in that store, and I let them all have it. You know my temper."

"I'm afraid I do," Celia said softly.

"I thought there were more good people in Piggville than bad, but I've begun to change my mind."

Celia hadn't said so aloud, but she felt the same disappointment. Why had everyone turned their backs on her so quickly? All because of a weak moment, and then the rumors, gossip, and out-and-out lies.

Finished with the unloading of the wagon, Huff took off his jacket, rolled up the sleeves of his linen shirt, and attacked—to Celia's disbelief—the kitchen. To look at him, she would have thought the man incapable of hard work, with his fine clothes and his neatly fashioned hair, but he didn't even hesitate when he was faced with the years of dirt and rot that awaited him in the kitchen. It wasn't long before the girls joined him, laughing and squealing at the same time.

Maybe making this place livable wasn't impossible after all.

Rosemary and Huff had been there perhaps half an hour when another wagon arrived. To everyone's surprise, it was Kay Anne Ascot and her husband, and the back of their wagon was as full as Rosemary's had been.

Lumber, tools, a small table, and a pair of chairs. And Kay Anne was carrying a covered basket.

As Celia met the new visitor at the door, Kay Anne smiled tentatively. She offered the basket, which was warm and smelled of fresh-baked bread. "I'm sorry," she said softly.

Her husband cut right to the heart of the matter. "How's the well look, Miss Celia?" he shouted from the wagon.

"Not very good, I'm afraid. There's a stream not far from the back of the house, if you need water."

He nodded thoughtfully. "I'll just take a look at that well."

To Celia's surprise, Kay Anne grabbed the third broom.

It wasn't long before the others began to arrive, the people of Piggville who had turned their backs on Celia again and again in the past couple of weeks. They brought food and mattresses, lumber and nails and hammers, even curtains and rugs and odd pieces of furniture. Four hens, a rooster, and two pigs. One lady even brought a vase of flowers from her garden, to brighten up the new home.

When it got dark, they hung lanterns all around the house, inside and out, and kept working. They fixed the roof, built a new outhouse, and scrubbed away years of dirt. Kids made a game of pulling weeds.

James Richardson was there, working with the men, casting glances toward Faye whenever he got the chance. Laura Richardson didn't come, but Celia told herself that Laura was busy at home with the youngest of her boys. It was gratifying that James and his father and the other Richardson boy was there.

There were no more girlish squeals from the twins after the arrival of the Richardsons.

Even Mr. Culpepper was there.

By the time they finished working, the old brick house was habitable. It was no mansion, no fine estate, and Celia had no doubt that on occasion a mouse would still peek around a corner . . . but it was home.

There were several offers of a place to stay for the night, since there was still work to be done, but Celia declined them all.

She was home.

"Where the hell is everybody?" Ben asked after he threw back another whiskey. The saloon, which had been filled to bursting last night, was all but deserted.

Jud polished the bar. Ginger played with a long strand of red hair, twirling her finger around a curl. A single drunk occupied the table nearest the stage.

"Maybe you scared everybody off last night," Ginger said huskily, "the way you closed up. Tossing that poor fella down the stairs and yelling and all."

"Chickenhearted bastards," he mumbled as he poured himself another drink.

Ginger sidled down the bar until she was leaning against his side. She slipped her arm through his and put her head on his shoulder. "Why don't you just close up early tonight, sugarplum. Send Jud and that old drunk home and let me cheer you up."

"I don't need to be cheered up," Ben said morosely.

Ginger sighed, and ran her fingertips over his

forearm. "You used to let me cheer you up, back in Denver," she cooed. "Remember?"

Of course he remembered. Ginger was very . . . enthusiastic about her job. "Maybe another time." He wasn't really in the mood tonight for enthusiasm.

"It's that other girl, isn't it?" Ginger didn't move away. She rotated her head against his shoulder, like a cat, either not recognizing rejection or preferring to ignore it. "I heard about her."

He didn't have to ask what girl. There was only one woman on his mind. "What did you hear?"

"I heard she was caught leaving your room this morning," Ginger said calmly.

"It's not how it looks."

"And I heard it's not the first time the two of you have been caught."

"It's not like—"

Ginger ignored him. "You know, there are some fellas in this town who are mighty cross with you for stealing that little girl right out from under their noses."

"I didn't—"

"Seems she's been playing Miss Goody-Goody for years," Ginger interrupted with her usual good humor, "and then along comes Ben Wolfe to prove them wrong."

"She wasn't playing."

Ginger hummed thoughtfully, and the hum transformed gradually into a purr. "In that case, why don't you just forget Miss Goody-Goody and let me cheer you up?"

Ben glanced at the redhead on his shoulder.

She turned her face up, and stood on tiptoes to kiss him lightly. It was tempting, but he really didn't want to be cheered up at the moment.

Heavy footsteps plodding across the floor saved him from rejecting Ginger again, and he released her to turn around. A customer, at last. He found himself face-to-face with his lawyer, his friend, a Huff he hadn't seen in years.

Huff was filthy. His hair was sweaty and slicked away from his face, all but a dark clump that fell over his forehead. Grime had ruined what had once been an expensive white shirt, and his trousers were ripped at one knee. There was even mud on his fine boots.

"You stink," Ben said as he looked Huff up and down. "What is that?"

"It's called hard work," Huff snapped. "It hasn't been that long for you, Ben. I'm surprised you didn't recognize the odor."

"It's gotta be the girl," Ben said with a smile. "What's she got you doing now?"

Huff looked harshly at Ginger, and she moved away, sliding down the bar to talk to Jud Lucas. When Huff turned his attention back to Ben, neither man was smiling.

"I quit," Huff said lowly. "I can't do this anymore."

"You're gonna tuck your tail between your legs and run back to Dallas," Ben chided. "I can't—"

"No." Huff shook his head, tired and determined at the same time. "I'm not running anywhere. I'm staying right here."

At that, Ben laughed out loud. "And do what? You just let your only client go."

Now it was Huff's turn to smile. "Who said you were my only client? Jud Lucas wants to sue the railroad." Huff nodded toward the bartender. "Seems a train hit his dog a few months back, and the mutt lost a leg. Jud feels he's due some compensation, and I agreed to represent him. There's a minor property-line dispute, which I am not at liberty to discuss, but I will be representing one of the parties."

"I don't believe what I'm hearing."

Huff lifted his chin and straightened his spine. "And as soon as I've established a profitable practice here in Piggville, I'm going to ask Rosemary to marry me."

Ben was truly stunned. This sure as hell was not part of the plan.

"Close your mouth, Ben," Huff said as he turned away. "Standing there at the bar with it hanging open like that, you look like an idiot. Or a drunk."

Huff was at the staircase before Ben thought to ask again, "Just where were you tonight?"

"At Celia Pigg's house," Huff called as he trudged up the stairs.

"*My* house?" Ben called.

"Nope," Huff said wearily. "*Her* house. It's small, it's run-down, and it's off the beaten path, but it's definitely hers. Sorry, Ben. I'm afraid I missed it in my initial investigation."

"You missed it?" Ben stepped away from the bar to yell at Huff as he reached the top of the staircase. "There's another goddamn house and you *missed* it?"

Huff turned and gave Ben a tired smile. "I'm afraid so. It was her mother's, I believe, and there's no mortgage for you to buy up."

"You're a lousy lawyer," Ben shouted as Huff turned away.

"Good night, Ben," Huff called dully.

"Good night, Celia," Floy said as she gathered the quilt to her chin.

They'd decided, just for tonight, to sleep together in the parlor. The girls were anxious about sleeping in a strange place, and Celia—wedged between them—didn't mind. She needed to be reminded that she wasn't as alone as she sometimes felt.

In the dark she smiled. Wasn't this what she'd always wanted? A simple life. A little house and a few animals. While it wasn't exactly a farm, there would be room for a big garden next year. Maybe even a small one this year, if she got busy.

Perhaps she'd arrived here in a roundabout way, but the realization had come to her as she'd watched her friends drive and ride and walk away. This was home.

Ben would surely be mortified if he discovered that he'd actually helped her achieve her dream, if he knew that his revenge had resulted in a new and simpler life for her. He'd said that everyone needed upheaval in their lives, and in this one instance, perhaps he was right.

The girls still had their trusts, they had this

house, and in a few weeks Margaret would be back. With that small inheritance in the bank, they'd have a cushion of sorts against disaster. Maybe the house was a little small for the four of them, but they'd make do.

So there, Benjamin Wolfe, she said to herself.

He could take her house, her businesses, her good name, but it seemed he couldn't take away all her friends, after all. Oh, there were some who'd helped today only grudgingly, joining in perhaps because Rosemary had made them feel guilty. There were still others who had looked her way more than once with out-and-out pity in their eyes, but even they showed signs of coming around, with an occasional smile or kind word.

There was no business to worry about, no mortgage to be paid, no salaries to dispense. It didn't matter if all the loans she'd made in the past year were paid off over the next several years with pigs and chickens and eggs. In fact, that might be just fine.

She didn't fool herself into thinking that this war with Ben was over. He wouldn't be satisfied until she had nothing left, of that she was sure. He was determined to see her chased from town with nothing . . . just as his father had been.

She wasn't going anywhere.

"Good night, girls," she said softly, and almost instantly she was asleep.

Chapter Thirteen

Thanks to the help of her friends, the house was tolerable. More than tolerable, it was quite comfortable. Still, even with all the cheerfully offered help she received, there was a lot of work to be done. Cleaning, arranging, moving their meager belongings into the house.

It was days before Celia even thought to look in the cellar.

It was a dreary place she and her mother had slipped into on their visits to the house, to explore old trunks that were stored there. A dark and ominous corner in an otherwise bright house, the cellar had always seemed magical to Celia. She'd been alternately frightened and elated when stepping into the cellar. Treasures were stored there, but was there danger in every shadow?

Celia put aside the fanciful ideas of youth and turned her thoughts to the months ahead. The brick house was sturdy, but in the event of a bad storm, the cellar would be the place to go. Since it was quite cool, it could also be used to store fruits and vegetables.

She threw back the trapdoor and, with an oil lamp in her hand, peered into the darkness below. She was prepared for almost anything as she stepped onto the stairs and descended into the dark cellar.

The air in the cellar was cool, but it was not as damp as she'd expected it would be. She held the lamp high, and cast light over the small cellar.

It hadn't changed in fourteen years. There were still several old trunks, a corner piled high with empty bottles Grandma Hart had saved, and a profusion of spiderwebs. The ceiling seemed lower, the room much smaller, but Celia knew the only proportions that had changed over the years were her own.

It would make a good storm cellar. Wasn't that why Grandpa Hart had dug it in the first place? Grandma Hart had been uneasy during storms, and the fury of Texas tornadoes had terrified her. The cellar was her safe haven when the skies became too dark and the wind shook the sturdy brick house.

One of the trunks could be emptied, and filled with candles and matches, a bit of dried meat, perhaps a jug of water. Celia wasn't scared of storms at all, but Faye certainly was. And in a new, smaller house, she'd be doubly nervous.

While the girls were at school, she could spend a little time in the cellar, fix the place up a bit. She didn't dare bring the girls down here until the spiderwebs and the spiders were taken care of. It was too dark and small to be a proper room, but it would be perfect for storage and for refuge during a storm.

There were three trunks, and she started with the one at the front. She suspected most of what she found would have to be thrown out, but she couldn't be sure. There might be a treasure in here somewhere. Not gold or silver, but letters from Grandpa Hart to Grandma, before they were married. She remembered her mother reading those sweet, romantic letters to her years ago. Grandma's wedding dress was probably in here somewhere, and goodness knew what else.

The first thing she found, there on top of the trunk's contents, was a small tattered rug that had been handwoven by Grandma. Perfect. Celia placed it on the floor and sat on it as she sorted through the rest.

There were a hundred chores to be taken care of, here and upstairs, but Celia took her time as she sorted through the contents of the trunk. There was a crushed hat she placed upon her head, the treasured pack of letters bound in blue ribbons, a dress. Not the wedding dress, but a special dress indeed. It was silk and lace, a silvery blue gown that had seen little wear. It was, of course, years out of date, but the material was in surprisingly good shape. With a pair of scissors and a needle and a few nights' work, this might make a decent dress for one of the girls.

Ben Wolfe had not sunk so low as to take the very clothes off their backs, though she imagined that if he could get away with it he wouldn't have a qualm. There were years ahead to think of. Floy and Faye had not stopped growing, and they would be mortified to attend school or church in clothes that were too small or tattered and worn. She'd have to think of such things from now on, watching her pennies whenever she could. Everything she could save would put her that far ahead.

There were more clothes, Grandma's and Grandpa's, some of them perfectly fine, others obviously saved simply for sentimental reasons. Most of them would be useful. She was especially interested in the calico she found, dresses and skirts in all colors, some in better shape than others. For cleaning the house and caring for animals, calico made a lot more sense than silk.

At the very bottom of the trunk there was a book, a thin journal, Celia saw as she lifted it carefully. In all their excursions, she couldn't remember her mother ever reading from a small leather-bound book like this one.

Grandma Hart's journal would make fascinating reading, she was sure. She'd been here when Piggville had been founded. Of course, it hadn't been called Piggville then, but Perfection. Perfection, Texas. A fanciful name for a small town situated in the middle of nowhere. The land must have looked perfect to the Harts and the Ascots and the Sanfords when they'd decided that this was the place they wanted to live and raise their families.

It hadn't been renamed Piggville until her father had moved in with his money and his big plans.

"Celia!" Rosemary's voice was high-pitched, frantic, and Celia tossed the journal on top of the trunk's contents as she stood.

"I'm down here," she yelled as she closed the trunk.

By the time she climbed the stairs to the parlor, Rosemary was waiting, standing by the opened trapdoor and tapping her foot.

"You won't believe what he's done now," Rosemary said indignantly as Celia climbed from the darkness. The bright light pouring through the open window hurt her eyes for a moment, and she shielded them with her hands.

"It's horrid . . . unthinkable . . . why, why," Rosemary twittered nervously, "Benjamin Wolfe should be shot."

Celia extinguished her lamp and sat on the sofa. She brushed a spot of cellar dirt from her gray serge skirt before lifting her eyes to her friend. Judging by the expression of revulsion on Rosemary's face, Ben had gone through with his latest outrageous threat. Goodness, he'd actually done it.

"You have to come to town with me, Celia. You have to stop him."

Stop him? She couldn't even slow him down. He'd come into Piggville and run over her like a runaway rail car. Without a qualm, without an ounce of decency. Stop him? The attempt would place her in his path again, and she just couldn't face Ben Wolfe at the moment. "There's nothing I can do," she said pragmatically. "And I have no desire—"

"But you don't know what he's done this time."

"He's turned my house, pardon me, *his* house, into . . . into . . ."

"A whorehouse," Rosemary supplied, her voice lowering to a hoarse whisper. "You should see the outlandish women who are living there. They came in on the train, and they paraded themselves right through town to your house, and they took up residence."

Celia dropped her head into her hands. How could she bear to go to the main street of Piggville again? And she would have to, eventually. She couldn't hide here forever, lovely as that sounded at the moment.

"There's nothing I can do," she admitted into her hands. "Nothing."

"But you have to do something," Rosemary pleaded. "Stop him. Huff says you're the only one who can."

By leaving town.

Hadn't he done enough? Wasn't it enough that she'd gone from the nicest, biggest house in Piggville to a cottage at the edge of town? That he'd taken her boardinghouse, closed her general store, ruined her reputation?

There was nothing left for him to take.

"Come with me," Rosemary pleaded. "Maybe you can talk some sense into him."

"Impossible," she muttered. "The man hasn't a lick of sense."

Rosemary took Celia's hand, grasped it firmly, and pulled her to her feet. "Try. I think you're the only one he'll listen to."

"What about Huff?" Celia said as Rosemary led her to the door.

"They're not speaking," Rosemary admitted as she pulled Celia through the front door and toward the waiting buckboard. "Huff told that man he wouldn't work for him anymore," she said proudly. "There's just one project he says he has to finish before he completely quits. Something to do with Cory Anders, I believe."

Celia shuddered at the mention of the banker's name.

"So," Rosemary continued, "it's up to you. Appeal to his sense of honor."

"He doesn't have one," Celia spat as she climbed into the seat of the wagon.

It was a lie, and she knew it as soon as the words left her mouth. Perhaps he had an odd way of expressing his good character, but he had saved her from Cory, and this entire calamity stemmed from Ben's vow to his father. A vow he couldn't or wouldn't break.

He was wrong; he just couldn't see it.

"All right," she said as Rosemary took off down the rutted path. "I'll speak to him. It won't do any good," she added quickly, "but I'll see what I can do."

*   *   *

It was almost perfect. Ginger's girls, all six of them, were seated in Hamilton Pigg's rocking chairs on the front porch of what had been the Pigg mansion. They laughed loudly, and crossed their legs so that a varied and generous view of legs long and short, slim and full, were on display, and they propositioned every male who walked by.

Ginger had placed two large marble cherubs on the porch, and was in the process of redecorating the interior of the house, as well.

It was just as he'd planned, and was almost perfect. If only Celia were here to see it. . . .

He couldn't get her out of his mind, and that fact drove him to distraction. He'd actually found himself worrying about her in the past several days, living away from town proper the way she did. There were just the three of them, Celia and the twins, and there was not a single close neighbor. And there was that bastard Cory Anders to worry about.

Half a dozen times, Ben had made his way to the brick house at the edge of town. He walked, so she wouldn't hear him coming, and he never got too close . . . just close enough to spy Celia through a window and know that she was all right.

He usually ended up standing behind that damn tree for hours, watching the brick house long after dark. The windows would glow with the warm light from within, and Ben stood there and watched Celia and the twins pass in front of those windows. He watched until the lights went out, and he was certain they were safe for the night.

He was surely demented.

If she could see what he had done to her home, she would pitch a fit. She could call him every name in the book, try to toss him out of town again, and then he could remind himself who she was . . . a Pigg.

He stood in front of the general store, his general store, and watched the reactions of the people down the street, as they saw what had become of Hamilton Pigg's fine home. The women gasped in horror and crossed the street. The men glared, some fascinated, some as openly offended as the women.

It was almost perfect.

"I didn't think you'd really do it."

He turned around to face her, the woman who had plagued him since the moment he'd seen her, the woman who could make this moment perfect. He smiled at Celia, a wide grin. "Now, what would make you doubt my word?"

He waited for her to explode, to lash out, to scream, but she was oddly and infuriatingly serene.

"No matter what your father did, he was a preacher. Perhaps he had his faults, his weaknesses, but—"

"He had no weaknesses," Ben snapped. Hell, she was perfectly calm, and *he* was losing control.

"Everyone has weaknesses," Celia said calmly. "We're ordinary people, not saints."

This wasn't at all how this conversation was meant to go. "Did you get a good look at the Piggville Gentlemen's Social Club?"

"I'm afraid I did," she said softly. "Is there any way I can convince you to send those . . . those unfortunate ladies home and close the Gentlemen's Club?"

He knew how to get to her, how to make her angry. "Any way?" he repeated with a suggestive lift of his eyebrows. "What are you willing to do to make me change my mind, Celia, sweetheart?"

"Don't," she said, a flash of anger in her eyes.

He reached out to touch her chin, and she jerked away before he could turn her face up. But when she was free, she lifted her face to stare at him. "I don't suppose it would matter," she said softly, her anger fading but still evident. "After all, everyone in town already believes that we were . . . that we were . . ."

"Lovers," he finished for her. She shuddered as he spoke.

"But it does matter to me," she continued when her shudder had passed. "I know the truth, and believe it or not I still have my honor."

"Is that a no?" Ben asked lightly.

Celia sighed. "That's a no, Benjamin."

She looked past him to the Pigg mansion down the street. "Would you do me one favor?" she asked despairingly. "Would you ask the . . . ummm, ladies, to stay inside when school is dismissed? The girls have to walk right past the house on their way home, and I don't want them to see . . . they'll hear, of course, but there's nothing to be done for that, I'm afraid."

He could say no, but using the kids to get to Celia seemed unfair. Anything else was fair game, but not the twins. "Sure," he said casually.

He waited for Celia to move away, but she stood there on the boardwalk, staring down the street. A few people nodded and said hello to her as they passed. They ignored Ben completely.

"Are you happy, Ben?" she asked softly, just when he expected her to move away.

The question caught him off guard. "Happy?"

"Content, cheerful. Happy," she said again.

"I'm always happy," he said with a smile.

She took her eyes from the spectacle that used to be her home, and pinned her gaze on him. "I don't believe you," she whispered. "Once, I did. When we first met I thought you were the most easygoing and contented person I'd ever seen, and I envied you for it. It's the smile, I suppose. It fooled me."

He knew how to make her nervous. A single step closer, and she had to crane her head to look up at him. "You should be happy now," she whispered. "But I can see that you're not. You've won, Ben. You've taken everything that was once mine and destroyed it."

"Not everything, and you're still in Piggville."

"Oh, yes," she answered quickly. "I still have a few friends, and my little house, and my sisters. And as for being in Piggville, the edge of town is practically at my back door."

"I swore—"

"Your father would be very proud," Celia interrupted softly.

How could he have ever thought Celia Pigg was weak? Helpless? She stared up at him with strength in her dark eyes and the lift of her chin.

"I pity you," she said so quietly that he almost didn't hear her. "You're the one who has nothing."

Before he could answer, Celia turned her back on him and walked away. Without anger, without looking back.

"Over there," Faye said in a hiss, and Floy followed the line of her sister's pointed finger. She saw nothing but a stand of trees and complete darkness.

"I don't see anything."

And then she did. It was a quick flash of orange, like fire, a flame in the darkness.

"He's smoking," Faye said unnecessarily.

They peeked from the window of their room. No light was burning, and yet they maintained a low position there beneath the window.

Celia was still up and about. She'd cleaned the kitchen earlier, banging pots and pans as she put them on the shelves above the stove, and now Floy could hear her muffled movements as she gathered up all her sewing materials and placed them into the basket she kept by her rocking chair.

Now that she knew where to look, Floy could see him, too. He was nothing more than an indistinct figure, a still and quiet watcher in the night. The form was unmistakable. It was Benjamin Wolfe.

"What do you think he's doing here?" Floy hissed.

"I don't know, but I swear he was out there last night and the night before."

It crossed her mind, briefly, that Benjamin Wolfe meant them all some harm . . . but it was a thought that came and went quickly.

The thought that came and stayed was that he was watching over them, protecting them somehow.

"We could shoot him and say he was trespassing," Faye suggested.

"No," Floy said in a hiss. "We most certainly can't."

"Why not?" Faye whispered harshly. "It's what he deserves."

"Perhaps," Floy agreed. "But I don't think it would be a good idea."

Faye didn't agree or disagree; she simply grunted softly and turned her eyes to the watcher.

"Do you know what I think?" Floy whispered. "I think we were right all along. No matter what's happened, I think Ben Wolfe likes Celia a lot. I think maybe he even loves her."

"Don't be ridiculous."

"Think about it. Don't you remember the way they looked at each other?"

"He was pretending."

Floy shook her head. "You can't fake a look like that."

Faye placed her arms on the windowsill and settled her head on her hands. "So what exactly are you suggesting? He took everything from us. Everything." Her voice softened to a whisper so low Floy had to lean her head to one side to hear clearly.

"A man who loves a woman wouldn't take her home and her business," Faye insisted. "He would court her and bring flowers and candy and ask her out for picnics and town dances. He would woo her with gifts and then ask her to marry him. That's the way it's done."

Faye's argument made sense, but Floy was not completely convinced. "Maybe Mr. Wolfe just doesn't know that he loves Celia, not yet."

Faye was not one to give in easily, but she was too tired to argue. Eventually she yawned and closed her eyes. "So what about Celia? Does she love him? How could she after what he's done?"

That was the question they had to consider carefully. It was true enough that Celia had once cared for Ben . . . but that had been before he'd taken everything from them. And now? How could she possibly love him? Faye was right about that.

But if she did . . . if somehow Celia could still love Ben after all he'd done, and if he really did love her . . . it would be an extraordinary kind of love.

It was the sort of romantic notion that made thirteen-year-old girls sigh.

Chapter Fourteen

Piggville was losing its charm.

Even though he was a pariah, business was good. The saloon, the general store, and the Piggville Gentlemen's Social Club were raking in the money. It didn't come in great amounts, like when he hit that silver strike, but it wasn't exactly hard work, either.

The men of Piggville who snubbed him by daylight didn't seem to mind frequenting the saloon or the social club after dark. It was as if everything changed when the sun went down, as if tolerating him was a price they paid for their pleasures.

And as for the women—well, hell, what were they going to do? Ride three or four hours to the next town for flour and sugar?

But it wasn't fun anymore. Without Celia watching, it wasn't fun at all.

He was headed for the social club, to see what kinds of changes Ginger had made to the interior. Ginger's tastes ran to the extreme. She liked bright colors and gold and anything with fringe on it. With all his heart, he hoped that he would find the Pigg house gaudy as hell.

"Mr. Wolfe?"

The sound of that sweet voice made the hair on the back of his neck stand up. He stopped there on the boardwalk, and turned slowly. How long had the little demons been following him?

"Girls," he said, unable to hide the suspicion in his voice.

"We were just wondering," Floy said casually. At least, he thought it was Floy. "About the puppy we gave you. Is he all right?"

They were too docile, too damn agreeable. "He's fine. What do you really want?"

The other one, Faye, he supposed, smiled grandly. "What did you name him? You never did say."

He didn't know what the game was, just yet, but if they wanted to play . . . "Lucky."

Their smiles faded. "You named him after a saloon?" Floy despaired softly.

"Actually, I named the saloon after him."

They looked at one another briefly, communicating in some silent, eerie way. He'd have to watch his back around these two.

"Well, I guess that's all right, then." Faye again. "Maybe you'll let us see him sometime. He's so cute and cuddly, and he did seem very smart. Maybe we could teach him a few tricks."

Ben was waiting for the other shoe to drop. Waiting cautiously for one of the girls to pull a gun or a knife from behind a full pink skirt or from under a wide sash. Neither of them made a threatening move. "Sure, anytime," he finally answered. "Lucky pretty much has the run of the saloon. You can find him—"

"Oh, Celia won't allow us to go into the saloon," Floy said, wide eyed and innocent.

Just the mention of her name sparked something inside him. He was no longer wary, no longer bored. "She won't? Well, I have to agree with your sister on this one. A saloon's no place for little girls."

"We're not little girls," Faye said indignantly. "We're young women."

"Of course," Ben said solemnly. "I didn't mean to offend you."

Their smiles told him he was forgiven. What was going on here?

"How is Celia, by the way?" he asked casually, leaning against a nearby post and striking an "I-don't-give-a-damn" pose.

"Celia?" Floy repeated. The twins looked at each other again. Not a word was said aloud, but it was spooky as hell. A warning tingle climbed his spine. "She's all right, I suppose, all things considered."

"I haven't seen her around town lately."

"No." Faye shook her head. "She doesn't like to come to town anymore. She says she's not ill, but . . ." Another one of those damn looks that excluded him completely passed between them.

"But what?" he snapped. "Has she been sick?" He was such a fool to ask, an even bigger one to care. "I should've had the doctor look at her after she bumped her head. Head wounds are peculiar; I told her that."

"I don't think it's her head," Floy said seriously. "She says it's nothing at all, but she's been a bit under the weather. Pale, circles under her eyes, and she just can't seem to shake that horrid cough. Celia has never been one to complain, so she wouldn't tell us even if she was sick. Daddy used to call her his little soldier."

Little soldier, hell. Celia was no goddamn soldier. She needed someone to watch over her, someone to take care of her. "If she doesn't get to feeling better, maybe you should talk to the doctor."

"We have to go," Faye said suddenly. "If we're late, Celia will worry, and she doesn't need any more worries right now."

"Yes," Floy agreed, and the two of them backed away a few steps. Before they turned to run, she had a few more words for him. "Sorry about the boots. It was all Faye's idea."

Most of the cobwebs were gone, and the crude plank floor her grandfather had laid in the cellar had been swept clean. Celia decided to rest for a moment before she climbed the stairs to the parlor. The girls would be home soon, and there was dinner to cook.

Best to steal a moment while she could.

She opened the trunk, the only one she'd had a chance to explore, and plucked Grandma Hart's journal from the top of the heap. It was such soft leather, even after all this time, and Celia ran her hands over it lovingly.

With care, since it was so very old, Celia opened the book. There was nothing on the first page, nothing at all, and she turned the page carefully. It would be a real disappointment if the journal was completely blank.

It wasn't, but what she found when she turned the page surprised her just the same. The neat handwriting, evenly slanted and painstakingly neat, was her mother's. She had even written her name—Priscilla Pigg—in the upper right-hand corner.

Celia considered closing the book and returning it to the bottom of the trunk. When she'd thought these were Grandma's writings, prying had seemed innocent enough, but as these were her mother's words—more a diary, perhaps, than a journal—it seemed an invasion of sorts.

Just a page or two, she decided. If the contents were too personal, she'd return the diary to its proper place and never give it another thought.

November 17, 1869

There's no one I can talk to, so I decided to try writing my thoughts down. Perhaps it will help me sort things through.

I love it here, in the house where I grew up. There's a peace here I never feel when I'm at home. Maybe I touch the past here, in this little house. Children are so innocent, so happy. They don't know what lies ahead, that life is not easy, that every decision they make has the power to change their lives. I miss the innocence. Perhaps I wish I was a child again.

Celia is in the front bedroom, trying on Mama's wedding dress again. She thinks perhaps she's grown enough since she last tried it on, less than a month ago, that it will fit her. Celia is the light of my life. She's wonderfully beautiful, and sometimes I look at her and marvel that Hamilton and I could have produced such an angel.

I love days like this one. Celia's much too serious, most of the time. I wish she would laugh more, play more, but I suppose it is her nature to be sedate, older than her years. If she had brothers and sisters, it would be different. Easier for her, I think. I would love to have a house full of children, daughters and sons, sisters and brothers for Celia. But of course, that is impossible.

Impossible? Celia looked at the date at the top of the page again. The twins were born little more than a year later.

Above her head, the girls announced their presence, slamming the front door and shouting their greetings. Celia placed the diary on top of the silver-blue silk, and closed the lid.

She felt like a meddler, a snoop, but she

wanted to know her mother better. Celia had been a child, not much older than Floy and Faye, when Priscilla Pigg had become ill and died. She remembered her mother as a caretaker, a comforter . . . a mother. What was she like as a woman? Celia wanted to know. Still, it would be best not to leave the diary lying around for the girls to find, at least not until she'd read it through.

"Down in the cellar again?" Faye said as Celia climbed into the well-lit parlor.

"There's a lot of work to be done there." Celia brushed at her skirt, making certain she brought none of the cobwebs into the parlor with her.

"You'll never guess who we saw today," Faye said brightly. "On our way home from school."

"Who?" Celia asked, her mind still more on her mother's diary than on the twins.

"Benjamin Wolfe," Floy answered.

The diary was forgotten. "You stay away from that man, do you hear me?" The girls stared at the finger she shook at them. "He's . . . he's . . . a ne'er-do-well, that's what he is. A rogue who has no business associating with decent young women."

Floy and Faye looked at one another, and Faye lifted her eyebrows slightly.

"He didn't look as though he felt well," Floy said as the girls faced Celia again. "He looked a little pasty, and there were dark circles under his eyes, and, well . . ." Floy sighed and cut her eyes to the side. "He just didn't look like himself."

"I don't believe he smiled at all," Faye added.

Celia turned her back on the girls. Sick? She should be glad. She should wish him ill. She should wish him dead. "Mr. Wolfe's health is none of our concern. Now, you can do your homework, or you can help me with dinner."

"We have lots of homework," Faye said quickly. Of course, Faye dearly hated cooking, cleaning, sewing, and other womanly chores.

Benjamin Wolfe! Why couldn't she simply put the man from her mind? Every time she thought she'd dismissed him from her thoughts completely, someone reminded her. Rosemary, and now the girls. Would he never leave Piggville? He didn't belong here. This was not his home.

Celia washed up quickly, and tried to rid her mind of the unwanted image of Benjamin Wolfe, pale and sickly.

Ben dropped his cigar and ground the stub with the toe of his boot. He was so far away from the house he couldn't see a damn thing. Every now and again Celia walked in front of the window. He'd seen her give the girls a hug and kiss them good night, and a few minutes later the light in the front bedroom had been extinguished.

There was still a light burning in one room, but he hadn't seen Celia for several minutes.

What if she was really sick? He took a step forward, out of the shelter of the trees. Lucky was with him, right at his heels.

Clouds covered the sky tonight, so there was no moon. The soft light that poured from the window lit the ground, but all around him was complete darkness. If he were careful to avoid the small area of light, Celia wouldn't see him even if she were to look out of the window. And, damn it, he had to know that she was all right.

He was almost so close to the house he could touch it before he saw Celia. She was sitting in a rocking chair to the side of the window, mending in her lap and her full attention on the task.

He couldn't see her face. The top of her head, a pale cheek with a strand of dark hair falling across it, her hands as she repaired the hem of a blue calico skirt—that was all he could see. Damn it, he needed to see her face.

Thunder rumbled in the distance, and Celia lifted her head. She was looking straight at him, straight at the window.

She didn't appear to be ill, not at all. She was tired, he could see that, but there was color in her cheeks and life in her eyes.

Thunder again, closer this time, and the first fat raindrops fell. They landed softly in his hair and on his shoulders, single, gentle drops of rain. He had no intention of standing in the rain just to watch Celia Pigg. It was a ridiculous notion.

Slowly, moving fluidly, Celia stood and placed her mending in a basket at her side. With the storm coming, perhaps she was going to turn off the light and go to bed. Maybe she was afraid of storms and wanted to hide under the covers.

He wanted to hide under the covers with her.

Instead of extinguishing the lamp, as Ben thought she might, Celia moved her rocking chair closer to the window. Once she was settled there she picked up her mending and began again, as intent on her work as before.

The thunder and lightning passed to the north, never more than a distant rumble and a faint flash of light in the night sky, but the rain came . . . a sprinkle and then a torrent.

As the rain intensified, Celia lifted her face more and more often. Finally, she dropped her mending into the basket and came to the window.

Lucky growled lowly.

"Go home if you can't take a little rain like a man," Ben whispered hoarsely.

Lucky didn't hesitate, but took off running across the yard.

Celia saw the movement. Ben saw her eyes follow Lucky's run to the path, but she didn't look concerned at all. Of course, in the night, in the rain, the ugly mutt could easily pass for a rabbit.

There was a small smile on Celia's face as she turned her eyes to the sky and placed her hands against the panes of glass. It was as if she were trying to feel the rain in spite of the barrier, as if she wanted to be outside with him, getting drenched to the skin.

She didn't look at all sick. In fact, she looked more beautiful than ever. Celia was warm, and serene, and as alone as he was.

Her fingers rocked back and forth on the glass, and in response Ben clenched his fists. This was ridiculous, bizarre, God's idea of a joke, right? That he should wait all this time for revenge, that he should come here and find her and be so damned besotted that he could stand in the rain all night and just look at her.

Without taking so much as a single step forward, he could reach out and lay his hands against the glass; he could lay his palm against hers with nothing but rainwater and glass between them, and all but touch her. But he didn't. He didn't move at all.

The rain soaked his clothes through and then soaked his skin. It ran over his head and down his face. And he didn't think once of slipping back to the shelter of the trees, or making his way to the saloon or his own warm, dry bed.

"I can't believe he's still out there," Faye whispered from the bed.

Floy knelt in front of the window and watched Ben Wolfe's motionless and broad back. Even though there was no longer even the far-off rumble of thunder, Faye refused to sit by the window. "Me neither."

"Why doesn't he just come to the door and ask to speak with her? I don't understand this at all."

"She likes him, too." Floy turned away from the window and toward the narrow bed where her twin hid from the storm. "Did you see her face this afternoon when she told us to stay away from him?"

"I know."

"What are we going to do now?"

Floy turned to face the window again, and through the misty and rain-splattered panes of glass she watched Ben Wolfe's back. She practically had to press her face against the glass to see him, he was so close to the house, so that was just what she did.

"They need to talk," she said, and the window fogged up where her breath touched the cool glass. "If we could just force them to sit down and talk . . ."

"I have an idea," Faye said quickly. The bed squeaked as she sat up.

Floy had heard this particular tone of voice before, and no good ever came of it. "What kind of an idea?"

"You won't like it," Faye promised. "It's very wicked."

Floy sighed and climbed into her own bed. Ben Wolfe might be able and willing to stand out in a storm all night, but she had school tomorrow. "I suppose you should tell me all about it," she said with a weary sigh.

Chapter Fifteen

Celia placed her hand over Floy's forehead. There was no fever, but Floy was pale and she clasped at her stomach fretfully.

"I can't possibly go to school," Floy said weakly. "I feel just terrible."

Faye danced into the room to stand by her sister's bed. She was dressed for school and carrying her books, apparently ready to make the walk to school alone. It was rare that one of the twins would be sick and the other not, but it had happened on occasion.

"Perhaps you'd better rest in bed for a while," Celia said, tucking Floy in. "If you're not better by this afternoon we'll visit Dr. Edwards."

"I'm sure I'll be better by this afternoon," Floy said weakly. A bit too feebly, in fact. "I just need to rest."

"I hope so." Celia patted her sister's hand. It wasn't like Floy to fake being sick. Maybe she was having trouble in school, or maybe all the turmoil of the past several weeks was catching up with her. In any case, it wouldn't hurt to let Floy curl up in bed for a single day. If it became a regular occurrence, well, then she would have to put her foot down.

Faye walked from the bedroom with her. There was a liveliness in Faye's step that was quite a contrast to Floy's lethargy. Odd, since one twin was usually affected by the other's mood.

"Will you be working in that yucky cellar again this morning?" Faye asked as she walked to the door. The rain had soaked the ground, but the sun shone brightly. It was going to be a beautiful spring day.

"I plan to," Celia said. "After I feed the animals and clean up the breakfast dishes."

Faye nodded thoughtfully. "That shouldn't take very long."

With that, Faye left quite happily for school. She was almost skipping over the rocky and grassy patches of ground so she wouldn't step into the mud.

Everything might work out after all. If she disregarded today's *illness*, the twins were adjusting well to the changes. There was a sturdy roof over their heads, and food on the table, and in a few years the girls would have their trust funds for security. Together, they could survive until then.

The morning's chores went quickly, as usual. Celia was already becoming accustomed to this new and simpler way of life. Feeding chickens and pigs instead of making numbers add up. Cleaning up the kitchen instead of sitting behind her father's desk.

She liked it.

When the chores were done, she peeked in on Floy, who was pretending to sleep. Celia decided to let her get away with her charade, for the moment. They'd have a nice, long talk over a cup of tea before Faye came home from school.

After a short rest, a few minutes to enjoy a cup of tea by herself, Celia threw back the trapdoor, lit a lamp, and descended the narrow and steep stairs to the cellar.

Perhaps today she'd have a chance to explore another of the old trunks, and to read a bit of her mother's diary. The prospect of reading her mother's words was exciting and daunting at the same time. She didn't want to pry, but this was an opportunity she couldn't ignore.

She wanted to know Priscilla Pigg as a woman—even if only through words written years ago.

But first, there was cleaning to be done. Did they really need all Grandma Hart's bottles?

Someone was going to be shot. Specifically, the someone who was banging relentlessly on his door.

Ben rolled up and brought his hands to his eyes. It was late in the morning, he could tell by the light, but then it had been nearly dawn before he'd gotten to bed. And he could feel a cold coming on. To prove himself right, he sneezed violently.

"Go away!" he shouted as he fell back to the bed.

"I can't, Mr. Wolfe. Please open the door."

At the sound of that voice, he was instantly awake. Hadn't he and Celia both told the twins that a saloon was no place for little . . . young women?

He swung out of bed, stepped into his pants, and grabbed yesterday's shirt from the back of the chair. He was still buttoning it when he opened the door.

"Thank goodness," she said, a desperate plea as she clutched her hands tight. "I don't know what I would have done if I hadn't found you."

All this time in Piggville, and he had never seen one twin without the other. "Floy?"

She nodded quickly. "You have to come with me, quickly. Celia's fallen."

"What?"

He stepped into his boots.

"She fell, down into the cellar. Faye's sitting with her. Oh, Mr. Wolfe, Celia's hurt, but I don't know how badly."

"You've already sent the doctor to your house, right?" he asked sharply as he left his room and joined Floy in the hallway.

"I couldn't find him," she said pathetically. "And besides"—she turned wide, innocent eyes to him—"Celia asked for you."

He stopped dead at the top of the staircase. "She did?"

Floy nodded her head slowly. "She said, 'Floy, you go get Ben for me. He'll know what to do.' She was a little groggy, and her voice wavered weakly, but I could understand her very well."

She'd asked for him.

He ran, down the stairs and the boardwalk, to the alleyway between the café and the doctor's office. This was the quickest route, he had discovered.

Floy was right behind him, keeping up quite well as he followed the narrow path that had become so familiar. The ground beneath his boots was sopping wet, the leaves on the trees he passed heavy and brilliant green. He didn't look over his shoulder, but he could hear Floy huffing and puffing as she kept up the pace.

His heart beat fast, and it wasn't the running; it wasn't the worry.

She'd asked for him.

He didn't knock, but burst into the little brick house. He could see the open trapdoor there in the main room. It was standing open, and beyond the opening, in the darkness below, he could see the glow of a lamp.

"Celia?" he said breathlessly as he dropped into the darkness.

She was crouched on the floor in front of an open trunk, and her head snapped up when she heard his voice. Faye was nowhere to be seen.

Celia didn't appear to be hurt, but she did look surprised to see him.

"What are you doing here?" she asked, her voice perfectly clear, not at all groggy or weak.

And then the trapdoor slammed down, and the hammering began in earnest. By the time he climbed the ladderlike stairs and pushed against the door, it was secure and wouldn't budge.

"Damn it!" he shouted. "Open this door!" He pounded his fist against the trapdoor. It gave, fluctuating just a little with each strike, but showed no signs of opening or splintering.

The hammering continued, and then stopped all at once.

"Girls!" Celia shouted, and Ben realized she was directly behind him, standing on the bottom step and lifting her head to the closed trapdoor. "Open this door at once, or I'll spank you both, I swear it."

"No, you won't," one of the twins said with certainty.

"I will!" Ben shouted.

There was dead silence for a long moment.

"Try it again," Celia whispered.

Ben pushed against the door, but it was securely fastened.

"What did you girls do?" he asked, trying for a friendlier tone. They surely wouldn't let him out if they thought he would really spank them.

"We placed a plank over the trapdoor and nailed it into the floor," one of them said proudly. "We used at least a dozen nails."

"Sixteen," someone whispered, and it was not Floy or Faye.

"James Richardson, is that you?" Celia asked sharply. "When I tell your mother what you've done . . ."

"It was all Faye's idea," he said miserably. "See?" he said in a hiss. "My mom's gonna skin me alive."

"You should've kept your mouth shut," one of the girls responded. Faye.

"Floy," Ben said sweetly, appealing to the obviously more genteel of the two. "I can't believe you lied to me. Let us out right now, and all is forgiven."

"Actually," an amused and completely unrepentant voice answered, "I was the one you spoke with. Floy is a terrible liar."

Ben slammed his fist against the barricaded door again, and someone above his head squealed.

"There's a sack in the corner behind that rotten old black trunk, and it's filled with food, and a couple of canteens of water, and candles and matches."

"Just exactly how long do you intend to leave us down here?" Ben bellowed. And then he sneezed.

"That's what you get for standing out in the rain half the night, nitwit," Faye said brightly. "We'll be back in a few hours, directly after school. Unless, of course, Mr. Culpepper decides to keep us after school for being tardy again. In that case it might be nearly nightfall."

"You will open this door right now!" Celia demanded.

"They're not going to open the door," Ben said in a low, resigned voice.

"You two need to talk," Floy said amiably. "And

if Celia won't go into town, and Ben stands outside the house all night like an idiot and won't even come to the door . . . well, what do you expect us to do?"

There was the shuffle of feet overhead. "Floy! Faye!" Celia shouted.

"We'll come straight home from school," one of the girls called merrily.

And then, with a shuffle of feet and the slamming of a door, they were gone.

Celia backed away, off the stairs, toward the lamp that was sitting on the floor by the opened trunk. Had she heard and understood what the twins had said about him standing out in the rain half the night?

"I'm so sorry," she said softly. "They're not bad girls, not really, they're just . . ."

He sneezed.

When she was in the cellar alone, it was small. Right now, with Ben standing at the bottom of the stairs, it seemed incredibly tiny.

"God bless you," she said habitually.

He glared at her in response.

What on earth had the girls meant by saying that Ben had been standing outside the house half the night? He wouldn't. And if he did, why? She remembered the animal that had gone scurrying across the yard in the rain. A rabbit, or a very large squirrel, she had imagined.

Lucky?

"They mean well," she said softly. "They just don't understand."

"I think they understand more than you know."

His voice was low, a growl from the shadows.

She'd avoided the possibility of so much as passing Benjamin Wolfe on the street, and she'd tried so hard to get him out of her mind. There were moments when it seemed she might succeed, others when she knew she never would. And now here he was. There was no escape, no place to run to.

"They seem to think we need to sit down and have a civilized conversation," Ben said, apparently accepting the situation. "And maybe they're right."

He took a single step forward and then stopped.

"Maybe we could start with a few simple questions," Celia suggested,

Ben nodded, then positioned himself at the bottom of the stairway with his legs spread and his arms crossed, as if he were getting ready for a fight. "Shoot."

There were so many questions she wanted to ask, and most of them she didn't dare voice. She would have to be very careful.

"Is this war of yours over yet?"

His face hardened. She could see that even in the dim light that didn't quite illuminate his features. "No."

"I see." She sighed. If she could, she'd lift the lamp and hold it high so she could see Ben's face. His eyes told everything when he was off guard. Such a move would betray her, though, and she had to be satisfied with what she could see.

"Don't you think you've done enough to satisfy the promise to your father?"

"No."

At least it seemed to be a reluctant *no*.

That reluctance spurred her on. She wanted to know . . . she had to know. "Have you been watching me?" Her voice was so faint she wasn't sure it would carry, not even across the small space that separated them.

"Yes," he answered just as faintly.

"Why?"

Ben shuffled from one foot to another. At last, she'd managed to make him nervous. "I don't know."

She believed it was an honest answer, perhaps the only one he was capable of offering at the moment. If he was going to be honest, if he was going to open himself to her, just a little, she should seize this moment.

"Do you hate me?"

"No," he answered quickly. "Now it's my turn."

"All right." Celia lifted her chin and waited for the barrage that was certain to come.

"Why are you so damned stubborn?" Ben took a step forward, and she could see his face more clearly. He was frustrated, and perhaps a little angry.

"I don't think that's a fair question," she said haughtily. "Please be more specific."

"Specific?" She could hear so much in his voice. Frustration. Uncertainty. Anger. "All right. Why are you still here?"

He took another step, and it brought him too

close. She had to look up to see his face. Goodness, he was much too handsome. Just the sight of him made her pulse quicken, and she remembered the kisses they'd shared before he'd revealed his true nature. These were certainly not the thoughts to be having as she faced him defiantly.

"This is my home. I belong here. Doesn't that mean anything to you?"

"No," he said darkly. "It means nothing to me."

For all his money and his determination and his blasted vows, Benjamin Wolfe had very little in this world.

"What are you going to do, Ben, when this is all over? When you run me out of town and your promise to your father has been fulfilled . . . what will you do?"

"I'm asking the questions now," he snapped.

"Sorry," Celia whispered.

Ben spun around and stalked back to the foot of the rickety stairs. Again, his face was lost in darkness. "You have every right to hate me," he said from the shadows. "You should hate my guts, you should want me dead, you should be planning right now to take your revenge."

"Ben . . ."

He lifted a hand to silence her. "Do you?" he asked softly. "Hate me?"

She should say yes, loud and firm and without hesitation, but she didn't. And besides, wasn't John always telling her she had to learn to say no?

"No."

225

Chapter Sixteen

"We might as well make ourselves comfortable,"
Celia said sensibly. She sat on a rug and leaned
back against the chest.

Comfortable? He couldn't possibly be comfortable while he was trapped in the same room
with Celia.

He sat down anyway, and leaned against the
post at the foot of the stairs. This was about as
far away from Celia Pigg as he could possibly get
in the cellar.

She was so damned calm. How could she?
How could she admit that she didn't hate him,
and then blithely suggest that they make themselves comfortable?

Perhaps she wasn't as calm as she appeared to
be. She rested her hands in her lap, deep in the
folds of her skirt, and he could swear she was

twiddling her thumbs. A flounce at the hem of that skirt danced, as if she were shaking a foot nervously.

She should be nervous. Did she know that he would give everything he owned, everything he was, just to have her? That he would gladly leave behind every dollar he'd sweated for to live in a little house like this with her, to hold her every night . . . Damn it, he could never tell Celia how much he wanted her.

There was no longer any doubt about Celia's nervousness. She fidgeted on her rug, and now she was staring raptly at her twiddling thumbs. Hours. They would be here for hours yet, and already he felt as if he would explode if she touched him, if she *didn't* touch him . . . if she so much as looked at him with a hint of longing in her eyes.

He'd seen that longing in Celia's eyes, before she knew why he'd come to town.

It entered his mind that what they needed was a nice, safe conversation, some harmless chit-chat to defuse whatever the hell was going on between them and pass the time.

He couldn't think of a single thing to say. At least, nothing harmless.

The extended silence grew more and more uncomfortable. He squirmed.

"Would you like something to sit on? The floor's awfully hard, I know. There's lots of old clothes in these trunks, and you could always make a cushion of sorts. There might even be another rug or an old quilt in one of them. I haven't had time to go through everything yet, but I'm sure—"

"Celia," Ben interrupted softly. "You're babbling."

"I never babble," she said indignantly, and then she blushed.

She surely couldn't see him very well, but with the lamp sitting at her side she was illuminated perfectly. Her hair was in a damn twisted-up braid again, and he wanted to crawl over there and free it. Every dark, silky strand. Her dress was another prim, plain, gray monstrosity, high necked and long sleeved and without a touch of lace or a single ribbon. The only frivolity was the small flounce at the hem.

He wanted to dress her in gold and blue, in lace and satin. Most of all, he wanted to peel that damned ugly gray dress off of her body.

What a shape she had, rounded in all the right places. Full, rounded breasts, small waist, curving hips. Even in that homely dress she was gorgeous. It occurred to him that perhaps she dressed this way on purpose. If she dressed properly there wasn't a man in the world who wouldn't want her to the exclusion of everyone, everything else.

How well he knew that fact.

"Ben?"

He almost jumped out of his skin at the sound of her voice. "What?" he snapped.

Celia hesitated, and he wondered if his tone of voice had scared her into silence. Maybe it would be best if that were true. Just the sound of her voice got under his skin.

But Celia wouldn't be scared into silence. She squared her shoulders and looked directly at him. He knew she couldn't possibly be able to see him well, not while he hid here in the shadows, and yet she stared unflinchingly. Her hands and her feet were finally still.

"Why can't you just let it go?" she whispered.

He could handle her anger better than he could handle this serene questioning. Far better. He never backed down from a fair fight.

It was on his lips to ask her, again, what she was willing to do to make him change his mind.

He couldn't.

"I swore to my father—"

"I remember your father," she interrupted. "Not very well, but I remember sitting in church and listening to him. I was just a child, and my mother liked to sit near the back, so I could never see his face very well as he preached, but I remember his voice." She smiled, a small, enchanting smile that made Ben's insides tighten.

"Everything came through in his voice. Fire, anger, love. Even when I didn't understand what he was saying, I . . . understood. I could feel it." She brought a small fist to her breast. "Here."

"He was a fine preacher."

"Yes, I believe he was," Celia agreed. "No matter what he did."

"He didn't *do* anything."

Celia sighed. Perhaps she realized this was an argument she could never win. "In all my memories of Ezekiel Wolfe, I don't remember ever hearing malevolence in his voice. Was he a vengeful man, your father?"

"Celia—"

She didn't allow him to continue. "Did he ask you to make this vow of yours? Did he request that you come here to ruin me?"

"Ruin you?" Ben rocked forward.

"Isn't that exactly what you set out to do? Isn't that exactly what you've done?"

Ben sprinted to his feet. "You're the one who's ruined everything."

"Me?" she asked innocently.

"Yes, you," Ben said angrily, stepping into the circle of light Celia's lamp cast. "You're not what you're supposed to be, and you don't fight fair. Hell, you don't fight at all."

She didn't even stand, but sat there at his feet and contemplated his knees. "I'm not a fighter, Ben," she said softly. "This is your war, not mine, and it has been from the beginning."

He dropped to his knees so he could see her face, her eyes. "You were supposed to be like your father," he accused. "Mean and spiteful and ugly—inside and out. You were supposed to pay for what he did."

Celia did fight, and it wasn't fair . . . not fair at all. She raised a hand and touched his cheek. Her fingers feathered over the stubble there, and then she delivered the final blow. She rocked up to her knees so that they were chest to chest, and she kissed him. Before he could react, before he could move away.

"Let it go," she whispered as she pulled her lips from his.

"I can't."

"You can." She kissed him again, and this time there was no thought of backing away. Celia was his weakness, his only weakness, and he kissed her back with just a hint of the longing that filled him. Again, she was the one to break the kiss and move away, rolling back slightly. "You say this is for your father, but I don't believe you. You're doing this for yourself. Your father wouldn't want to see you like this. Angry. Unforgiving. Alone. Surely he wanted more for his only child."

Ben wanted to argue with her, but he couldn't. She was right. He lifted his hands to her face and held her, his palms against her cheeks, his fingers in her hair.

She was so beautiful, and warm, and he wanted more than anything to be a part of her life. Now and forever.

"Help me," he whispered. "Help me let it go."

Her answer was a smile, and then another kiss. A kiss that made him forget all the pain and the promises of the past.

With a sigh of surrender, Ben lowered her to the floor. Celia shivered, deep inside, as he followed. Her bones, her heart, her blood, everything she was, trembled.

He brought his mouth to hers, and Celia closed her eyes. It was delicious, this kiss that went on and on. His tongue teased and then invaded her. His arms tightened around her. There was no one else in the world but the two of them, nothing that mattered beyond this cellar.

This was pure, potent pleasure, and with every second that passed it grew and changed into something new. A quickening of her heart, a hunger of her mouth, an ache so deep down she couldn't identify it. She couldn't allow this to stop.

Ben's hands slipped from her back to her sides and danced up slowly, over her ribs, over her heart that beat so hard and fast, until he touched her breasts.

The gentle touch was tantalizing and thrilling. She arched up and into him, instinctively wanting more.

Ben drew away from her ever so slightly, and the buttons down the front of her dress flew through his fingers, exposing her chest to the chilly air. She wasn't chilled for long, though. Ben covered her breasts with his hands, his palms touching bare skin and the thin linen of her chemise, and it was as if he gave her heat, as if the warmth from his hands grew until it surrounded her.

She wanted, needed, his mouth against hers again, and she took his face in her hands and pulled him gently downward until his lips met hers.

This time when he pulled away he brought her with him, with a hand at the back of her head. She was sitting up, and Ben straddled her hips with his knees against the old rug.

He removed the pins from her hair, his hands

sure and unhurried. When her braid fell Ben ran his hands through the strands. Everywhere he touched her, she was branded. Her scalp, the back of her neck, down her spine to the small of her back.

"I want to see you," he breathed as he took his hands from her hair to slip his fingers beneath her dress and peel it from her shoulders and her arms.

"Yes," she whispered against his lips.

"Everything."

"Yes."

The short chemise was stripped gently from her skin, baring her breasts for Ben's eyes, and his fingers, and his tongue.

When he sucked a nipple into his mouth, Celia jerked up and against him.

"Did I hurt you?" he asked softly, pulling his mouth away from her flesh, but continuing to caress her with his hands, those gentle fingers.

"No," she whispered.

Ben brought his mouth to hers again, and kissed her softly while his fingers stroked soft skin and hardened nipples. His lips brushed hers, slipping away and coming back again, teasing, enticing.

She wanted Ben in a way she'd never imagined was possible. The ache was unrelenting, and undeniable, and it was growing with every moment that passed, with every stirring of his hands and his lips. This ache was in her chest, in the pit of her belly, between her legs.

"Celia," Ben whispered hoarsely. "Do you

know what's happening, sweetheart?"

"Yes." Mercy, she could barely talk, she was so breathless.

"Do you want me to stop?" he breathed as he kissed her again. "If you do, tell me now and I will. I'll stop touching you, and I'll stop kissing you, and I'll move away." He drew his mouth from hers and took a deep, stilling breath. "Do you want me to stop?"

"No."

She pulled his mouth back to hers. Imitating him, she plunged her tongue into his mouth and unfastened the buttons of his shirt. She ran her hands against his skin, found the tiny nipples nestled in a sprinkling of fine chest hair, and teased him mercilessly.

He pushed her skirt to her waist and gently spread her knees and her thighs. Resting between her parted thighs, he touched her with tenderly probing fingers.

Her reaction was intense, as unexpected and pleasurable as the sensation of having her nipple in Ben's mouth. More.

"You're wet for me," he whispered as he brought his mouth to hers and kissed her. He kissed her as he stroked the wetness between her legs, and then there was more.

A touch of something hot and hard, pressure, an urgent push, and then he was inside her. He was still as her body adjusted to his, and then he pulled away and thrust again, this time driving his manhood just a little farther inside her. He waited again, kissed her deeply, and then he thrust hard, pushing deep, breaking past her maidenhead and filling her completely.

It hurt. He had invaded her body and her heart, had joined his body to hers. It hurt, and it was wonderful, and she wrapped her arms around Ben's neck as he began to move within her, stroking gently and as surely as he had with his hands.

Gradually her body adjusted to accept his, and the pain faded. He kissed her, and he pushed deeper inside her than she'd thought possible. He was a part of her, in body and in spirit. The intense longing that had begun when she'd first kissed him grew and changed, until she felt as if she were coming undone.

"Ben?" She whispered the plea against his lips.

"Easy," he answered. "Let it happen, Celia. Let it go." He was relentless in his assault. His lips moved over hers, his hips thrust against her again and again.

She listened to Ben and relaxed. She didn't think, she didn't wonder, she just *was*.

Unraveling. Falling apart.

And then she did. In a burst of sensation too fierce to deny, she came apart.

Ben came with her. He drove deep one last time, trembled in her arms, and came undone.

He didn't pull away, didn't leave her body or her arms, but encompassed her and held her tight.

She whispered his name, so softly she didn't know if he would hear her or not. How miraculous, how frightening, how undeniably right this was.

Celia smiled and wrapped her arms around his waist. The war was over.

Ben raised himself up and looked down. He and Celia were a tangle of limbs and clothes that hadn't quite made it all the way off. She was dark silky hair and flushed cheeks, sensitive skin with a sheen of sweat that glistened in the lamplight.

She was everything he'd imagined and more. Passionate, loving, and, as he'd always expected, far from the prudish maiden she pretended to be.

"Are you hurt?" He didn't want to hurt her again, not ever. He would make up for everything he'd done by making sure no one and nothing ever hurt Celia again.

"A little sore," she admitted, but a smile took away the sting of the words.

He left Celia there on the rug—beautifully glowing, half-dressed, and a little dazed by love-making—to fetch the survival pack the twins had left behind. All he took from the burlap sack was a canteen of water.

From the trunk Celia had leaned against earlier, he took an old linen shirt. It was well worn, and there was a long rip in one sleeve. The sleeve came off with an easy tug, and he dampened the linen with a splash of water from the canteen.

Celia sat up when he knelt between her knees with the damp cloth in his hands.

"What are you doing?"

"I'm taking care of you."

He didn't allow her to object, but placed the cool, damp cloth between her legs and held it there. Celia didn't pull away, didn't look down or away and pretend to be shy, but allowed him to attend to her.

She was the only woman he had ever known who was completely without artifice. Celia didn't lie, and she didn't amuse herself by playing with other people's lives. She said exactly what was on her mind, and expected everyone else to do the same.

It would be nice to live in a world like that.

He discarded the cloth and pulled Celia into his arms. Sitting on the rug with his back against the trunk, he held her. "You know," he said softly, "I hardly think this is what your sisters had in mind. They didn't mention anything but conversation, and it seems that you and I, Celia, sweetheart, are dismal failures when it comes to harmless chitchat."

She stiffened in his arms and turned her face up. Her clothing was still more off than on, and he had a generous view of bare skin below the neck. "You won't tell them, will you?"

"Of course not." He couldn't be insulted because Celia thought he might. He'd done worse since she'd met him.

"They just don't know . . . they don't have any idea." She sighed and placed her head against his chest. "Goodness, *I* didn't have any idea it would be like this. I mean, I wasn't completely ignorant, but no one ever told me it would be so wonderful."

Ben turned her face up and kissed her quickly. "If you don't be quiet," he promised, "I'll end up taking you again, and I'm not sure you're ready."

"Will you?" she whispered.

It was the touch of hope in her voice, the longing in her eyes, the way she parted her lips as she lifted her face to his that got to him.

He had no choice but to kiss her. Wasn't this a fine turn of events? Nothing mattered at this moment, not revenge, not justice. He didn't ever want to leave this damp, dark cellar.

Celia rested in his arms, nestled there, fitting so perfectly it was as if she'd been made just for him. Her head rested against his arm, and thick, dark hair spilled across his sleeve. Celia, unkempt and reclining in his arms, was the sort of picture dreams were made of. The sort of picture a man would remember until the day he died.

"You confuse me," Celia said softly. Her fingers played against his arm, feathery, uncertain touches.

"Do I?"

"Yes," she whispered. "I didn't know it was possible to feel so very strongly about a person one minute, and then have my emotions whirl and change completely the next."

"I know what you mean," he admitted.

"Do you?" She leaned her head back to look at him. "Do you really?"

He answered her with a kiss.

"You made me so angry," she said as she drew her lips from his. "No one's ever made me angry before. And then . . . and then . . ."

Another kiss and she forgot her gentle protests. She came to him as if she experienced the same undeniable draw he did. Nothing else mattered but this, and they both felt it.

This time, neither one of them would wear a stitch of clothing. Ben peeled the dress off Celia's body, slowly, carefully, tasting skin as he progressed. He wanted to feel her skin pressing against his, wanted to kiss every inch of her.

In a matter of minutes he was wonderfully, magically lost.

It was Celia who pushed his unbuttoned shirt off his shoulders, who pushed his Levi's over his hips and down.

And this time when he made love to her they were lying on a cushion of discarded clothes. There was nothing between his body and hers, nothing to keep him from feeling the pulse of her beating heart and the quiver of her flesh.

How was it possible that he could be so desperate for her so soon? That he should need her like this?

As if his very life depended upon being a part of her.

And he realized, as he released his seed into her a second time, that if this was war, he'd just surrendered.

Chapter Seventeen

"She's going to kill us," Floy whispered hoarsely.

Faye was kneeling over the trapdoor, her ear to the floor. "No. *He's* going to kill us."

Either way, it didn't look good.

"Well, we have to let them out. They can't stay down there forever."

"Do you hear anything?" James asked softly. He waited several feet away with a crowbar cradled in his arms.

"Shhh." Faye pressed her ear flush against the floor and listened hard. "Nothing. Nothing at all."

They had killed each other, Floy was certain. Celia and Ben Wolfe were both dead, probably with their hands locked around one another's throats. If they were alive there would be some sound, some sign of life below.

This had been a dreadful mistake. What would

they do without Celia? They would surely be arrested and charged with something dreadful.

"James?" Faye said solemnly.

Reluctantly, James stepped forward and shooed Faye out of the way. Kneeling on one knee, he slipped the flattened end of the crowbar under the plank that held the trapdoor closed. A good shove, and they'd be on their way.

He hesitated, and lifted an uncertain face to Faye. "Now?"

Faye nodded soberly, and James put his weight on the steel bar. With a resounding crack, one side of the board and a good number of nails rose up. He moved the tool to the other side and repeated the simple move, and the plank was gone.

Standing in a tight knot, the three of them waited, watching the door that was set in the parlor floor. Nothing happened.

Celia and Mr. Wolfe were surely dead.

It was Faye who was brave enough to reach out and lift the trapdoor. James backed away, but he didn't leave. Faye had told him earlier that he had to stay until this ordeal was over with. Something about a witness.

The door opened fully, and there was Ben Wolfe. He was standing on the stairs and looking up at them, an odd expression on his face. Not angry, not smiling, just . . . bland acceptance.

"Good afternoon, girls."

With that perfectly agreeable greeting, Ben Wolfe climbed into the parlor. Floy didn't remember him being quite so tall and menacing, but he was as he rose slowly from the depths of his temporary prison. Celia was right behind him, a candle in her hand that Mr. Wolfe took as he held her other hand and helped her up.

Floy had expected Celia to be livid, at least for a while, but she appeared to be as calm as Ben Wolfe.

"Well," Celia said as she brushed at her skirt, clearing off a bit of dirt. Goodness, there was dirt all over her dress, and a few strands of hair were falling from a crooked braid, and there was a single smudge of dirt on her cheek. Those cheeks were quite red. When she lifted her eyes, Floy knew they hadn't gotten off scot free. There was a dark fire in Celia's normally kind eyes. "What am I going to do with you girls?"

That didn't sound good at all.

"We were only trying to help," Faye said stridently.

"That's right," Floy agreed, but with less vigor.

Ben Wolfe smiled. Not widely, but one of those sneaky half smiles Faye got when she knew a secret and was trying to decide how much to share. Floy noticed that he was in the same shape as Celia. His shirt was dirty, smudged here and there with dirt from the cellar floor. His boots were dusty, his trousers wrinkled. Like Celia, he had a single smudge of dirt on his face. Oh, this had been a bad idea.

They'd been stuck in that nasty cellar for hours. She and Faye should've taken a while longer with their plan and thought of a more comfortable place to strand the stubborn couple.

"I'd be happy to take them back behind the

woodshed and whale the tar out of them." Ben Wolfe's words were harsh, but the tone was oddly mellow.

"That won't be necessary," Celia said with a sigh. "Go to your room, and stay there. No supper for you girls tonight."

"But, Celia . . ." Faye began. Celia silenced her with an almost stern glare.

James was backing slowly and quietly toward the door.

"James Richardson," Celia said sweetly. "Don't you go just yet."

James's face went white, but he stopped and waited.

"I should tell your mother just what you've done," Celia said cordially.

"She'll whup me good, Miss Celia," James said with a shake of his head. "Please don't tell her." He could have told Celia right then and there that this was all Faye's idea, that she had commanded him to assist in their plot, but he didn't.

"Well." Celia glanced up at Mr. Wolfe. "What do you think?"

He seemed to think the problem over carefully. "You need a lot of help around the place. Maybe James could volunteer to chop wood and feed the animals and do a bit of fixing up around the house for, say . . . a month?"

"A month!" James said, and the color rushed back into his face. "I'd rather get a whupping. I've got my chores at home, and school, and—"

"I can walk James home," Mr. Wolfe volunteered cheerfully, interrupting James's whining.

"It'll save you the trip. You mentioned speaking to his mother, but I think I'd prefer to talk to his father."

"All right," James said quickly. "A month."

Mr. Wolfe decided to walk James part of the way home anyway, leaving the Pigg women alone. Floy waited for Celia to explode, but she didn't.

"Go on to your room," she said when the men were gone. "You can do your studies and then get to bed, and when you're hungry you remind yourself how rude it is to trick people, to lie and scheme and . . . imprison them, even when you have your so-called reasons."

She was maddeningly calm, though she tried to be stern. Was that a good sign or a bad one?

Faye grumbled as she went to the bedroom she shared with her twin, but Floy was silent. Celia had never been able to punish them, not really. Twice before she'd sent them to their room without supper, and both times she'd slipped them something to eat not long after their regular suppertime.

Had it worked? Celia and Ben Wolfe hadn't killed one another, and they hadn't been arguing or silent or pouty. Upon their release they had been, in fact, almost serene.

That had to be a good sign.

James Richardson hurried off toward home, glancing back twice to see if he was being followed. The second time, Ben smiled and waved.

Ben wanted to spin around and run back to

Celia's house. He wanted to hold her and make love to her again, and tell her that she had changed his life, but of course that wouldn't work. The twins were there, and besides, there were plans to be made.

The Piggville Gentlemen's Social Club would have to be closed, and the saloon converted back into a boardinghouse. Should he make arrangements to close Zeke's and reopen the Pigg General Store? Two general stores in this town didn't make much sense, but after they were married it wouldn't make any difference which store was in operation. Either one would be theirs.

Theirs. Married. A smile crept across Ben's face. They hadn't discussed marriage, not yet, but it was inevitable.

He had never even imagined that a woman like Celia could want him, or that he could need anyone like this. Could she really love him? The word hadn't been uttered by either of them, as they'd come together in the cellar. They'd spoken of want and need and pleasure, but not love. It was the kind of commitment you couldn't take back.

But Celia wasn't the kind of woman to give herself to a man she didn't love. Even if she hadn't said the words, even if she'd been holding back, he knew it was true. He'd felt what could only be love coming from Celia. Could he love her back?

Yes. Without reserve, without a single doubt. Heaven help him, it was true.

His father would approve.

He'd sworn to drive every last Pigg out of town,

and he'd come to Piggville with just that purpose. Of course, when he married Celia she wouldn't be a Pigg any longer; she'd be a Wolfe. And the twins?

The Ezekiel Wolfe he remembered wouldn't approve of waging war on little girls. Even little girls like Floy and Faye, who were more than capable of fighting back. Celia had reminded him of that fact, when she'd asked him if his father had ever been a vengeful man.

Maybe someday, when the twins were older and wiser, he would thank them for taking him prisoner.

When the girls were closed in their room, Celia could finally smile.

She had often wondered what true love would feel like, on stormy, sleepless nights. As the thunder and lightning broke the night, she closed her eyes and wondered what it would be like to be kissed properly, to trust her heart and her soul to a single man. Forever. True love had been a part of her dream of a better, simpler life, and at times it had seemed as impossible as that dream.

It had cost her her home, her businesses, her very security . . . but it was worth it.

Ben was so perfectly wonderful. She dismissed the niggling doubt that entered her mind as she opened the trapdoor to reenter the cellar. He had taken terrible revenge on her, deceived her and ruined her financially, as well as making sure that she'd never be able to hold her head up in

Piggville again, but that was before . . . before love had changed everything.

With the lamp in hand, she made her way to the open chest. The diary was on the top, but was almost hidden in the folds of the blue silk dress that was lying across the contents. Celia took the diary, closed the trunk, and returned to the stairs.

At the foot of the narrow stairs, she turned to survey the cellar. Such a dingy, dirty place. Small, cramped, musty. And beautiful.

Ben had loved her here. She fairly tingled with the memory. It was as if she could still feel the heat and the comfort of his hands on her, his lips molded to hers, his chest pressed to her breasts and the pressure and the pleasure of his body joined with hers.

She left the cellar with a sigh and a smile, and settled herself in the rocking chair with her mother's diary. Why had she thought of it so urgently? Maybe because she couldn't walk to the cemetery this late in the day to tell her mother how she'd finally found love. Maybe because holding this diary made her feel close to Priscilla Pigg, the woman, in a way that a child's remembrances or a visit to the graveyard couldn't.

For whatever reason, Celia held the book lovingly. With the girls ensconced in their room, this was the perfect opportunity to read a bit farther in the journal.

January 21, 1870
I spoke to Ezekiel Wolfe this afternoon.

He's such a nice man. Kay Anne Ascot has suggested an addition to the church, an expansion, really, of the existing building. She has great plans. A bell, an organ, a new parish house. Since Hamilton is the only citizen of Piggville with the funds to take on this proposition, she came to me. It seemed a good idea to talk to the Reverend Wolfe and see what he wants for the church.

I never realized what magnificently piercing blue eyes Reverend Wolfe has until this afternoon.

Celia felt a cold prickle of warning.

He was very kind, as usual. It appears he wants nothing for himself and his son Benjamin, though he was excited at the prospect of a new bell and an organ. I think I shall go talk to him again tomorrow. These things cannot be rushed. Whatever changes are made to the Piggville Baptist Church will be long-lasting, and we must be very selective. The Reverend Wolfe has suggested that I meet him tomorrow afternoon at the parish. This is rather exciting. I need a new project to occupy my time.

Celia flipped past several pages, through several neatly composed pages, until a name jumped out at her, nearly coming off the page. *Zeke.* Not Ezekiel, or Reverend Wolfe, but *Zeke.*

Zeke came to the old house again this afternoon. We only had an hour, but it was heavenly. I know it's wrong. If anyone knew the truth it would be scandalous, a disaster for us all. Some nights I am able to convince myself that I must be strong and tell Zeke this madness must stop. It is a kind of madness, I know. A brain-muddling, life-altering insanity that makes me forget everything I've ever believed in. Adultery is a sin. When I am alone I tell myself that this must end. I have a family to think of. My good name. My very soul. But I find I cannot think of sending Zeke away when he is near. When he touches me I forget about my family, my good name, my soul. I never knew love could be so wonderful.

Suddenly ill, Celia covered the offensive page with her hand, hiding the damning words. It was too late, of course. The words were burned into her brain, and she couldn't erase them.

Ben's father, the womanizer, had seduced her mother. Just the way he'd seduced those other women. Just the way his son had seduced her.

A horrifying thought occurred to her, and she peeled her fingers from the page. This suspicion was just a product of her overactive imagination. It couldn't be true. It couldn't possibly be true.

She turned the page, and then another, and then another, searching for the words that would turn her entire world upside down.

And then she found what she was looking for.

I am terrified, I am ecstatic. I am going to have Zeke's child.

Celia slammed the diary shut and closed her eyes tight. The curly blond hair, the blue eyes, the enchanting brightness that had never been a part of Hamilton Pigg or his wife Priscilla.

The twins were Ben's sisters.

"But why are you closing us down?" Ginger asked angrily. It was a bit too early in the morning for her, and for the girls who followed her—yawning and grumbling and catching the eye of every passing gentleman.

"Change of plans," Ben said brightly. He didn't mind telling Ginger everything. Half an hour from now she'd be on the train and headed, in a roundabout way, for Denver. "I'm getting married and we'll be living in that house, I imagine."

Celia might have other ideas. Would she live there after the short and scandalous occupation of Ginger and her girls? If living in that house made Celia uncomfortable, he'd build her a new one. It would be twice as big as the old Pigg place, if that was what Celia wanted. Either way, the Piggville Gentlemen's Social Club was out of business.

"She finally got you, huh?" Ginger asked. "What did it?" She looked up at Ben's impassive face, and after a moment's study she smiled. "I see. Hmmm," she cooed contentedly, in that seductive way she had. "Sugarplum, I never figured you as a sucker for a virgin."

Ben didn't take the bait.

"I admire her," Ginger continued. "I certainly do. She saw what she wanted and went after it. We women do what we have to do to get what we want, and our options for persuasion are, shall we say, limited."

"Celia's not like that," Ben said easily, knowing that a woman like Ginger could never understand. "She's . . . she's different."

Ginger laughed. At him, Ben supposed, but he didn't really care.

"We all have our failings, sweet pea," Ginger said with a smile. "There's no need to be embarrassed just because yours is something so conventional as a virgin."

Ben ignored Ginger's honey-sweet comments. When he glanced away from her he spotted Huff and his lady friend, Rosemary Cranston, standing on the boardwalk and watching the parade of fallen ladies through Piggville.

Huff had been right all along. Ben had allowed vengeance to rule his life for too many years. He'd lost all perspective.

Hamilton Pigg was dead, and Celia had done nothing to deserve what he'd done to her.

As the ladies continued not-so-merrily on to the train station, Ben said a quick and general good-bye and changed course to head toward Huff and his lady friend.

"Good morning," Ben said brightly, wondering if Huff would return the greeting or simply shake his head and walk away.

Huff returned the greeting, suspiciously.

"What's all this?" he added, nodding to the retreating girls.

Rosemary was so interested she was holding her breath and leaning forward very slightly. Her eyes were wide, her cheeks flushed a becoming pink. Ben gave her a smile.

"I'm sending Ginger and the ladies back to Denver."

Huff raised his eyebrows, in a condescending and superior expression of surprise. "Is that right?"

"Yes it is."

Rosemary was obviously relieved. She took a deep breath and grinned widely.

"I'm glad you've had a change of heart on that front," Huff said cautiously. "What about Lucky's?"

Ben shrugged. "I suppose I'll have to close the saloon, too, turn the place back into a boarding-house." He didn't want to have this conversation in front of Rosemary, but he had a suspicion that Huff told her everything anyway. "You know how I hate to say this, but you were right. I went too far."

"I knew it," Rosemary said with a grin of satisfaction.

"You knew what?" Huff asked before Ben could.

"That Celia could change his mind." Rosemary tilted her head back and gave Huff a look of wide-eyed innocence. "You said yourself that she was the only one who could bring Ben to his senses, and see? You were right about that, too."

Huff said nothing, but he did have the good manners to look embarrassed. Rosemary, on the other hand, was not embarrassed at all. She looked at Ben and gave him a wide smile.

"She didn't believe me at first, when I told her she was the only one you would listen to. Poor Celia, she was so upset over everything that's happened, and she was certain there was nothing she could do or say to change your mind." Rosemary ignored the stilling hand Huff placed on her arm. "I'm so glad. . . ."

Ben didn't hear any more. There was noise, there were words, but they didn't make any sense. Unfortunately everything else—Celia's affection, her soft pleas, her ardor—suddenly made perfect sense.

Rosemary stopped speaking abruptly as Ben spun on his heel and headed for the depot.

He was such an idiot. Such a gullible fool. Celia *knew* he wanted her. That was a fact he'd never been able to hide. She'd known it all along, and yesterday she'd used that knowledge to get exactly what she wanted.

Celia Pigg was no better than Ginger and her girls. At least a whore was honest about the arrangements she made. Sex for money, a straightforward deal.

Not Celia. She offered love for control, for the return of her life as she'd once known it.

The girls were waiting for the train to arrive. A single ticket taker stared—not quite open-mouthed—as they lounged and yawned and grumbled, sat on hard benches and leaned against the walls. All but Ginger. She was standing ramrod straight in the middle of the room, and watching the door.

"I changed my mind," Ben snapped. "Get back to the house."

One girl, a busty blonde, groaned. "You mean you dragged us out of bed at the crack of dawn for nothing?"

"Call it a momentary lapse," Ben said, forcing a smile. "I hope you'll accept my apologies, along with an extra twenty at the end of the week."

It was the offer of money that made the ladies forgive him. Ginger even smiled. As she passed, she dragged her hand across Ben's arm. "Glad you came to your senses before it was too late, sugarplum."

"So am I," Ben growled.

"Do you think the little woman will want to stay with us after you're married?" There was a touch of malice in Ginger's voice. "There's a vacant room on the second floor, that bedroom you told me not to touch. Why, a sweet little thing like your bride Celia would be right at home there, I'm sure."

"I'm not getting married." Ben said as he followed her from the depot.

Ginger wrapped her arm through his as he stepped onto the boardwalk. "Glad to hear it."

This time, as Huff and Rosemary watched the parade, Ben didn't even look their way.

Chapter Eighteen

The insistent banging on the door made Celia jump. Even before he started yelling, she knew who it was.

"Celia," Ben shouted as he knocked on the door continuously. "Open this door." The handle wiggled, and upon finding that the door was locked Ben apparently kicked at the barrier. Celia jumped again.

She couldn't let him in. She couldn't face him, not with what she now knew. His father had been the womanizer he was accused of being, and Ben was no better.

"Go away," she said to the door. "I don't want to see you. What happened yesterday was a mistake. A terrible mistake."

"You've got that right, at least," Ben growled, lowering his voice only slightly. "I just wanted to let you know that your scheme didn't work. Nothing has changed, Celia Pigg. Nothing. Did you really think I would forget the vow to my father simply because you spread your legs for me?"

Celia clapped her hands over her mouth. How dare he? Her legs were trembling, her hands shaking.

"It was just sex, Celia, a roll in the hay," Ben said, his voice much calmer now. "The kind of amusement any man can buy at the Piggville Gentlemen's Social Club."

"Go away," she whispered.

"Not yet," he answered just as softly. His voice was perfectly clear. "Let me in."

Celia shook her head.

"Come on, sweetheart. Don't play the shy one with me now. You're not the bashful and demure prude you pretend to be. You're actually quite talented." Celia reached for the latch on the door. She wanted to look into Ben's face, wanted to see if he was lying to her. "I talked to Ginger just this morning. There's a vacant room at the social club, and she thought you might be interested in a job. It's your old room, of course. Now, wouldn't that give the gentlemen of Piggville a kick, screwing the respectable Miss Pigg right there in her little-girl bedroom in the Pigg mansion."

Her hand flew to the latch and flipped it back, and she threw the door open, startling Ben so that he stepped back as she confronted him. "Are you suggesting that I take a job as a . . . as a . . ."

"The word you're looking for is *whore*, sweetheart," he said calmly.

Celia strode forward and slapped him as hard as she could. Her hands were no longer trembling, her legs were perfectly steady, and the sound of her palm against his cheek resounded sharply, like a shot.

The attack didn't seem to affect him at all. He didn't move, didn't snap his head back or wince or make a sound. So she hit him again.

This time Ben grabbed her wrist before it could swing completely away from his face.

"Don't ever hit me again," he ordered lowly.

"You deserved it. After what you did to me . . ."

"What I did to you?" he interrupted, incredulous. "Hell, you set me up like I was some kinda greenhorn sucker, and I fell for it like the fool I am. You were in on it all along, weren't you? Admit it. You and those demon twins . . ."

She wanted to hit him again, but he held her wrist tight. As she lifted her left hand to strike out at him, he grabbed that wrist, too.

"Admit it," he whispered.

He yanked her hands down, forcing her against his chest. Celia lifted her face defiantly. "That's a ridiculous accusation."

He looked her over boldly, taking in the yellow calico dress she wore with a surprised lift of his eyebrows. "Admit it." His entire body was tense, hard and unyielding.

Poor Ben, he didn't believe in anything. He certainly didn't believe in love or honesty. He couldn't, or wouldn't, trust his heart. If he believed that she was capable of deceiving him, then he didn't believe what his own eyes told him, either.

She lifted her face, attempting to present a calm and untroubled front. "If this is the time you choose for confessions, perhaps I should ask you to go first. Really, Mr. Wolfe, they say confession is good for the soul. Yesterday's . . . misjudgment was a part of your plan all along, wasn't it?"

His eyes narrowed, as he lowered his face slightly. Those eyes were close to hers, clear blue and piercing and angry. "It was a clever trick, Celia, sweetheart, tempting me with that luscious body of yours. Offering everything in a pathetic attempt to make me change my mind. Everything you say, everything you are, is a lie."

Celia shook her head. Did he really believe that she would deceive him? "I've never lied to you," she said softly. "How dare you accuse me after what you've done? You've bankrupted me, ruined my reputation, and . . . and seduced me. I hate you, Benjamin Wolfe," she whispered, telling him her first lie.

"And I hate you," he said as he lowered his mouth to hers.

She tried to turn away, to break the contact, but Ben wouldn't allow it. He claimed her mouth with his, thrust his tongue between her lips, and kissed her until she melted against him and began to kiss him back.

Her body responded quickly, reacting to his

touch, and she forgot her anger, her disillusion, her very soul.

With a groan Ben lifted Celia off her feet and carried her into the house, kicking the door shut behind him.

"You make me insane," he whispered against her lips as he carried her to her bedroom.

Madness. Celia was shocked into reality as his words brought back her mother's journal. She couldn't want Ben like this, so hard it made her forget everything, just as her mother had.

"We can't," she whispered as he set her on her feet at the side of the bed. "I . . . I hate you. I don't ever want to see you again." Another lie.

"I know," Ben breathed against her lips as he kissed her once more.

Celia lifted her hands to push Ben away, but those hands settled on his shoulders. She wanted him so bad she couldn't deny it, couldn't send him away. And he wanted her. The arousal that was pressed against her was hard, insistent, even through layers of clothing.

He undressed her, shucking away her calico dress, and her chemise, and her petticoat. When he tugged at the drawstring that held her drawers up and let them fall to the floor, he lowered her to the bed.

She pulled Ben with her, even though he was still fully dressed. After one long, deep kiss he left her.

With his eyes on her, Ben undressed. His shirt and his boots, his denim trousers. She never would have thought it possible for her body to take the hardened length that was revealed, but she knew it was possible. More than possible, it was perfect.

When he came back to her he touched her, pressing insistently with a roughened hand, driving a finger inside her. She arched against him, spread her legs wider in invitation, and closed her eyes. Sensations flooded over her, remarkable, impossible sensations.

"Do you want me, Celia?" Ben whispered into her ear. "Do you want me inside you?"

"Yes," she breathed.

"How much?"

She opened her eyes to find him staring down at her. There was no smile on his face, no joy. Only pain and desire. "More than anything."

He pressed against her lightly, his manhood touching her damp folds. "Now, Celia, sweetheart, will you let me come in?"

"Yes," she whispered, and as she spoke he filled her with a single thrust.

There was no gentleness in Ben's lovemaking, and Celia neither gave nor asked for grace. This was passion, pure and simple, a primitive force that banished thoughts of hate and betrayal, of right and wrong. It was a faultless mating of their bodies, a primal transaction.

When she shattered, reaching fulfillment with an arch of her back and the whisper of Ben's name, Ben came with her. Unlike yesterday, he said nothing. There was no whisper of her name, no soft words.

And then he collapsed on top of her. She was

trapped between the soft mattress and Ben's warm body, and it was heavenly. With Ben inside and around her, she wasn't alone. She felt, in moments like this, that she would never again be alone. Ben was a part of her, he belonged to her, and there was not another man who could make her feel this way.

She wanted this, and she wanted more. She wanted Ben to love her. That was impossible.

This could never happen again.

Her need for him, this obsession that she kept trying to call love, would be her ruination. Perhaps it already was.

"All right," she said breathlessly. His hair was pressed against her cheek, and she turned into it. Blond waves that were almost as fair as the twins' curls brushed her face. "You win."

He lifted his face and frowned down at her. "I didn't realize it was a race."

"I'm leaving town."

Ben rolled off of her, leaving her suddenly empty and cold. "Great. When?"

With his back to her, he began to dress. "When Margaret gets back from Boston."

She wanted him to turn and look at her, but he didn't. She wanted him to ask her to stay, but he wouldn't. Ben sat on the side of the bed and buttoned his shirt, his stiff back to her.

She had to leave town. This was a man who was willing to take everything from her. Everything she owned, including her heart and soul. If he knew the twins were his sisters, he would take them away, too.

And they were all she had left.

She reached for the quilt and used it to cover herself, thinking that perhaps if she weren't exposed she wouldn't feel so vulnerable. It didn't help at all. She simply felt as if she were hiding.

Ben finished dressing, had even stepped into his boots, but he remained there on the side of the bed. He kept his back to her, and after a long moment Celia reached out and touched that broad back.

"You can't come here again," she whispered, and the muscles in his back tightened.

"I know."

"We'll be gone in a few weeks," she promised. "Until then, if you could just leave us alone . . ."

He twisted to look at her then, and there was a trademark Benjamin Wolfe grin on his face. He tried to fool her, but he couldn't. That smile didn't touch his eyes. "Do you really want me to leave you alone, Celia, sweet—"

"Don't," she interrupted softly. "No matter what happened in the cellar yesterday and here today, I know you don't . . . care for me. All you care about is your blasted vow. Your revenge. Well, it's over. I have nothing. You've taken my money, my home, my reputation, my virtue, my . . ." She almost said *my heart*, but stopped herself in time. "My goodness, isn't that enough? Give me a few weeks. When Margaret returns from Boston, the twins and I will leave town. Isn't that what you've wanted all along?"

Ben leaned over her quilt-covered body. "It doesn't matter what I want, Celia, sweet." She thought he was going to kiss her, but he didn't. His face hovered over hers, but he didn't touch her. "You said I can't come back here, and I know that's true. At least, I know I shouldn't come here again, but to be honest I don't know if I can stay away. Every time I look at you, I want you. Even though you're who you are. Even though you tried to trick me by pretending to . . ." He stopped speaking and slipped his hand beneath the quilt.

"I've never pretended anything with you," Celia swore as his hand found her hip.

He didn't believe her, that much was clear. There was a touch of anger in his eyes, and he shook his head almost imperceptibly. "It doesn't matter."

Celia sat up and the quilt fell to her waist. Ben's hand was resting against her hip, and his eyes were on a blue square in the quilt.

He was a womanizer like his father, an unreasonable and selfish man, and he had purposely ruined her life. And she loved him. If all they had was this, even if it couldn't last, she was going to take all she could. Memories. She would make wonderful memories to keep her warm on stormy nights.

"Ben?"

He lifted his head to look at her, and the hand at her hip slipped to the small of her back.

"What I said about you not coming back?" she said softly. "I didn't mean it."

Ben leaned forward to kiss her. "I know."

*　　*　　*

He did love the saloon.

Ben leaned on the bar, a glass full of whiskey cradled in his hands. The mirror behind the bar reflected quite a picture. Tables crowded with men laughing, drinking, playing poker. There were no women here, not since the Piggville Gentlemen's Social Club had opened. The stage was deserted, and Jud's cousin Hugo was busy serving whiskey and beer.

He should be deliriously happy. Celia would be leaving town in a matter of weeks. He didn't doubt her word on that matter. The money was pouring in, replenishing what he'd spent to bankrupt Celia. Huff, in his usual quiet and efficient way, was well on his way to bankrupting Cory Anders. The banker would never know what had hit him. He'd just wake up one day and have nothing.

And back to Celia again. He had not intended to end up in bed with her when he'd gone to confront her this morning. He wanted her to know that he wasn't a fool, that she wasn't able to wrap him around her little finger, that he was still in control.

His pecker had proved him wrong again.

He'd never wanted any woman like this before, to the point where he was damn near blinded. It didn't help matters any that she came to him so easily, that she so obviously was a victim of the same desire that consumed him.

In the weeks before Celia left Piggville he'd have to work that desire out of his system. He'd make love to her day and night, fast and slow, every way he'd ever heard of or could think of, until he could look at her and feel nothing.

He got hard just thinking about it. The whiskey burned his throat as he tossed it back in a futile attempt to forget Celia. He'd head over that way right now, but of course he couldn't. The twins were with Celia now, and there was no way she'd let him in while they were around.

Maybe Huff could find a way to get the twins out of town, like Margaret.

Ben grinned at his empty glass. He was a long way from working Celia out of his system.

"Damn mutt!" a coarse voice shouted. There was a loud scraping of chair legs and a crash against the floor.

Ben spun around to see that Lucky had marked his territory right on an unsuspecting gambler's leg. The lanky man who still held his cards in one hand was a stranger, but then there had been a lot of strangers in Piggville lately, thanks to the saloon and the social club. The sheriff had even taken to wearing a gun.

The puppy danced around the enraged man, happy as could be as his victim glared and swore and tossed his cards to the table. Ben grinned at the comic scene, until the gambler kicked at Lucky.

"Hey!" He stepped away from the bar. "That's my dog you're taking aim at with your boot."

Tired of messing with a frolicking puppy, the man turned his attention to Ben. "The damn mutt pissed on my leg."

Ben grinned widely as he stepped closer. Nobody called Lucky a damn mutt but him. "He must like you. Lucky doesn't piss on just anybody."

The man turned a scowling face to the puppy, and in answer Lucky launched himself at the gambler's leg and grabbed hold with teeth and claws.

Ben almost laughed, and then the gambler drew his gun.

Ben launched himself across the table, knocking playing cards and silver coins to the floor. As he reached for the six-shooter, the other patrons ducked or jumped away.

He was able to grab the gun, but the gambler wouldn't loose his hold. At his feet, Lucky growled and intensified his own attack.

They struggled for several long minutes, getting nowhere. The gambler was strong, for a scrawny man, and he wasn't about to let go of his weapon. There was not another sound in the room, but for Lucky's pitifully high-pitched snarl, the gambler's heavy breathing, and the shuffle of their feet.

And then the gun went off, a roar that stilled everything.

Ben waited to feel pain, but there was nothing. The gambler seemed to hold his breath, and then they both looked down. On the floor, between the toes of their boots that weren't more than two inches apart, there was a perfectly round bullet hole.

Lucky was hiding beneath the table, his tail between his legs.

The gambler released his hold, and Ben came away with the six-shooter. He wagged it in the man's direction, butt first. "Get out. If Lucky doesn't like you, I don't want your business."

The gambler left, but not until Ben removed the bullets from the six-shooter and returned it. Just in case. Piggville had always been a quiet town, not the sort of place a stranger would linger. There had never been much in the way of entertainment here, until Ben had opened his businesses.

Before the saloon returned to normal, Ben lifted his eyes and saw Huff standing just a few feet away, there at the bottom of the stairs.

There was a small smile on Huff's face. "The Ben Wolfe I remember wouldn't risk getting shot over a dog."

"I didn't get shot," Ben said casually, ignoring the fact that his heart was beating a mile a minute. He turned away to coax Lucky from under the table. The mutt came to him easily, jumping into his arms and hiding a fuzzy head in the crook of Ben's elbow.

"There now," Ben said softly. "The bad man's gone." He forced Lucky to look at him. "From now on, be careful about who you take a leak on. Some people are not as forgiving as I am."

Huff laughed and turned to climb the stairs.

"What's so damn funny?" Ben snapped, and Huff stopped there on the stairs, spinning about to look down into the saloon.

"The fact that you're talking to a dog like it's a child, or the fact that you're the most unforgiving man I've ever known. Take your pick."

"I am not the most—"

"Good night, Ben," Huff said as he resumed his climb. "Try to keep it down, how about it. Some of us need to sleep."

The girls were sound asleep, but Celia wasn't tired at all. She took her mother's diary from the drawer in her room, where she'd hidden it beneath a silk petticoat, and she sat on the edge of the bed and opened it.

August 22, 1870

I told Ezekiel about the baby today. We met here at the old house late in the morning, as we often do. I was afraid of what his reaction might be, but he was truly happy.

We've talked of leaving together before, here in this very house, and now I'm sure we will. Hamilton hasn't touched me in years, so he will know this is not his child. We will take Celia, of course, and then we will disappear. Zeke and Benjamin, Celia and me, and in a few months the new baby. We'll be a real family. My only fear is that Hamilton will follow us and try to take Celia away from me. I'm not worried that he will try to force me to come back. He doesn't love me and never has.

I have never been this happy.

Celia flipped past several pages. Words jumped out at her now and again, and she tried to ignore them. *Love. Zeke. Heart. Soul.* It was too intimate.

And thanks to Ben, she understood too well.

And then everything changed. The words were smaller, neater, though this was obviously still Priscilla's handwriting.

October 15, 1870

I wish I were dead. All this time I thought Zeke loved me. He said he did. He showed me how he loved me. But it wasn't me. At least, not only me. When Rizpah Tucker, that filthy woman, stood at the altar with Hamilton and claimed to be carrying Zeke's child, I didn't believe it. And then Elizabeth Holt stood up and cried out, and then Susan Woodbury. And I sat there without a tear, without saying a word.

It would hurt less if he had killed me. He's gone now, run out of town. I watched him ride away. What else could I do? Hamilton insisted that I stand at his side and show my support for his decision. Once, Zeke looked over his shoulder to me, as if he were asking for forgiveness, almost as if he wanted me to stand up for him. I was strong, but it was so very hard. I had to turn away. I didn't cry, but it was difficult. In fact, I did my best to display no emotion at all.

I feel sorry for Benjamin, who is an innocent victim in this tragedy. He's a sweet boy who doesn't understand any of this.

Tonight, when Hamilton comes upstairs, I will be waiting in his bedroom, in his bed. He has shown no interest in sharing a marriage

*bed for the past five years, but tonight I will
beg him to make love to me if I have to, and
he will never know that this child is not his.
I have no pride left. I have nothing left, but
Celia and this child.*

The remainder of the pages in the thin journal
were blank.

Celia slammed the diary shut and tossed it
across the room. No wonder her mother had
stopped coming to this house. No wonder there
had been no more happy days here, no more picnics or laughing afternoons spent trying on
Grandma's old clothes.

This was *their* place. Priscilla and Ezekiel met
here when they could and carried on their illicit
affair. The twins had been conceived here, in this
house, the product of adultery, a preacher's lies,
a woman's dreams.

The tears that came were in anger . . . for her
poor father, for her miserable mother . . . for Ben
and for herself.

Chapter Nineteen

Celia hadn't been sleeping well. Floy glanced over her bowl of oatmeal, lifting her eyes slowly to Celia's face. There were dark circles under her eyes, and she was much too pale, and she fidgeted nervously and barely ate her own breakfast.

She'd started wearing Grandma's old calico. The bright colors, like the pink she wore today, should have made Celia look younger and prettier, but today she simply looked exhausted.

Locking Celia and Mr. Wolfe in the cellar hadn't been such a brilliant idea, after all.

Faye seemed not to notice how unwell Celia looked, but then she was chattering on about Mr. Culpepper and how unfair he was. A really good teacher, she said, would recognize that her genius in English overshadowed her failings in arithmetic.

"James will come directly home with us this afternoon," Faye said brightly, and that statement got Celia's attention.

"Whatever for?" she asked crossly.

Faye finished off the last of her oatmeal before she answered. "You know, to chop wood and help with the animals, like Mr. Wolfe suggested. I might help him, since locking you and Mr. Wolfe in the cellar was my idea, after all, and I did insist that James help us. Floy and I would never have been able to nail that board down fast enough without James."

Now Celia really did look ill. Pale and unsettled. "Faye, how old is James?"

Faye smiled as she delved into her favorite subject. "James is exactly ten months and four days older than I am."

Celia closed her eyes.

"Are you all right?" Floy asked, leaning forward.

"I have a horrid headache," Celia said softly. "That's all. As a matter of fact, I don't want James Richardson here this afternoon. With this headache I don't need another body knocking around the house." She fixed her eyes on Faye. "Since this was all your idea, perhaps James shouldn't be punished at all. You can tell him that I release him from his obligation."

Faye looked very disappointed, but she couldn't possibly argue.

"Maybe I should stay home with you," Floy suggested. She was not one to worry unnecessarily, but she didn't like the look of Celia at all.

Celia shook her head. "No. You need your education more than I need someone to sit with me. I'm sure Mr. Culpepper would agree with me on that point. I'll be fine. It's just a headache."

"You should spend the day in bed," Faye suggested brightly.

"I have a feeling I'll be doing just that."

Ben waited until he was sure the twins were gone, and then he presented himself at Celia's door. Arriving so early would give him away, but he found he didn't care. He was anxious to see her, so anxious he'd barely gotten a wink of sleep.

At his feet, a perpetually delighted Lucky danced, jumping and bouncing happily.

"Go away, mutt," Ben growled, but Lucky just lifted his head and . . . could dogs smile?

This morning Celia didn't shout at him to go away. She opened the door at his first knock, almost as if she'd been waiting for him.

Ben's smile died as he looked down at her. She was ashen and her eyes were puffy, and she was staring at his chest as if she were afraid to look him in the face.

"It's not a good idea for you to be here today," she said weakly.

"You're sick," Ben said, stepping around her and into the house, shooing Lucky away when he tried to come into the house. The mutt yelped once when Ben closed the door. "What's the matter?"

"I have a headache." Celia turned her back on him. "And I didn't sleep very well last night."

"Neither did I," Ben rumbled.

"So please, Ben," Celia pleaded softly as she headed for the kitchen. "Leave me alone. Take your little dog and go home."

He didn't tell her that this old brick house felt more like home than his comfortable room over the saloon. Than anywhere he'd lived in fourteen years. "You should go back to bed."

She went directly to a basin of water and began to wash the breakfast dishes. "While that sounds lovely," she said sarcastically, "I have other things to do with my life besides . . . besides . . ."

"To sleep, Celia," he clarified. "You look like you could use a few hours of good, deep sleep."

She laughed, but it wasn't the lilting laugh he was accustomed to from Celia. It was dark and low, and full of pain. "Unfortunately there's cleaning to be done, and chickens and pigs to feed, and we're almost out of firewood for the stove, and . . . what are you doing?" she snapped as he grabbed her wrist and forced her to drop a tin plate back into the water.

"Putting you to bed," he insisted. Celia pulled weakly against his grip, but it was useless and they both knew it.

"I can't—"

"I'll feed the chickens and the pigs, I'll chop some wood, I'll even wash your dishes."

"You can't—"

"I don't sweep or mop, and I never dust," Ben said as he led her into the bedroom where he'd made love to her yesterday. "And if there's any mending to be done, forget it."

"You're teasing me," Celia said as Ben pushed her gently and she sat on the edge of the bed.

"I am not." He bent down on one knee and removed her shoes. She wanted to struggle, but was obviously too tired to put up much of a fight.

Celia reclined on the bed, fully dressed, and closed her eyes. Ben leaned over her, placing his face close to hers. "And when you wake up, you can tell me if you had a sleepless night for the same reason I did."

She opened her eyes, and he brushed his mouth against hers. Anything more than that, he knew, and she wouldn't get any rest at all.

He rolled up his sleeves and finished her dishes first, grumbling and muttering the whole time. This was woman's work, pure and simple.

But Celia looked so tired. More than tired, she looked like someone had sucked the spirit right out of her. He ignored the knowledge that if anyone had damaged her spirit, it was him.

It had been a while since he'd left the Huffmans' ranch, but he was more at home in the small barnyard than in the kitchen. The chickens and pigs were ready to be fed, aggressive and hungry little monsters. He cursed at them softly while he did that chore. Lucky joined him, running around the side of the house and barking happily. Ben silenced the mutt with a glare and an order. Celia didn't need that sharp barking outside her window.

Once he'd located the ax in the barn, Ben took off his shirt and tossed it over a fence post. From all he remembered, this was hard, sweaty work.

Who'd been doing this chore since Celia and the girls had moved out here? With more than a twinge of guilt, he realized that it had to be Celia. She wouldn't ask the girls to do it, and there was no one else.

He'd make sure they had enough chopped wood to last them—the blade of the ax came down on a righted log—for the next few weeks. When Margaret came home, Celia would leave. Just as he wanted, just as he'd planned all along. The vow to his father would be fulfilled. The last of the Piggs would be destitute and run out of the town that was named for Hamilton Pigg—that good-for-nothing liar.

And Ben would have everything he'd ever wanted. His promise kept, his bank account healthy, the people of Piggville filling his pockets with their vices. He would have . . . he would have . . .

Nothing.

"Damnation." He brought the blade down again, and the log split with an earsplitting snap.

If only Celia hadn't used his weakness for her body to try to manipulate him into giving back everything he'd taken from her. She'd almost managed it. He'd been set to reverse everything before Rosemary's words had made him realize what was happening.

She's the only one who can make you change your mind.

He chopped enough wood to last Celia and the twins a month. They probably wouldn't be here that long. The lawyers in Boston couldn't delay

Margaret much longer than that. She'd come home with a small but healthy sum of money, enough to get the four of them off to a start somewhere else.

The inheritance had been Huff's idea, but Ben had heartily approved. Ben had even suggested a higher sum than was first proposed. He didn't ask himself, more than once, why he worked so hard to bankrupt Celia, and then turned around and made sure that she was provided for.

When the chores were done, Ben let himself in through the rear door of the house, a narrow door that opened onto the kitchen. Once again, he had to close a cavorting Lucky out.

He took off his boots and left them there by the back door, and slipped silently through the house to Celia's bedroom. He needn't have worried about being quiet. Celia was out, curled on her side and sound asleep. Dead to the world.

When he lowered his body to the bed, she didn't move at all. When he placed his head on the pillow beside hers, she shifted slightly. When he put his arms around her and drew her wonderfully warm back to his chest, she sighed.

And in a matter of minutes, he was asleep.

Celia woke slowly, wonderfully, and for a moment there was nothing but warmth and comfort. Such a change from last night when she'd tossed and turned.

Then she realized that the source of that warmth and comfort was Ben Wolfe, as he cradled her in his arms.

Deep, steady breathing in her ear assured her that he was asleep, and she relaxed, allowing herself to fall deeper into his embrace.

Had he really done all her chores for her while she slept? Surely not. Washing dishes and feeding animals? It wasn't his style. Besides, she couldn't allow herself to believe that there was any kindness in Ben Wolfe's heart.

He moved against her, brushing her spine with his chest, rotating the arm that encircled her, brushing an indolent hand against her breast.

"You're awake," he breathed into her ear.

"Yes." She tried to rotate so she could see his face, but he held her tight.

"Not just yet," he growled, and then he began to kiss the back of her neck, slow, lazy kisses that feathered across her sensitive skin. His palm barely brushed a nipple, and beneath the fabric it hardened against his hand. She reacted to his touch so quickly, so completely.

As if they had all the time in the world, he lavished attention on her neck and her breasts, flicking buttons open until he could slip his fingers inside and touch her bare flesh.

When she didn't think she could take any more, he slipped that hand beneath her skirt and to the open crotch of her drawers. She was already wet for him, and with his touch she arched against the hand that teased her.

"You're mine," Ben whispered hoarsely into her ear.

"Yes," Celia breathed.

"You need me."

"Yes."

With that, he gently turned her onto her back, and his mouth came to hers with a hunger that held none of his earlier lethargy. His kiss was deep and tender, as his tongue danced with hers. When he reluctantly pulled away he glared down at her.

"See what you do to me, Celia?" He took her hand and guided it from his bare chest to the hardened length beneath his denim trousers. "All I have to do is look at you."

She fumbled with the buttons that held his trousers closed. One at a time, they came undone, and she came closer to revealing the evidence of his need for her.

When the last button came undone and his shaft was free, Celia wrapped her fingers around it. Ben practically leaped out of her hand.

"You're mine," she whispered.

"Yes."

"You need me."

He answered her with a deep kiss. Celia slipped her hands beneath Ben's waistband and shoved the trousers over his hips. Her hands brushed against his hot flesh as she skimmed the fabric down.

He did need her, more than he realized, more than he would ever know. How much true love had Ben had in his life? How much tenderness? Maybe it was too late to break through that tough shield he'd built around his heart—but she had to try.

Ben pushed her skirt up and out of the way,

and then he thrust inside her. How quickly her body had adapted to his, as if this was right and true. One more thrust, and he filled her. For a moment he was still, resting deep inside her, his body joined with hers.

She touched his face, tracing his jaw with gentle fingers, memorizing the feel of him, the warmth and the strength, the bristly beauty. She smiled and closed her eyes when he began to move within her, slowly, deliberately. For now, in this moment, Ben was hers and she was his, and she could love him as deeply and truly as she desired.

Ben didn't offer her tender words, words to echo the love she felt. He loved her hard, completely, and with an instinctive gentleness Celia knew he tried very hard to ignore. There was only *this*.

What a marvel this was, the sensations that grew and changed with the stroke of their bodies.

She came apart too soon, shattering in breathless wonder and holding Ben tight as she lifted her hips to take everything he offered. As the intense pleasure faded, Ben drove deep and found his own completion.

She could hardly breathe, and it wasn't because Ben was pressing her into the mattress. Physically, she had given him everything, and she was exhausted.

It was nothing like the exhaustion of this morning, after a sleepless night.

"You don't play fair," Ben grumbled as he lifted his head to look down at her.

"I didn't know we were playing." She looked down, and laughed lightly. "Goodness, I'm still dressed, and your pants are down around your knees."

"I was planning to peel that pink calico off of you and kiss you all over, and make you beg me, and what happens? You touch me and I can't wait to be inside you." There was reluctant wonder in his voice.

She brushed her hands across his wonderfully naked chest. "And you wanted so badly to hate me."

"That I did."

She moved her hands to Ben's jaw and forced him to look at her. She had no choice, did she? She couldn't stay in Piggville, no matter what she wanted to do. There was no future for her here, and this morning, over breakfast, she'd entertained the horrible notion that James Richardson, Faye's supposed intended, might be the twins' half brother.

How many women had found themselves in the Reverend Wolfe's bed? Would she forever wonder if every fair-haired child of a certain age was his offspring? She had to get the girls and herself out of town.

But she didn't have to leave Ben miserable. He was so much more than the smiling rounder he presented to the world, and he had so much still to discover. "You must forget what happened in the past. What your father did has nothing to do with you."

"I can't have this discussion with you again."

He rolled away. "My father didn't do anything."

She could prove him wrong right now, get the journal from her top drawer and read a few key passages to him. But then he'd know about Floy and Faye, and that could never happen.

"Would it be so horrible if you found out that you're wrong about him? For you, I mean. You're not your father. You don't have to prove anything to anyone."

He stood up quickly, shooting off the bed and pulling his pants up. "Am I supposed to betray my father just because you—"

"Don't say it," she warned softly.

Some of the fire went out of him, and he sat on the edge of the bed. "You were too young to remember what he was like," Ben insisted. "He was a good man."

"Good men make mistakes."

That wasn't what he wanted to hear. "You're so sure the tales were true, you prove it. You think I'll change my mind about what happened to my father?"

"I'm not trying to change your mind, Ben. I'm just trying to help you let this thing go. For you, not for me. I'm leaving town, no matter what."

Ben put his weight on one arm and leaned over her. The smile on his face was not happy. "I'm a gambler, Celia, sweet. You want to make a bet? You prove to me that my father did anything wrong, that he's guilty of the crimes your father accused him of, and I'll give it all back."

"Give what all back?"

"Money, the house, the saloon . . . which I

imagine you'd quickly convert back into a boarding-house. All you have to do is prove that my father turned his back on everything he believed in to screw a good number of the respectable women of Piggville."

"You can't give everything back."

"Why not?"

Her heart, her virtue. "You've ruined my reputation, Ben. Even if you returned everything else, I could never live in Piggville and hold my head up. What kind of a life can I have? What respectable man will ever marry me?"

"I'll marry you."

"What?" She was certain she'd heard wrong.

"We'll make it part of the deal. Prove my father was a womanizer out to ruin the women of Piggville, and I'll give back everything I've taken, including your good name. I'll make an honest woman out of you, and then I'll get the hell out of town."

He meant it, every word. There was such fire and determination in his eyes. Eyes a darker blue than the twins', but somehow the same. And all she had to do was take her mother's diary from the top drawer and show it to him.

And then he'd know about Floy and Faye, and he'd tell. Everyone in town, no doubt. It would be devastating to the girls.

"I can't."

The front door slammed, and Ben jumped off the bed.

"Celia!" Faye called. "We're home!"

"What time is it?"

Ben reached into his pocket for the watch he always carried with him.

"Never mind," Celia snapped as she leaped from the bed. "Obviously I slept much longer than I realized. I'm in here," she shouted as she hurried to the door to close it. "I'll be right out."

Ben was standing in front of the window in nothing but his denims.

"Where are your clothes?" Celia hissed.

"I left my shirt outside," he said softly, "and my boots are just inside the back door."

"Great," Celia mumbled.

"I was trying to be considerate."

He didn't take this seriously, not at all. "Quick. Out the window," Celia ordered, brushing past him to open it wide.

"You must be kidding," he said in a hiss.

"Not at all."

"Celia?" Floy was knocking at her door softly. "Are you all right?"

"I'm fine," Celia shouted. "I'll be right out."

With a mumbled curse, Ben slipped through the window.

"I'm going to toss your boots out the back door," she said, shoving lightly as she tried to assist him through the window that was almost too small for his large body. "You grab the shirt and get out of here. Don't let the girls see you."

When Ben was finally all the way out of her room, he simply turned to face her stoically. Celia leaned out of the window slightly. "Go!"

He grabbed her face and kissed her quickly.

"I think I saw Lucky on the way home," Floy

shouted through the closed door. "What would he be doing so far away from the saloon?"

Celia stepped slowly to the door, gaining strength and serenity with each step. This was a disaster that could be averted.

When she opened the door, Floy was looking at her expectantly. "You look so much better."

"Thank you," Celia said as she stepped into the hallway and closed the door behind her. "I was able to get a nap, and it helped tremendously. Now, you put your books away, and I'll get started on dinner."

Very calmly, she walked to the kitchen. The boots were right there where Ben had said they'd be, big, brown, battered boots sitting by the back door. Without changing her step, she lifted the boots, opened the back door, and tossed them out.

"Thanks a lot," Ben whispered dryly, and a hand reached out to snag the boots.

Her focus went from the boots, to the hands, to the enormous stack of firewood just beyond.

"No, thank you." She stuck her head out of the portal to watch Ben step into his boots. The shirt he'd retrieved had been slipped on, but hung open. "I likely won't have to chop wood again before I leave town."

Ben took a step toward her, a single long step. "Celia, sweet—"

"I'm starving," Faye said dramatically as she burst into the kitchen, and Celia slammed the door shut.

Chapter Twenty

Ben was leaning against the bar with a glass in one hand, a cigar in the other, and Lucky resting at his feet. For the first time in years, for the first time that he could remember, he knew what it was to be content. It was a temporary oddity, he knew, but while it lasted he was going to enjoy it.

He should be angry, with Huff for turning on him, with Celia for drawing him into this curious and inexplicable relationship for her own manipulative reasons, and with himself for forgetting what had brought him to Piggville in the first place. But he wasn't angry. He was strangely complacent.

It was the memory of Celia in his arms that chased away everything else. Standing at the bar all alone, Ben smiled. She might dress like a prim-and-proper lady, but beneath those prudish clothes there was a body that could give as good as it took. For the past week and a half she'd been doing just that. How long before he worked his fascination for Celia out of his system? A couple more weeks, a month, perhaps.

Forever.

Hell, he didn't have forever. Margaret would be back in a matter of weeks, days perhaps, and Celia—true to her word, he was sure—would pack up and leave town.

His smile faded. It was what he wanted, right? It was what he'd wanted all along. Everything Hamilton Pigg had once owned was his, and the last remaining Piggs would soon be leaving town. This was the goal that had brought him to Piggville, and it was almost accomplished.

Too soon. Ben had prepared himself mentally for years to do battle with Hamilton Pigg. It was the old man he'd wanted to break, Pigg he'd wanted to watch cower on his way out of town with nothing but the clothes on his back.

Not Celia. Not the twins.

He didn't see Ginger until she placed her hand on his arm, and it was with the greatest control that he kept from leaping out of his skin.

"Hello, darlin'," she said as she wound her arm through his.

"What are you doing here?"

She raised her finely shaped eyebrows at his brusque question, but a smile quickly followed. "It's a slow night at the club, boss. I hope you don't mind that I wandered on over to keep you company."

He didn't need or want company, unless it was Celia's. In a few minutes he'd head over that way, slip past quiet buildings to the path, sneak through the night like a thief, and all just to watch her place for a while. To stand at a distance like the outsider he was and simply watch. He told himself, as he did every night, that someone had to make sure that Cory Anders and those like him stayed away from Celia's isolated brick house.

"Sure," he said casually, and Ginger ordered a whiskey.

"Phoebe ran off with a cowboy," Ginger said as she wrapped her fingers around her glass.

"Which one was Phoebe?"

"The short blonde with the big tits." Ginger was obviously perturbed that he didn't remember. "It's a real inconvenience. Phoebe was a popular girl."

Ben refilled his glass, watching the light play on the golden liquid.

"And that's not all," Ginger said, removing her hand from his arm and backing away a half step. "The dotty old preacher has finally figured out what's going on, and he's mounting a crusade. Business is down, sugarplum. A good number of the regulars are afraid of what the good preacher might think."

Ben knew what his father would think.

"The girls are getting restless."

Ben glanced down at the woman by his side.

Her features, usually so relaxed and easy, were tensed, and the toe of one foot tapped impatiently. Ginger was a bit restless herself.

"So," Ben said softly. "When are you headed back to Denver?"

Ginger's finely shaped eyebrows lifted subtly. "You're not mad?"

He couldn't tell her he was actually relieved. That admission would reveal too much. "No."

"The only reason I came to Piggville, Texas," Ginger admitted in a low voice, "is because I thought maybe you and me might . . . well, I didn't know about your virgin at the time."

Ben didn't know what to say. He and Ginger had had some good times in Denver, but that had been long ago, and there had never been anything to compare with what he felt for Celia.

Ginger leaned close and smiled, and for a moment Ben was afraid she was going to suggest one last night for old times' sake before she left town. She'd be riled when he said no thanks. "You love her, don't you?"

"No," Ben said quickly.

Ginger's smile brightened. "Are you lying to me, or do you just not realize yet what's goin' on here?"

Ben wondered if there was a way to protest without sounding like a complete ass. Love was for foolish romantics. It wasn't real. Passion he understood, commitment, logic. Love had nothing to do with any of that. He drained what was left in his glass.

"You ever been in love before?" he asked.

Ginger's smile faded and she looked away from him. He could see her face in the mirror behind the bar, could see the pain she didn't want him to see. "You mean with someone besides you?" she quipped.

Ben placed his empty glass on the bar and, with his hand on her cheek, forced Ginger to look at him. "Who's lying now?"

He'd always thought Ginger was tough as nails. Nothing touched her, and she didn't care about anything but having fun and making money. His kinda gal. She didn't look particularly tough at the moment.

"I was married once," she said as she shook off his hand. "Made stupid plans for kids and a house and a flower garden and crap like that." Her eyes hardened. "And then he died. We had no kids, no house, no nothing. There wasn't enough time."

He, she said. Not even a first name.

"What was his name?"

Ginger shook her head. "Don't do this to me. I was another woman then, and I can't go back there. I can't remember or talk about or even dream about that time in my life. It hurts too much."

He wanted to ask her so many questions. Why she had chosen this life, why there had been no other husband since then, why she looked at him and assumed he was in love with Celia.

"When are you leaving?" he asked instead.

"Tomorrow," she said, and then she sipped at her whiskey. He realized, as he watched her drink slowly, that although he had often seen her with a glass in her hand, he rarely saw her drink.

"Taking the other girls with you?"

"I don't know. You could ask them to stay, if you want." She relaxed. They had returned quickly to her world, a world she was comfortable in. "I suggest you put Lizzie in charge. She's the only one of the girls with any kind of head for money."

He didn't have to think about it for long. "Take them back to Denver with you." It was for the best. "And do me a favor. If anyone asks, tell them the Reverend Rivers ran you out of town."

Ginger laughed, transforming her face. Once again she was the carefree, happy woman he'd always known her to be. "That old geezer?"

He didn't want anyone, not even Celia, to know that he was capitulating on this one.

She turned her back on him, leaving a half-emptied glass of whiskey on the bar. "If that's what you want, sugarplum."

"Ginger?"

It was a wary face she presented to him as she spun slowly around. "Yes, boss?"

Now that he had her attention he didn't know what to say. It wasn't like him to pry into other people's business, unless he considered it *his* business. "You don't have to go back to Denver."

She grinned. "It's much too dull for me here. I need excitement."

"You could go someplace else. Back east or out west. You've done me a real favor coming all this way. I'd be happy to stake you."

Her smile faded quickly. "When did Ben Wolfe turn into a crusader? I'm who I am, *boss*," she said bitterly. "And so are you. Don't forget that, when your virgin tries to turn you into a respectable citizen or a farmer or one of those disgustingly obedient men who follow after their women muttering 'yes, dear, whatever you say, dear.'" She took a single step in his direction. "The wolf doesn't become the lamb, ever, so stop kidding yourself."

He wanted to grin at her as if he didn't have a care in the world and ask her what she meant by all that gibberish, but he didn't. It was more than he could handle at the moment.

And besides, he knew exactly what she meant. Nothing on this earth could transform him into the kind of man Celia needed and wanted. He had no roots, no patience, no dreams of settling down with kids and a house and a flower garden. All he had was his good fortune, his anger, and his passion for Celia.

Passion, he wanted to tell her, not love. Love was just a word people used to fool themselves into thinking that committing yourself to one person for a lifetime made any sense at all.

He'd never told Celia that he loved her, and she'd never asked. Of course, she'd never made that particular declaration either, though he'd convinced himself on at least one occasion that it had to be true.

Ginger departed before he could say anything at all, and Ben was left at his bar with an empty glass in one hand, a cigar in the other, and Lucky at his feet. And whatever peace he had enjoyed earlier was gone.

Margaret would surely be back any day now, Celia told herself as she rocked slowly and ignored the pile of mending in her lap. Any day. And then she would pack their bags, load the wagon she'd bought with the last of her cash, and head out of town.

She still needed two strong horses to pull that wagon. It was terrible to start this new life guided by horses bought with Margaret's inheritance, but there was nothing to be done for it, not unless a few of the loans she'd made in the past year were suddenly and unexpectedly paid back. In cash, not livestock.

Outside the parlor window all was dark. Was Ben out there, hiding beyond the line of trees and watching? A few times in the past couple of weeks she'd looked out that window late at night and been certain she saw something, and then she convinced herself that it was Ben. On more than one occasion she'd been tempted to open the front door and ask him to come in.

If she showed him the diary, would he really give everything back? The house she would never live in, the boardinghouse he had converted into a saloon, the general store that was closed up tight? Maybe, maybe not. It was a risk she was not willing to take.

It was cruelly ironic that she should have fallen in love with the man who had made it his life's work to destroy her. When he came to her, while the girls were in school, she could almost convince herself that there was something in his heart besides revenge, but when she was all alone, when she wasn't influenced by his touch and his warm voice, she knew she was fooling herself.

Everything was a game to Benjamin Wolfe. Pleasure, revenge, her very life.

This was a very dangerous game they were presently playing. That first time, in the cellar, she hadn't given any thought at all to the possibility that their lovemaking would lead to a baby. And then that next day, well, he hadn't given her an opportunity to think at all.

She told herself that she should send him away when he came to her door, but she never did. She reasoned that her mother had been married five years before she'd been born, and then it had been another eleven years before the twins came.

Of course, she knew now that Priscilla and Hamilton Pigg had not had an exactly passionate relationship. But there was Kay Anne Ascot and her husband, who had despaired of ever having a child, and then, eight years after their wedding, she'd given birth to a baby girl.

She'd allowed herself to forget the fact that Rosemary had been born nine months to the day after her parents married, and that there had been a good number of perfectly healthy "premature" babies born in Piggville in the past few years.

In quiet times like this she found herself wondering. Would there be a baby? Was there already a child, Ben's child, growing inside her?

The idea alternately thrilled and terrified her. She could very well find herself an unmarried woman, in a new home, bearing and raising a child on her own. It would be difficult, the hardest thing she'd ever done, but she found it was not a completely unpleasant thought.

Of course, if there was a child and Ben knew about it, would he allow her to have and raise it alone? One moment she was certain he wouldn't care . . . and the next she was certain he would care very much.

She returned to her mending, trying to put the questions from her mind. It was just a possibility, one she couldn't afford to dwell on.

Ben fell back onto the bed fully dressed. He'd stood for too long outside Celia's window, remaining there long after the house had gone dark. Even Lucky had fallen asleep in the grass at his feet.

Now, as Ben was ready to strip off his clothes and fall asleep, the mutt wanted to play.

He kicked off his boots, and the mutt chased after them, one and then the other. When Ben sat up and shucked off his coat, Lucky leaped onto the bed and tried to help, taking a sleeve in his teeth and shaking his head. And as Ben reached for the buttons on his trousers, Lucky caught the watch fob and yanked his head back.

Ben reached out as the mutt leaped to the floor and the watch followed, and he cringed as the watch hit the floor with a sickening thud.

It came open to reveal the face of the watch, and Ben scooped it off the floor, muttering a curse to the prancing puppy. This was all he had left of his father, the only possession Ezekiel Wolfe had held on to after he'd been kicked out of Piggville.

Ben held the watch to his ear, and sighed with relief at the reassuring sound of rhythmic ticking.

Nothing seemed to be broken, but there was a loose round of metal that might scratch the face when the cover was closed. Ben pushed at it, trying to gently return the thin metal to its place, and the small round piece practically jumped into his hand.

The secret that was revealed when the metal fell away was enough to make all thoughts of finding a restful night's sleep vanish.

At first glance it looked like Celia, the miniature portrait that had been concealed beneath gold. The dark hair, the wide eyes, the high cheekbones. But he knew it wasn't Celia who stared back at him. It was the mother, Priscilla Pigg.

His father had carried this watch with him always, had died with it in his hand.

It all came together, too cleanly, too neatly, the pieces falling into place even as he tried to deny what his own eyes saw. His father hadn't been carrying on with half the women in town: he'd been carrying on with Priscilla Pigg. No. Carrying on was wrong. Ezekiel Wolfe had not been the sort of man to take affairs of the heart lightly. He'd loved her.

And Hamilton Pigg had found out.

Did Celia know? Surely not. Ben placed the tip of a finger that suddenly seemed fat and clumsy against the face in the portrait.

It seemed his father had not been a saint after all. Celia was right. He'd had weaknesses, like any other man. Human faults. Ezekiel Wolfe was not the rogue he'd been accused of being. He hadn't wooed half the females in town, and he had certainly never forced his attentions on any woman, but neither was he . . . perfect.

Priscilla Pigg had been a married woman when Ben and his father had come to Piggville, the wife of a prominent town leader. How long had it gone on, the affair between Ezekiel Wolfe and the pretty Priscilla? Weeks? Months? Years? And how had Hamilton Pigg found them out?

Another, more horrible thought occurred to Ben as he studied the tiny portrait. Priscilla Pigg had dark hair and eyes like Celia. The old man had, in Ben's memory, a sparse head of hair that was black or so dark a brown it might as well have been.

So where had the twins come by their fair hair and blue eyes?

Ben propped the open watch on the bedside table so he could study Priscilla Pigg's face in the light of the lamp while he undressed. Lucky, perhaps sensing the change in mood, had settled down and was resting quietly on the rug where the watch had popped open.

Had his father pined away for her after he'd been chased out of town? There hadn't been any other women; Ben was more certain of that fact than ever. He was certain, because he knew what his father had felt. Celia was doing the same thing to him.

There might as well not have been another woman in Piggville, in all of Texas.

It was not devastating to discover that his father was human, after all. It was, in fact, rather comforting. Ben didn't remember his mother. She'd died when he was a baby, so he'd never seen his father in love. He'd never seen his father relent in anything, and especially not in his fixed beliefs of what was right.

It had often been hard to live up to the expectations of a man who was perfect, a man who expected perfection of those around him. Especially his son. Little Benjamin had never been quite smart enough, and he'd certainly never been good enough. He'd possessed a mischievousness that was normal in most children, but that was unacceptable in the Reverend Ezekiel Wolfe's only child.

Maybe that was why he felt obligated to exact revenge on the Piggs.

Remembering the conviction of Ezekiel Wolfe's beliefs, Ben knew it had not been easy for him to put aside all he believed in to have this woman.

Thanks to Celia he understood all too well what it meant to want a woman until everything else you believed meant nothing. Ginger called it love, his father would have justified the affair by calling it love, but Ben was more inclined to call it passion.

Was it possible that the twins were his sisters? It was a question he would have to keep to himself. It would kill Celia to discover that her beloved sisters were, perhaps, the result of an adulterous affair between his father and her mother.

Impossibly, he smiled. Sisters. He looked for clues to confirm or refute the possibility. There was the physical resemblance, but he couldn't be sure that the likeness went any deeper than hair and eye coloring. The twins were fair and soft, and he found it impossible to find any similarity between the hard countenance he saw in the mirror and those purely feminine faces. Was his smile as fiendish as Faye's? Did his eyes ever flash like Floy's had when she'd rushed at him to protect her sister Celia?

Celia couldn't know. Not about her mother's fall from grace, and not about the possibility that Floy and Faye were his sisters as much as they were hers. Her family was important to her. It was her heart and soul. He'd taken everything from her. He wouldn't tear her family apart with this revelation.

Ben doused the light and fell onto the bed, but he wasn't naive enough to expect that sleep would come.

Chapter Twenty-one

"Look!" Faye shouted brightly, and then she was running down the street. It took Floy a minute to realize what, or rather who, Faye was running toward. She'd never thought the day would come when Faye would be so delighted to see Margaret.

Margaret was stepping across the street, a small bag in each hand. She looked tired, but then it was quite a trip from Boston.

The smile she gave them wasn't tired at all, and she dropped her bags in the street to give them each a proper hug. "I've missed you girls so much," Margaret said as she released Floy and hugged Faye again. "I thought they would never give me my money and let me leave that darn big city."

"We missed you, too," Faye said brightly. "And

so much has happened since you left."

Margaret picked up her bags, and together they headed down the street. "Tell me all about it," she said sensibly.

"Well," Faye began, "we moved."

Margaret stopped and stared at Faye. "Again?"

"To Grandma and Grandpa Hart's house," Floy added. "Mr. Wolfe turned the boardinghouse into a saloon."

Together, the twins pointed to the offending business. It was rather quiet this time of day. It was still early afternoon, and the place didn't really get busy, they had heard, until well after dark.

But there was that big sign out front, the one that was embellished with an illustration of playing cards, Aces and Kings, and in the middle of it all there was LUCKY's painted in big blue letters.

"How's Celia?" Margaret asked as she resumed her pace without another glance at the saloon.

"Fine," Faye said quickly and brightly.

"Not so fine," Floy amended. "She's tired and upset, and I just know she's not sleeping well. And the past couple of days she's been ill."

"Ill?"

"Sick to her stomach."

Margaret sighed deeply. Actually, it was more of a despairing groan than a sigh. "I never should have left her here alone."

Floy wanted to protest. Celia wasn't alone. She had her sisters to watch over her.

Margaret sighed and increased her speed. Evidently she knew the way to the old Hart place.

"What's done is done. But everything will be different now that I'm back," she said with confidence.

Floy didn't doubt that was true.

The house was quiet, as always, the light from the windows warm and inviting . . . and still Ben watched from the cover of a stand of trees.

He wasn't worried about Cory Anders bothering Celia anymore. Cory's financial problems had driven him from Piggville, and the bank's owners had sent in another manager just last week. It had been almost too easy for Huff to find Anders's debts and call them in, to buy out a company he'd invested in and close it down. Cory had slunk out of town like the dog he was—apologies to Lucky.

Still, Ben found himself wandering over this way each and every night. Like a moth to the flame, he was drawn to this little house, to the bright light that poured from the parlor window. Like the defenseless moth, he was drawn to his destruction.

Had he really thought that taking Celia day after day would cure him of this obsession? Days passed, and then weeks, and nothing changed. He wanted her more every day, it was harder to leave her each time he came here, and the dreams wouldn't stop.

She crossed in front of the window, her arms full of folded clothing. Wash or mending, he supposed. Celia was always doing something. She was never idle, never still. Except, of course, for the moments she lay quietly in his arms. Those moments were rare, much too fleeting. It seemed that just as they became comfortable, one of them moved abruptly away. Some days he was the one who pulled away; other days it was Celia.

They both knew this couldn't last.

His dream turned into a nightmare when another figure passed before the window. Too large to be one of the twins, too old and mean to be Celia, Margaret's arms were as full as Celia's had been.

Celia wasn't mending and she wasn't doing laundry. She was packing.

Why was he so angry? This had been his goal all along, to run the last of the Piggs out of town. Celia hadn't lied to him about this. She'd told him, more times in the past month than he cared to admit, that she would be leaving soon.

He'd done it. As Celia liked to remind him, he had won.

So why did he feel as if he had nothing?

With luck, they'd be gone before Ben arrived. Celia paced, unable to sleep, unable even to close her eyes. Margaret had arrived and immediately set about making things right. Huff had assisted with the purchase of two horses, ugly but sturdy animals that would easily pull their wagon to Austin.

She wanted to slip quietly from this room she shared with Margaret, and make her way to Ben's saloon and up the stairs to tell him goodbye. She wanted him to kiss her and hold her and tell her that he didn't want her to leave Piggville after all.

But Ben Wolfe didn't change his mind.

It would be easiest, she knew, just to ride away and not look back. To make a new life in Austin with Margaret and the girls. That was the plan. Margaret had decided that they needed to get back into business as quickly as possible. A boardinghouse or a small mercantile, she'd suggested, depending on what opportunities they found in Austin.

The girls were upset about the move, about leaving their friends and their home behind. They'd adjust, Celia assured herself. They were young and energetic and bright, and they would make friends and a home wherever they went.

As for herself . . . well, it wouldn't be easy. It was too soon to be positive, but it seemed there was a baby on the way. Ben's baby. It would no doubt be yet another blue-eyed blonde, another bright and beautiful child, and so she couldn't be sorry.

Rosemary had suggested she lie when they reach Austin, and invent an absent husband. A soldier, perhaps, or an exotic world traveler. Celia didn't think that would work. She was a terrible liar, after all.

Of course, she'd been able to keep the truth about the twins' parentage from Ben, and from everyone else. No one suspected that she loved Ben with all her heart, that just the thought of leaving him felt a little like dying.

Perhaps she wasn't such a terrible liar after all.

* * *

Ben threw open the door and stepped into Huff's office. The lawyer stared up at him with slightly surprised eyes. It was, after all, quite early in the morning, much earlier than Ben was ever seen around town.

"She's leaving," Ben said in a low voice that rumbled threateningly through the small office.

"And you're surprised?"

Huff certainly wasn't surprised. Not surprised at all. "When did you find out?"

"Yesterday afternoon." Huff returned his attention to the papers on his desk. "Margaret Harriman arrived, with the *inheritance* you so generously provided for her. They bought two horses, and from what I understand they spent half the night packing so they could leave at first light."

"You knew," Ben breathed.

"Yes."

"And you didn't tell me."

Huff threw his hands up in surrender. "Celia asked me not to. Hell, Ben, after what I've done, what I've helped you do, if she asked me to cut off my right hand I'd probably do it without question."

How had this gotten so turned around? Huff was his friend, his ally . . . and Celia was the enemy.

"So," Huff said, leaning back in his leather chair, "when are you leaving town?"

Leaving town. The war was over, and there was no reason for him to stay here in Piggville. He had money, and plenty of it. He could go anywhere, do anything. "I don't know."

Ben sank into the closest chair. He'd lived his whole life for this moment, and it had come and gone and left him feeling as terrible and lonely as the night his father had died.

"You got what you wanted, Ben. Come on, where's that big Wolfe smile I've grown so accustomed to?" Huff reached into his drawer for a couple of fat cigars. "Sweet revenge, after all these years." Ben refused the cigar Huff offered.

Huff took his time lighting his cigar. "Yes, sir, you did everything you set out to do, and more."

There was a bite in Huff's voice that alerted Ben. "More?"

Huff exhaled, and stared up at the cloud of fragrant smoke. "You captured her home, her general store, and her boardinghouse, and then you ruined her reputation. You humiliated her at every opportunity, turning her home into a bordello and her boardinghouse into a saloon. And then, as if that wasn't enough, you knocked her up before you ran her out of town."

He felt as if his lungs had been ripped from his chest. He couldn't breathe. "I did what?"

"You captured her home—"

"Shut up, Huff." Ben stood and leaned over the desk. "You know what I mean. Is it true? Is Celia really going to have a . . . a . . ." His knees went weak, and he resumed his seat.

"The word you're looking for is *baby*, and the answer is yes."

A baby. That changed everything, didn't it? It

didn't matter what he wanted, and it didn't matter what Celia wanted. He had to ask her to marry him, and Celia had to say yes. Didn't she?

"You look stunned," Huff observed. "Did it never occur to you, during one of those many mornings or afternoons you spent at her house, that she might get pregnant?"

"It wasn't the foremost thought in my mind, no."

Huff looked oddly satisfied. "You're not usually stupid. Has it occurred to you that maybe you wanted her to get pregnant? Maybe you wanted to take your revenge that far, and you couldn't admit, even to yourself, that you are so disgustingly shameless."

"How do you know?"

"How do I know what?" Huff asked calmly.

"Cut the lawyer crap," Ben snapped. "How do you know she's going to have a baby, and how do you know I was seeing her in the morning and the afternoon?"

"In that order?" Huff was amazingly calm, and Ben wanted to fly across the desk and take the man's throat in his hands.

"Just answer the questions."

Huff seemed to consider the smoke above his head. "I shouldn't be telling you any of this, but after all, Rosemary is my girl, not a client, and you are, technically, I suppose, still my client."

"Rosemary," Ben growled.

"Celia confided in her about the baby, and Rosemary told me. I think she wanted me to kill you, but I told her that wasn't really a lawyer's job." He sounded quite apathetic about the subject. "Of course, I already knew about the near daily visits. Really, Ben, this is a small town. You can't carry on like that and expect no one to know."

"Who knows?"

"Damn near everybody in town over the age of eighteen," Huff mumbled. "Personally, I was hoping you'd come to your senses and work this mess out, but it seems that was foolish optimism on my part."

Foolish optimism. Funny, but until he'd come to Piggville, Huff hadn't possessed a single optimistic bone in his body. Of that, Ben was certain.

He thought of Celia and his baby and the twins—his sisters?—out there on the road with only Margaret Harriman for protection. If they hadn't been safe in Celia's little brick house, they sure as hell wouldn't be safe out there on some deserted trail.

"Where did she go?"

Huff was shaking his head. "I'm not supposed to tell. I swore."

"I swear I'll break your nose and then your neck if you don't tell me."

Huff simply raised his eyebrows. Of course, he knew Ben would never carry out such a threat. "I understand the bit about breaking my neck, but why the nose?"

"It hurts."

Huff nodded, as if this was something to consider. "I see."

"Where?" Ben whispered.

*   *   *

Celia ran through the street, her eyes cutting first to one side and then to the other. She kept expecting to see the girls, to catch a flash of pink gingham and fair hair cutting around the corner.

How could they do this to her? Looking into their room and finding the bed empty had sent her heart leaping into her throat. Didn't they know that she would be worried sick?

All her plans to slip away before anyone knew she was leaving, ruined because the girls were heartbroken at the thought of leaving their home.

Her path took her directly to the lawyer's office. She didn't know where else to turn.

She threw Huff's door open and practically fell into the room before she realized that he was not alone. Ben was standing over Huff's desk with a forbidding expression on his face. She didn't have time to deal with him, not now.

Facing Huff and ignoring Ben as completely as possible, Celia drew in a long, calming breath. "The girls are missing."

"What?" It was Ben who exploded. "What do you mean they're missing?"

She had no choice but to turn to him. "I think they ran away. I've already looked at their friends' houses, and even at the school, but no one's seen them."

All of a sudden, her panic subsided. Ben would help her.

He exploded. "They ran away because you

were planning to leave this morning, isn't that right?"

"Yes."

Huff looked down at his desk and ignored the exchange.

"Well, what do you expect?" he thundered. "I know what it's like to be uprooted from your home. They're scared, and they're angry, and they don't understand—"

"Need I remind you," Celia began, "that you're the one who—"

"No," he interrupted. "You need not remind me."

A few moments ago she'd been frightened, but now she was furious. How dare he try to blame her for this?

"Might I suggest," Huff said calmly, "that we organize a search. We can keep it small, for now. If we've had no luck in a couple of hours, we'll expand the search."

"They're here in town," Ben said with certainty. "Close."

"I think he's right," Celia said. "They were very upset about the move. It wouldn't make sense that they'd leave town."

"The saloon, maybe," Ben suggested. "There are empty rooms on the third floor, and they know their way around the place."

"They know that's the last place I'd look," Celia confessed. Finally calm, she was able to think clearly. "If they're not there, they're at the house. The . . . the old house." The place had been standing empty since Ginger and her girls left town. As far as she knew, Ben was still living at the saloon.

"We don't need a search party," Ben said calmly. "Celia and I will find the girls. Let's go." Ben swept past Celia, took her arm, and practically dragged her out the door. They didn't head for the saloon, but cut across the street and straight for the house Ben had first taken from her.

"Maybe we should check the saloon first," she suggested.

"No." Ben didn't even look at her. "You were right. They're in the house. Plenty of places to hide there, it's empty, and we already know they can get into the place whenever they want."

The honey incident. Celia instinctively glanced down at Ben's boots.

They stepped into the house quietly, straining to hear a sound, a whisper or a shuffle of feet. There was nothing.

As they stepped past the parlor, Celia glanced into the altered room. A naked marble cherub stared at her from a table that had once held a vase of flowers. A large red scarf had been draped across the back of the sofa where Ben had first kissed her. Gilt-framed mirrors, paintings of ladies as naked as the cherub, a bar where half-filled bottles of whiskey still sat. The changes Ginger had made remained, long after the madam was gone.

Ben had to tug at her arm to hurry her along to the stairs.

He stepped quietly for a big man, making not

a sound, and Celia was careful as well. If the girls were upstairs, it would be best to catch them unaware. Otherwise, it would take the better part of the morning to look under every bed and in every wardrobe.

Ben stopped at the first door—her old bedroom—and pressed his ear to the door. He listened for a moment before he moved on down the hall. Celia tried, twice, to slip her arm from his hand, but he refused to release her as he checked each room in the same way. At the end of the hall, he hesitated, and then he began opening the doors, quickly and with a burst of noise.

"Get on out here, girls," he shouted as he threw open first one door and then another. "The game's up."

"Maybe they're not here," Celia said as he threw open the door to her old room. A quick glimpse showed her that nothing had changed. The furnishings had not been touched, the blue coverlet and lace curtains and embroidered pillows were just as she'd left them. Unlike the rest of the house, this room was unchanged. "Maybe they're at the saloon, like you said."

Ben faced her and grinned. "You're probably right." As he agreed with her, loudly, he pointed straight up. The attic? "There's certainly no one here."

"What do we do?" Celia whispered.

"I think you're right," Ben said clearly and just a bit too loudly. "Ginger ruined this place, and I understand why you'll never want to live here again. A fire is the perfect solution. With the straw insulation in the walls, it'll go up in a matter of minutes."

She heard it, a small squeal from above their heads. Ben must've heard, too, because his grin widened.

"And won't the girls feel silly when we find them and tell them that you're not moving after all."

It would be cruel to get their hopes up and then make them leave anyway. Celia shook her head, but Ben seemed not to get it. Above, there was a very faint scuffling of feet, and then the small square door in the ceiling opened.

"Don't burn the house down," Faye insisted. "We can fix it up just the way it was, I know we can."

"Are we really staying?" Floy asked softly.

Celia started to answer, to tell them that nothing had changed, when Ben jumped in.

"That's right. Celia and I are getting married, and we're going to live right here—"

"We are not!"

"In town," he continued. "Maybe not in this house . . ."

"Not at all," Celia clarified sharply. "Ben, I can't marry you."

He ignored the girls, who watched from above, and looked straight at her. There was no devilish grin, no sparkle in his eyes. "Why not?"

It was another of his jokes, a ploy to get the girls out of the attic. But he looked, staring down at her like that, perfectly serious.

Faye lowered the narrow ladder from the attic

and climbed down. "Married? Really? Oh, I just knew it. The first time I saw Mr. Wolfe, I said he was perfect for you. Ask Floy, if you don't believe me."

She threw her arms around Celia and then around Ben. Poor Ben looked as if he were surprised, and didn't know quite what to do. Finally, he decided to hug her back. Floy had to get in on all the hugging, after she stepped cautiously from the ladder.

"I knew it, too," Floy whispered.

How would she break it to them that this was just another of Ben's schemes?

"Oh, Mr. Wolfe," Floy began as she turned to him.

"Maybe you'd better call me Ben, since we're going to be related."

Celia's heart did a flip in her chest. Related? He was their half brother, as close a relation as she was.

"We're not getting married," Celia said softly, and they all three turned to look at her. When they stood together like this she could see it so clearly, the Wolfe coloring and features. Could other people see it, too? Or did she see it because these were the three people in the world she loved? She couldn't take the chance that others would see. "We're moving to Austin, you girls and Margaret and me, just like we planned."

"But, Celia," Faye wailed.

Ben placed his arms around their shoulders. Together, they formed a strong and impenetrable wall, all fair and beautiful and nefarious. It was like facing an invincible army of three.

"You girls go tell Mr. Huffman that we found you," Ben said calmly, "and then you get yourself home. Margaret must be worried sick."

"She is," Celia said softly.

"We'll be along shortly, just as soon as I convince your sister to marry me."

Too bad the days of kidnapping and carrying off the woman you picked as your own were gone. That would be a whole lot simpler and faster than convincing Celia that she had to marry him.

"Have you lost your mind?" she said after the girls had slammed the front door behind them.

"I don't think so."

"Why on earth would you tell the twins that we're getting married? That's the most preposterous—"

"Is it?"

She appeared to be considering his question. "Yes."

Ben paced the hallway. They couldn't go into one of the bedrooms, not even the one he'd insisted Ginger not change. The parlor was out of the question, and the office was just as outlandishly refashioned as the parlor. So he stayed right there in the upstairs hallway, blocking the stairs and Celia's only route of escape.

"We had a bet," he began.

"I haven't even attempted to prove anything," Celia snapped quickly.

"This is true. But I did unveil a fact that proved

315

to me that my father was not all I thought he was. I'd rather not go into the details, but I'm willing to give back everything I took. And I'll marry you."

She was maddeningly calm. "Oh, you will?"

"Yes."

"Am I supposed to be grateful? Impressed? Should I cry now and fall on my knees to thank you?"

He gritted his teeth. "All you have to say is *yes*."

"No," she whispered.

He wanted to reach out and grab her. At times it seemed they could communicate only when they touched, only when they allowed their bodies to speak for them.

"Why not?" He didn't touch her, and he didn't mention the baby. She had to say yes. She *had* to.

"No," she said again, just as faintly and surely as before. "I know you, Ben. Everything is a game to you, including me. I don't know why you've decided on this new form of punishment, but I won't—"

"Punishment?" he interrupted. "Marrying me would be punishment?"

"You don't really intend to marry me," she said, stepping back, looking at the space between him and the wall as if trying to decide if she could make it. "You're just trying to make me think . . . and then it'll all turn out to be some kind of joke. Another game. I've had enough."

"I was wrong," he said, and he kept his hands to himself. "Thinking that making you pay for

your father's sins would make things right, thinking that my father was a saint. Thinking that the
pain would go away if I got my damned justice."

"Ben . . ."

He lifted a hand to silence her. "Let me finish.
None of that matters right now. All that matters
is that . . . is that . . . I need you."

"Ben, don't—"

"I need you. You were right all along. You're
the only one who can help me let it go."

She wanted to believe him, but she didn't. He
could see that truth on her face, and in the ten-
sion in the hands that were clenched at her sides.

Was it too late?

"I want to make it up to you," he said, and Celia
closed her eyes, trying to shut him out. He
couldn't allow her to do that. Not now. "The
house, the saloon, the general store, it's all yours.
I can give that back to you, and I will. Huff can
draw up the papers today."

She was apparently unaffected by the offer.

"All I can do to repair your reputation is make
an honest woman of you." He swallowed hard.
What would it take to make Celia say yes? Perhaps the idea of a lifetime with him was more
than she could stand. "And if you want," he said
calmly, "the original deal stands. I'll marry you
and then I'll get out of town."

She opened her eyes and stared at him. "Why
are you doing this to me?"

"Marry me, Celia."

She stared at him for a long and much too

quiet moment. Was she searching for the truth in his face?

"This is your way of making reparation, isn't it?" she finally said. "You've finally discovered that you have a conscience, and by offering to marry me you're making amends."

No. It was more than that. It was much more. "You can put it that way if you want."

Perhaps she was thinking of the baby she hadn't told him about, and maybe, just maybe, she needed him as much as he needed her.

"And you'll leave town, once we're married," she added.

Was that what she wanted? His name for the baby and nothing else. "Yes."

She took too damn long to consider the prospect, and Ben wanted to grab her up and shake her. He wanted to kiss her and hold her and shake her up. She was too calm as she contemplated his proposal.

But he didn't. He was silent and motionless as he waited for her to make the decision that would affect the rest of his life.

"All right," Celia said softly, and then she slipped past him and flew down the stairs.

Chapter Twenty-two

"You can't marry that man," Margaret said as Celia set aside her alterations.

"I can and I will," Celia said firmly. "Please don't make this more difficult than it already is."

"See?" Margaret shook a finger in her direction. "It's difficult, you say so yourself."

The girls were in school, but of course Ben would not be dropping by today. Margaret's presence changed everything. There would be no more scandalous visits, no more kisses, no more shared passion.

It was for the best. After the wedding he would leave town for good. He would leave her. She would have his name, the baby would have his name, and that was all that mattered. Perhaps it would be easier to watch Ben ride away if the memory of his touch had time to fade away.

"Margaret, please . . ."

"Not *him*," Margaret said angrily. "You just don't know . . . I have my reasons. . . . You can't marry Ezekiel Wolfe's son."

There was something in Margaret's voice that convinced Celia that the woman knew everything. About the affair, even the twins. Margaret's hatred of Ben had nothing to do with him, and had everything to do with Ezekiel Wolfe.

Margaret collapsed onto the sofa. "It's like some demon's loop, where the same disasters befall us again and again, no matter what we do to prevent them." Her voice softened to a whisper. "Do you think I don't know? Do you think I can't see the changes in you? You're just like your mother, in that respect. I knew she was expecting you before she did, and with the twins. . . ."

"I know." Celia dropped her mending. "You don't have to do this."

It was obviously painful for Margaret to remember the past, but she refused to let it go. Just as Ben had always refused to do. "You don't know. . . ."

"About Ezekiel Wolfe and my mother?"

Margaret's head snapped up.

"It has nothing to do with Ben and me," Celia said calmly. "Nothing."

"The same thing's happening all over again." Margaret said softly. "The two of you, and now a baby. No good can come of this, I tell you."

Celia was actually able to smile. "There are a few important differences to consider. First of all, I'm not a married woman. Secondly, Ben doesn't know about the baby. With any luck, he'll be gone before anyone knows. Well, besides you and Rosemary and me, of course."

"Gone?"

"The third and most important difference is that I haven't fooled myself into believing that Ben loves me, and therefore he cannot break my heart."

She wondered if Margaret could see the lie in her eyes. Ben had already broken her heart, by not loving her the way she loved him. It wasn't his fault; he just didn't have it in him to trust his heart.

"Gone?" Margaret repeated.

"Once we're married, Ben will leave town. It was part of the deal."

The insistent knock at the door startled her, and Celia jumped out of her chair. Surely Ben wouldn't make an appearance today . . . surely not. And still her heart beat fast at the possibility of opening the door and seeing him standing there with a wide grin on his face.

She was even more startled to find John standing at her door.

"At last," he said as he stepped into her house. "Really, Celia, I come back to town to shut down my office and take care of a few details, and spend near half a day tracking you down. For the most part, no one will speak to me at all, and Jud Lucas actually spit on my boots." He looked horrified at the memory.

How many telegrams and letters had she sent to him at that Dallas law firm? She'd lost count after ten. Had she had so much as a reply? So much as a scribbled note to "leave me alone"?

"And why are you looking at me like that?"

"Where have you been?" Celia asked softly. "Why didn't you come home when I wired you and begged you to?"

"Wire? Celia, I haven't heard from you since I left." He looked genuinely befuddled. His spectacles had slipped down almost to the end of his nose, so that he peered at her over the rims. "I thought you were mad at me for leaving, when you didn't answer my letters."

Margaret joined them, and the expression on her face was one of pure anger. "You! You're no better than the other one. How can you stand to look at yourself in the mirror, you deserter, you traitor."

John looked more confused than ever. "Would someone please tell me what's going on here?"

It suddenly made perfect sense. Somehow, Ben had made certain that John didn't receive her pleas for help. He'd even stopped John's letters from reaching her here in Piggville. No doubt he'd been the one to arrange for John's time with the Dallas law firm. Did he think his money would buy anything and everyone?

"Come into the parlor," Celia said calmly. "I have quite a story to tell you."

She shooed Margaret from the room and settled herself in her rocking chair. John, as confused as ever, sat on the edge of the sofa and pushed his spectacles up with a pale and soft forefinger. As she told him a fair portion of what had happened, his bewilderment changed to animosity.

Throughout, Celia maintained her calm. She wouldn't take her anger out on John. He'd been duped, just as she had, and none of this was his fault.

She'd see Ben later.

John didn't sit for long. He paced the room while Celia told him all that had happened, excluding, of course, the more scandalous aspects of Ben's *war*. She didn't tell him that she was pregnant, and she didn't tell him that she had actually thought herself in love with the scoundrel.

"Oh, Celia," John said as he paced before her. He'd repeated those two words countless times in the past half hour. "I'm so sorry. I should have been here to help you. I should have known. . . ." He stopped suddenly and knelt before her. "I know it's too late to make up for everything, but I have a solution. I've been offered a permanent position with the Dallas law firm I've been working with. The money's good, the work is exciting. . . . Come with me."

"What?"

John reached out and took her hand. "Will you marry me? I always intended to make you my wife, when the time was right. You and the girls can come to Dallas with me. It's the perfect solution."

It did seem to be the perfect solution. She liked John, and she trusted him, and he would take care of everything for her.

"Will you marry me, Celia?"

*   *   *

"You snake!"

Ben had been leaning, quite contentedly, over the bar, when Celia's sharp voice reached his ears. Everything within him screamed a warning. Celia never came into the saloon unless she had no other choice.

"Talking to me, sweetheart?"

She didn't hesitate but came straight to him. "You lied to me."

"Countless times."

"You tricked me."

"Guilty."

She wanted to fight, his sweet Celia. Her hands were balled fists at her sides, her face was red, her eyes like dark fire . . . this couldn't be good for the baby.

"Maybe you'd better calm down," he suggested, and that only made her madder.

"Calm down! How can I possibly calm down after what you've done?"

"What have I done this time?"

Even his calmest voice didn't pacify her.

Her hands flexed and she leaned toward him slightly. "John Watts is back in town," she said lowly. "There was a time when I would have thought that name meant nothing to you, but I know differently now."

"Oh."

" 'Oh.' Is that the best you can do? You . . . you stripped away everything, including the one man in my life who might have helped me through the hell you planned for me."

"Yes, I did," he admitted. "And I won't apologize for it."

Her eyes grew, impossibly, wider and deeper. "You have no shame."

"Not when it comes to you," he admitted. Celia was more than ready at this point to marry him and send him on his way. The only problem was, he had no intention of leaving. "I wanted to make certain you didn't have anyone but me."

"That's so . . . so . . ."

"Pathetic, I know." He reached out and took her hand, and with a brave smile drew her closer.

"Cruel," she whispered. "That's what it is."

Ben lowered his head to kiss her gently, and he felt her anger fade as his mouth moved over hers.

"It's not right," she said as she drew her lips away. "How could you . . ."

He kissed her again.

"I can't live like this," Celia whispered as she pulled slightly away again. "I need faith and honesty in my life. Not this. Not some physical attraction I can't control."

Ben grinned down at her. "I kinda like—"

"John asked me to marry him."

Ben's grin died. "And you told him no, right?"

"I . . . I told him I didn't know," she whispered.

Ben released her quickly. "You're going to marry me, or did you forget that fact when John Watts proposed? You can't be engaged to two men, Celia, sweet."

"I know."

It hit him, then. She was here to break off the

engagement, to tell him that she was going to marry her safe and reliable lawyer friend. She was going to pass *his* kid off as Watt's, just like her mother had passed the twins who were most likely his sisters off as Hamilton Pigg's children. He couldn't allow her to do this.

"You have to marry me."

"Ben, we can't—"

"I came here to destroy you, and somehow you turned everything around. I came here prepared for battle, and you welcomed me with open arms. You let me into your home, your heart, your body. . . ."

"Ben, don't . . ."

If he said nothing, if he allowed her to have her say and leave, she wouldn't ever look back. She'd be miserable; he'd be miserable.

"Let me into your life. Now and forever, Celia, sweet. Let's face it, we're good together. In bed, out of bed, we're *right*." He grabbed her wrist and pulled her close. He slipped his arms around her and held on tight. "I have to confess, I lied to you again. Just this one last time, I swear. Right now I think you need to hear the truth."

"Please," she said softly.

"Once we're married I'm not leaving town. I'm not leaving you. I won't. You're going to be stuck with me forever, and being married to me won't be easy. I'm not an easy man."

He'd opened his heart to Celia, as much as he could, and if she said no—if she turned her back on him and married John Watts—it would destroy him, as effectively and surely as he'd meant to destroy her.

"No, you're not an easy man," she agreed softly. She didn't move away, and the expression on her face was oddly serene. A moment ago she'd been ready to toss him aside without a single misgiving. And now?

"So, Celia, sweet, what do you say?"

In two days she would be married. Celia placed a container of salt in her basket, there with the cinnamon and sugar. The prices in Zeke's were no longer outrageously low, but they were fair. They'd decided to keep this store open, and Ben had put Jud and Ophelia Lucas to work here.

The saloon was still operating. Poor Ben, he was having a hard time parting with that particular operation. He had developed an inordinate fondness for Lucky's.

"Celia, there you are."

Celia recognized Kay Anne Ascot's voice. As usual it was tinged with urgency. There was always a disaster of some sort in Kay Anne's life.

"I saw you come in, and then I stuck my head in the door and you were nowhere to be seen."

Celia held her basket with both hands, and allowed the half-filled container to swing in front of her. "Well, here I am."

Kay Anne ran her eyes up and down Celia's simple yellow calico dress. "You look different."

She wasn't about to tell Kay Anne that Ben had insisted she dress in brighter colors and wear her hair down. It was none of her business, and besides, it wasn't always safe to mention Ben's name in the presence of others.

"You were looking for me for some reason?"

Kay Anne nodded her head slightly. "I received the wedding invitation yesterday."

Celia forced a smile. Ben had insisted on inviting the entire town to their wedding. Everyone. The twins had spent an entire day delivering hand-lettered invitations. Goodness, her husband-to-be was a perverse man. "I hope you'll be there."

"Well . . ." Kay Anne was noticeably distressed. "This is partly my fault, I know. I should have seen what he was trying to do, and then I should have stood beside you. I remember what his father was like, and still I allowed him to work his wicked ways. Oh, Celia, we don't want you to sacrifice yourself to that man."

"Sacrifice?"

"Don't tell me that's not what you're doing." Kay Anne raised a slender hand to stop any protest Celia might make. "He took everything, and now you're destitute and you're marrying him because you feel you have no other choice. It's just not right."

"I'm not—" Celia began.

"Here." Kay Anne withdrew a wad of greenbacks from a deep pocket that was hidden in the folds of her skirt. "Everything we owe you."

"You don't have to—"

"The new banker allowed us to take out a loan. We'll make regular payments and pay interest." She actually smiled. "I doubt the bank will be as forgiving as you were if no payments are made."

Celia shook her head. "Kay Anne, I don't know what to say." How could she explain that her situation had nothing to do with her acceptance of Ben's proposal? When she didn't reach out to take the cash, Kay Anne dropped the bills into Celia's basket.

"There, I feel much better now. You don't have to marry that awful man."

Before Celia could explain that she didn't find Ben awful in the least, Bob Casson appeared at the end of the aisle. He wore a big grin on his face, and in his hands were a battered hat and a rolled-up wad of cash.

And behind him, the line stretched to the door.

They came to her, one at a time, and repaid loans old and not so old. They'd taken out loans at the bank, or sold prized horses and cattle, and they all offered their condolences.

Surely this was not what Ben had had in mind when he'd invited everyone in Piggville to their wedding.

It was very sweet. They wanted to save her from a forced marriage to the man who had come to town to ruin her, and they all seemed to feel some guilt that he'd very nearly succeeded. The pile of money in her basket, greenbacks and gold and silver, grew steadily. Goodness, this was a small fortune.

And no one wanted to listen when she told them that she wasn't being forced to marry Ben. She thanked them all, and they left—each and every one—with a wide smile on their relieved faces and a renewed lilt in their step.

Ben came in as Annie Lowell left, after repaying a three-year-old loan her father had made for fifteen dollars. Celia had forgotten about that one.

"What's going on in here?" he asked, glancing over his shoulder to the retreating Annie. "There's been a steady crowd in and out of here for the past . . ." He was silenced when he glanced into her basket.

Celia waved the basket daintily, so that it swayed before her. Should she tell him everything? "Repaid loans," she said honestly. "So I won't be forced to marry you."

He lifted his eyes from the basket to her face. "Oh, really."

Celia nodded slowly. "This is your chance, Benjamin. You can walk away right now and know that I'm financially sound. No guilt, no reparation necessary. What do you say?"

There was not even a spark of response in his cool eyes. "I don't think so. What about you?"

In spite of it all, Celia smiled. Maybe he didn't love her, but he was right about one thing. They were good together. Happy and lasting marriages had begun with less than that. "I don't think so."

"Dearly beloved," the Reverend Rivers began in a booming voice, and then he stopped. For a moment he looked quite confused, as he stared at the bride and groom and then to the crowd beyond.

Floy stood between her sisters. Celia was beautiful in Grandma Hart's wedding dress, with her hair curled and piled softly on top of her head. Faye was wearing her best pink muslin, as was Floy, and they all carried flowers, colorful mixed bouquets.

Ben looked magnificent in a new black frock coat and white vest, and he didn't seem to be nervous at all. At least, not until the preacher forgot the ceremony.

No one was doing anything. Floy glanced over her shoulder to the occupants of the filled church, and saw that no one had moved or showed any sign of stepping forward to assist.

When she faced front again, she leaned forward and whispered, "It's a wedding, remember?" she prodded.

"Of course," Reverend Rivers answered with a bright smile. "We are gathered here today to witness the marriage of Priscilla . . ."

"Cecilia," Faye said in a hiss.

"Oh, yes," Rivers said softly. "Cecilia Pigg and . . . and . . ." He glanced at Ben, and obviously drew a blank.

"Benjamin Wolfe," Floy whispered loudly so the near-deaf Reverend Rivers would be sure to hear.

This was terrible. People were laughing, soft but unmistakable laughter that rumbled through the church.

Floy hadn't been to a wedding in more than a year, and even then she hadn't paid much attention to the actual ceremony. She looked to Faye, and found her twin as confused and lost as she was. Maybe the reverend would suddenly remember and carry on.

She waited, but nothing happened.

"I know they kiss at the end," Floy muttered.

"You may kiss the bride," Reverend Rivers said solemnly.

With a smile and a shrug of his shoulders, Ben obliged.

"But that's not all," Floy hissed as Ben and Celia came apart. "There are vows. 'Do you, Benjamin Wolfe, take Celia . . . ' Surely you know the rest."

There was also supposed to be something about if anyone objected they could speak up. Floy decided it would be best to skip that part.

"Do you, Benjamin Wolfe," Reverend Rivers said in a booming voice, "take Celia . . . surely you know the rest."

"I do."

The wedding continued in this fashion. Floy and Faye supplied the lines, and Reverend Rivers repeated them faithfully. Ben and Celia exchanged rings at the wrong time, and kissed again before they were pronounced man and wife and then again after. The reverend called Ben "John" once, but Floy corrected him quickly. It was a good thing. *That* mistake made Ben livid.

As the disastrous ceremony continued, everyone else was amused. But Floy was mortified.

Of course, once it was all over Celia and Ben were married, and neither of them seemed to mind that the doddering old preacher was having a bad day. They laughed as much as anyone else.

How odd it was to sleep with Ben in this bed while it was dark outside.

Celia rolled onto her side and wrapped an arm around her husband.

Margaret and the girls were back in the Pigg mansion, and they were in the process of scrubbing the place from top to bottom and undoing everything Ginger had done. Celia didn't know if she could ever live in that house again, but leaving the girls and Margaret there would give her a day or two alone with Ben, and they needed that time.

Eventually—soon—she would have to tell him about the baby.

He circled in her arms to face her. "You never sleep," he rumbled softly.

"Of course I do, just . . . not tonight."

He opened his eyes, and by the light of the moon that gleamed brightly through their window he smiled sleepily. "You're a wanton woman, Cecilia Wolfe."

"You made me this way," she said as she kissed him lightly. His hands skimmed across her body, and she knew she had to do this now, before he distracted her. "I have something to tell you. Something important."

She had his full attention, and his eyes were no longer sleepy.

"Maybe I should start with a question," she began uncertainly. "Do you like children?"

"Not particularly." He sighed. "They're bothersome and noisy, and from what I've seen they're ungrateful monsters, for the most part."

Celia's heart sank. She so wanted him to be happy about the baby.

"Unless, of course," he continued, "they're *our* children. Our children will be perfect, naturally."

His grin was too smug, too sure. "You already know, you . . . you . . ."

"Daddy?" he finished for her.

She couldn't be mad at him, not while he was smiling like this. "How did you find out? No one knows but Margaret and Rosemary." Margaret had been attempting, until the last possible moment, to talk Celia out of marrying Ben. She surely wouldn't have shared the information with him. Rosemary, of course, she should have known as soon as the name left her mouth. Chattering Rosemary, who'd told Huff, who'd made sure Ben knew.

"When did you find out?"

He tightened his arms around her, "Right before you came charging into Huff's office to tell us that the twins were lost."

"Right before you told the twins we were getting married." She shouldn't feel sick, but there was a part of her that wondered if Ben would have insisted on this marriage if he hadn't known about the baby.

"It's so early. What if I was wrong?" she whispered. "What if there is no baby?"

Ben propped his head in one hand and stared down at her. "I'll be disappointed, and then I'll try really hard to make another one."

"I just wouldn't want to think that you only married me because—"

Ben silenced her with a kiss. "Don't ever say that. I married you because without you I have nothing."

His hand traveled up her side, a big, rough hand that touched her with love and tenderness. Ben seemed to study her, fingers tracing every line, every shadow. She wanted him, as fiercely as when they'd fallen onto this bed hours earlier.

He kissed her, more gently and patiently than the first time, and Celia slanted her head to deepen the kiss. She would never get enough of this, his mouth moving with hers, his bare flesh pressed against hers.

She loved the feel of his body, hard and rippled and warm beneath her roaming hands. The way he responded to those hands roused her as surely as the dance of his fingers on her own flesh.

He didn't come to her quickly as he had before, but lingered over this sweet game. Slowly moving hands caressed, down her spine to the dimples low on her back, across her flat belly to her breasts. His mouth left hers to sway across her skin as surely as his hands had, and Celia could only lie back and revel in the sensation.

How much could she take before she came apart in his hands? How much of this could she endure?

When Ben parted her thighs and moved to rest between them she expected the quick thrust that would fill her, but he hesitated. His manhood pressed against her lightly, touching the hot flesh that throbbed for comfort and release. She opened her eyes to find Ben staring down at her.

"Don't ever doubt that I need you," he whispered hoarsely.

"I won't."

He thrust to fill her and then he lowered his lips for a kiss that was at first gentle and then demanding.

She wanted to hold on to this, this world of sensations that chased away every doubt and every fear she'd ever had. She wanted this to last all night, but Ben's assault quickly became too much for her and she came undone. She unraveled, fell apart, holding on to Ben as if without her arms around him she would truly fly apart and disappear.

Ben tightened in her arms as the last of the rippling sensations flowed over her, and with a low growl he came undone himself.

Ben took his weight from her, rolled onto his side with Celia in his arms. He didn't leave her, but gave her a kiss, a soft, slow melding of their mouths.

"Tell me," he whispered a few moments later. "Was it a mistake? About the baby?"

"No." She settled against his chest, lay there nestled in his arms warm and happy and safe. "I'm sure."

"Good."

Sleep was far from her mind, but Ben seemed to be relaxing. He could fall asleep, and she would lie all night in his arms and be perfectly content. His breathing slowed, his arms relaxed, and he whispered in her ear.

"I have something to tell you," he breathed. "A surprise of my own. I was going to wait until morning, but while you're in a good mood . . ."

He hesitated, and Celia pulled away from him slightly so she could see his face. So often he'd been angry, or beguiling, or coolly insolent. Right now he looked uncertain, maybe even a little scared.

"What is it?"

He placed a hand in her hair, as if he were afraid she'd back away, twining his fingers through the tangled strands. "We're leaving tomorrow morning for a short trip."

"A honeymoon?" Celia asked with a smile. "Where—"

"Not a honeymoon," he interrupted. "I plan for the rest of our lives to be a honeymoon, Celia, sweet." He kissed her, delaying the news once again.

"Then what?" she whispered as he drew his mouth away.

"Huff's located Rizpah Tucker."

"Ben . . ."

"You keep telling me to let it go, but I have to do this," he said gruffly, "and I want you with me. I need you beside me when I do this, Celia."

That admission warmed her heart, more than she dared to reveal. "What if she tells you that it was all true? Everything. Every horrible rumor. It happened a long time ago, Ben." Celia placed her palm against his cheek. "Can't we just forget the past and get on with our life together?"

"I have to know."

There was such pain in his voice, such agony, and she realized that he was right. He needed to see this finished, once and for all, and he needed her beside him. She would be there, no matter what.

"All right."

Chapter Twenty-three

Though she'd been, she thought, well prepared to travel to Austin, this was not easy. All day long, Ben had made frequent stops, for the horses and for her, but there always came the moment when they had to climb into their saddles and begin again. It was just the two of them, and Ben seemed quite accustomed to the constant riding, the wind and the dust, and now—the hard ground Celia sat upon.

She didn't dare tell him that she hurt all over.

After they'd stopped for the night, Ben had taken care of the horses, two animals much more beautiful and able than the nags she had purchased to pull the wagon, and built a campfire, and prepared a simple dinner of dried beef and beans, and laid out a bedroll. All the while Celia had remained motionless.

She still didn't understand why he needed this so much. He'd admitted to the discovery that his father was not perfect, though he refused to elaborate. He was doing his best to make things right, to move forward instead of back, and yet here they were, making their way to the home of one of Ezekiel Wolfe's women.

According to Margaret, only she knew about Priscilla's fall from grace. She hadn't shed a tear that night as her world fell apart, nor had she joined the other women in their accusations. She'd kept her heartache to herself, never hinting to the others that she'd been one of the straying reverend's conquests. What pain she must have suffered, how horribly alone she must have felt.

Celia didn't want to tell Ben about the tryst that had resulted in the twins. He was so certain that his father was a good and decent man, though not—he'd admitted lately—a saint. If she were to tell Ben about the affair and the twins he would likely not believe her anyway, and they didn't need another battle.

And if he did believe her, if he looked at the twins and saw the resemblance she did, would he use that knowledge? Would he tell the girls, and everyone else in Piggville, that Floy and Faye were his sisters?

"Tired?"

She glanced up at the sound of his soft voice. Ben was demanding and difficult, and he seemed to view those faults as positive character traits. Every resident of Piggville, but for the twins, had assured her that marrying him was a disastrous mistake. He was a scoundrel, they said, like his father, a man who could bestow that heavenly smile while he lied and connived. How could she argue with that when she knew better than anyone else in Piggville what Benjamin Wolfe was capable of?

Yes, there had been moments in the past couple of days when she'd wondered what had possessed her to marry this man. This was not one of those moments. She didn't love him because he was handsome and strong and tall; she didn't love him because of the passion they shared. In fact, when Margaret had asked her why she had to fall in love with Benjamin Wolfe, of all the men in the world, Celia hadn't been able to come up with an answer.

It was just there. Love, a tenuous connection, the knowledge that this man was meant to be hers.

He was looking down at her with a frown on his face. "We shouldn't have ridden so far today." He dropped to his haunches and reached out to touch her face. By the light of the fire, he was the angel she had once thought him to be, bright and golden and beautiful.

She smiled. Benjamin Wolfe was a man, no more and no less. He made mistakes, he was disturbingly single-minded, and he had quite a temper when he was crossed.

"I'm tired, that's all," she said as his fingers traced her jaw. "I'll be fine."

Ben sat beside her and placed his arm over her shoulder. It was a possessive and protective move, and he seemed to think nothing of it. "Tomorrow we'll make it an easy trip. If it takes an extra day to get to Rizpah Tucker's house, well, I reckon she'll still be there."

She leaned into Ben, absorbed what heat she could from his body. He did need her, more, perhaps, than he realized. Had anyone ever tried to protect Ben? Surely not. He gave the impression of being invincible, fearless. But he wasn't. "No matter what she says, I want you to promise me that you won't be upset."

"I just want the truth."

She couldn't lift her face to his, couldn't look him in the eye at the moment. The proof that his father was a womanizer was locked in a trunk in the cellar, right where she'd hidden it. She didn't want to be the one to shatter his illusions about his father, didn't want to break his heart. If Rizpah Tucker told him that everything he'd heard about his father was true, that her child was his half sister or brother, what would he do?

"If the truth Rizpah Tucker tells you isn't what you want to hear, I want you to promise me that you'll let it go. We'll walk away together, and put this behind us. I want you to forget the past once and for all and start making plans for the future."

She waited for an argument, but it didn't come. "You make that easier than I ever thought it would be." As he spoke, Ben placed his hand over her belly.

He wanted this baby, wanted a family of his own. Was he trying to build for himself the home he'd never had? Ben needed her, he felt responsible for her, maybe he even liked her. Marriages were built on less than that every day, as she continued to remind herself.

But would Ben ever love her?

"Then this is the last of it," Celia whispered. "It has to be. We hear what Rizpah Tucker has to say, and when we leave her behind we leave all of it behind. No matter what she says."

Ben cupped his hand beneath her chin and forced her to look up at him. The firelight flickered over his face, golden and warm. "I never thought I'd rest until I knew what happened. All of it, every lie, every truth. But right now, I can see the end. It's like glimpsing home after being on the trail for so long you've forgotten what civilization looks like. Light at the end of a tunnel so long you thought you'd never get out. You did this for me, Celia."

"That's good," she whispered as he kissed her.

She knew then that she had to tell him. Like it or not, he needed to hear this from her.

"There's something I have to tell you," she whispered as he took his lips from hers. "I don't want to hurt you, but I don't know how to say this except straight out."

He pulled away from her slightly, and from the expression on his face he was prepared for the worst.

"After I moved into Grandma and Grandpa Hart's house, I found a diary. My mother's diary. It was hidden in a trunk in the cellar." She pressed herself against his side and stared into the fire. "Your father and my mother . . . they were having . . . she was . . ." She took a deep breath to clear her head and gather her strength. Ben held her tight. Goodness, this was so difficult to say aloud.

"I didn't think you knew," he whispered.

Celia tilted her head up. Ben was surprisingly calm as he reached into a pocket for his watch. There was no surprise, no shock, no denial.

"You knew all along," she accused.

Ben shook his head. "Not until I found this."

He flipped the watch cover open and held it so the firelight illuminated the miniature portrait that had been concealed there.

"My mother."

"I think he must've loved her very much," Ben said softly. To comfort her? Perhaps. Perhaps believing that there was love involved made it easier for Ben himself to accept the fact that his father was an adulterer.

"If he loved her then why did he carry on with those other women? She adored him, and he left her with . . . He broke her heart. He left her." She regretted her impulsive and angry words when she saw the pain on Ben's face. How much did he know? It didn't matter. She could hold nothing back. He deserved the truth, all of it.

"He left her with Floy and Faye. Can you imagine how she felt every time she looked at them and saw the man who had used and abandoned her?"

"He wouldn't have—"

"He did."

Ben closed the cover on the watch and slipped

it into his pocket. "I don't understand everything that happened then, but I do know my father died with this watch in his hand. It's the only possession he kept after he left Piggville. There was a thin sheet of gold covering the portrait. She was his secret, and he didn't want to share her with anyone else."

"He left her."

"He loved her."

Ben seemed so certain, and suddenly Celia didn't want to be the one to shatter the last of his illusions about his father. She had a feeling Rizpah Tucker would take care of that. No matter what, she would stand beside Ben. He said he needed her, and she wouldn't disappoint him.

"Maybe you're right," she conceded. "I know she loved him more than anything. She loved him enough to risk everything she had just to be with him." Everything. He could read the diary for himself, when they returned home, but for now it was all up to her. "They talked of leaving Piggville together, after my mother got pregnant with the twins. Of taking you and me and starting fresh in another place."

"Did they?" He sounded touched and somehow delighted.

Celia simply nodded her head. "The girls don't know any of this, and I'm afraid it would be difficult for them to understand."

Ben didn't argue. He just held her close and whispered in her hair. "Maybe when they're older. We'll know when the time is right."

He became awfully quiet. What could she say?

That the time might never be right? That Floy and Faye would adore having him as a brother, when that day came? She didn't know what to say.

Celia lifted her head to look up at Ben, and found that he was smiling. Not a bright, devilish grin, but a warm and gentle smile.

"I always wanted brothers and sisters," he said. "A real family. My mother died when I was a baby, and it was always just me and my father, and then just me. Now I have two difficult sisters, a wife, and a child on the way."

He wanted this so much . . . would she always wonder if he had married her only because he felt he had to? She was carrying his child, and he wanted a family and roots and a home. Was he making amends for his father's treatment of her mother? He'd known . . . all this time.

"Ben." When she whispered his name he looked down at her. "I don't want to live the rest of my life wondering if you only married me because—"

He placed a finger over her lips. "Huff is a smart man."

It was an odd way to change the subject.

"He suggested that I had purposely set out to get you pregnant. At first he thought it was part of the plan, some sort of revenge, and then he decided that I wanted to make certain you had no choice but to marry me."

"And what do you think?"

"I only know that I wanted you from the first moment I saw you."

It wasn't exactly an avowal of love, but it was a start.

"When you saved me from the horses?"

"Before that."

Celia scooted around and wrapped her arms around Ben's neck. "And now?"

"Always."

He kissed her, and she forgot her aching muscles and her doubts about Ben's motives. They had this, and it was a bond that couldn't be denied. If she told him that she loved him, if she told him right now that she loved him with all her heart, would he laugh at her? He needed to be loved, but she wasn't certain he was ready to accept that fact just yet.

All these years, and Rizpah Tucker didn't live a full two days' ride from Piggville.

Her house was a small but sturdy-looking place set down in the middle of a good-sized farm. From all he'd heard and remembered about the woman, Ben had expected a filthy shack and a dozen filthy children. Maybe that was why he'd ridden so slowly today, not to accommodate Celia, after all, but because he didn't want to face this part of his past as much as he claimed.

"Are you all right?" Celia asked as she pushed her horse forward so that she was directly beside him.

He tried to smile, to flash a grin to show Celia that none of this mattered . . . but of course she knew different. The grin never quite materialized, and his weak attempt at a smile did nothing to reassure her.

A child, a young man, stepped onto the porch to watch Ben and Celia approach, and Ben felt his breath catch in his throat. This would be the one, the child Rizpah Tucker claimed was his half brother.

This boy wasn't fair, but had dark hair and eyes. His build was stocky, rather than lean, and his square face was lifted in silent expectation. They probably didn't get many visitors out this way.

"Who is it?" He heard the voice from just inside the door, a perfectly normal and pleasant female voice that was nothing like the desperate squall he remembered from that night.

Rizpah Tucker stepped onto the porch to stand beside her son.

This was not the woman Ben remembered. Of course, fourteen years had passed. Rizpah Tucker was older, her hair graying and her middle thickening. She even had a peacefulness about her, until she lifted her head and took a good look at him.

Ben dismounted, and before his eyes the woman paled. She brought a hand to her heart and clasped it there. He went to Celia to help her from the saddle, and when they faced the porch together, Rizpah Tucker sank to her knees.

Was it true, then? If just the sight of him, so much like his father, did this to her, she must have terrible memories of Ezekiel Wolfe.

"What do you want?" she rasped.

"Ma?" The boy was staring down at his mother, fear and puzzlement on his not quite bright face.

"Seth, get in the house," she ordered.

"But, Ma . . ."

"Now!"

With only a quick glance in their direction, Seth obeyed his mother.

For a long and silent moment after Seth had entered the house, closing the door behind him, Rizpah Tucker remained motionless. On her knees, she stared at Ben as if he were the devil. It took him a minute to realize that she stared at Celia with the same awe.

"Miz Tucker, we don't mean you any harm. We just want to ask you a few questions."

"I knew you would come, one day," she said softly. "I waited for a long time, jumping at every noise in the night, cowering every time a rider approached. And then I almost forgot. I guess that's what you were waiting for, ain't that right, Reverend?"

The sun was at their backs, and Ben realized that her vision was badly hampered by the setting sun. "I'm Ben Wolfe, not Ezekiel," he clarified. "I just want to ask you a few questions."

She squinted, as if trying to make out his features more clearly, and then she turned those narrowed eyes to Celia. "And you're not *her*?"

"I'm . . ."

Ben put his arm around Celia's shoulder. "This is my wife."

"Go away," she rasped, forcing herself to her

feet. "Get off my land. I have nothing to say to you."

"Just a few questions," Ben insisted.

Rizpah took a deep breath. She was trembling, a sure, deep tremble. "What kind of questions do you have for me?"

After all this time, all his plans and machinations, here was the woman who could answer his questions. Proof that his father was an honest man, proof that Hamilton Pigg had all but killed Ezekiel Wolfe with his lies.

"You accused my father of getting you with child and then abandoning you," Ben said calmly. "Was that the truth?" His heart beat much too hard, his breath didn't come easy, but no one would see his anxiety. Not Rizpah Tucker and not Celia. He couldn't allow it.

The woman on the porch seemed to sway where she stood. "The truth?" She lowered her voice.

"Is Ezekiel Wolfe the father of your child?"

He could see the Rizpah Tucker he remembered in the hardened woman before him. There were more lines on her face, and she was heavier, but there was still something about her that was more animal than human. Something feral and unnatural. She apparently wasn't any brighter than the dull boy who'd greeted them. When she realized that they truly meant her no harm, that she wasn't facing a threat, her fear fled.

"The truth of the matter be known," she said lowly, "I don't know who Seth's father is. I look at him sometimes and wonder which one might have got me with child, but I can never be sure. Might be any one of a half dozen men from Piggville, none of them the good reverend."

He knew it, had known it all along, but the relief that washed over him was powerful. "Then why?" He realized he was hanging on to Celia too tightly, but he didn't loosen his hold. Couldn't. "Why the accusations against my father?"

She stepped to the edge of the porch, but didn't make a move to join them. "Why? What difference does it make? If the reverend wants an explanation, he can come to me himself and I'll—"

"He's dead," Ben interrupted. "He's been dead thirteen years. The explanation is for me."

Rizpah squinted in his direction again, and then stared at Celia. "Don't matter now. It's done."

"It's not done until I know the truth."

She sat on the top step, as if she couldn't bear the strain of standing any longer. She was weary, more tired than any woman should ever be. "I don't suppose it matters anymore. That was such a long time ago, and if he's dead, well then I reckon the deal is off, right?"

She looked to Ben for confirmation, and he nodded his head once.

"The reverend was carrying on with a married woman," she said, "and her husband found out about it. Saw 'em slipping off together one day, and decided to follow and see what was going on. Well, he found out what was going on, all right, and then he came to me."

Rizpah smiled, a lost, lonely smile. "In the beginning, he came to me for what other men came to me for, but he wasn't able to . . . he couldn't . . . let's just say he was wasting his time and mine."

"And then?" Ben prompted when she seemed to get lost in her own little world.

"And then he decided to get rid of the good reverend. I was well along, and didn't know just what I was going to do. I wanted a good life, for myself and my baby, but people don't want you to have a second chance." She sounded more lost than angry at her lot in life. "You make a mistake and you have to pay for it forever and forever."

"Ben," Celia whispered. She was tugging at his sleeve, but he didn't look down. "Ben, that's enough."

It wasn't enough. He wanted to know everything. "So he suggested that you accuse my father of getting you pregnant and abandoning you, and then—"

"Yes, but that wasn't good enough," Rizpah interrupted. "He got two other women to do pretty much the same thing, stand up and lie. One of them even suggested that he forced himself on her, that he raped her when she refused him. That whispered lie was the final undoing of the reverend. Truth is, if he'd wanted every woman in town, he coulda had 'em. They woulda lined up and fallen on their backs so fast it woulda made your head spin."

"But they didn't, did they?"

"No. Only the one."

It was enough.

Celia stepped out of his embrace, pulling slightly when he held on. "The man who came to you, the man you lied for, who was he?"

Rizpah Tucker cringed as Celia approached.

Ben stepped forward. "It's okay, Celia. Let's go."

"No." She shook off his hand and stepped forward again. "We've come this far, we've learned this much. You wanted to know it all, Ben, every sordid detail. Now I want to hear her say it."

She knew the answer as well as he did. No wonder his father had cursed Hamilton Pigg until his dying day.

Celia didn't need to hear this. "Forget it, Celia. Let's go," Ben said softly.

Rizpah Tucker glanced from Celia to him and back again. "Hamilton Pigg," she said hoarsely. "He paid me and them other women plenty to make sure the reverend was run out of town, and then he chased us out on the reverend's heels." She grimaced. "We were the only ones who knew what was going on. The worst of it that I remember was that night, when they run the reverend and that kid of his"—she glanced at Ben—"I guess that would be you . . . out of town. Priscilla Pigg was standing right there beside her husband. And the reverend, he looked at her, just once, and she turned her back on him. Probably nobody saw it but me, and maybe Pigg. That was the only time, through the whole night, that the reverend looked wounded."

That had done it. That moment had killed the

father he knew. Priscilla Pigg turning her back on him, believing the worst, believing the lies, had been more than Ezekiel Wolfe could stand.

"I bought this place with the money Pigg paid me," Rizpah continued. "I don't know what happened to them other women."

Ben took Celia's arm and pulled her away from the porch. She was pale, and beneath his hand she trembled.

"Don't you have any more questions?" Tucker called as they backed away. "Is Doc Edwards still livin'? Boy, do I have some stories about him."

Celia jerked her arm from his hand and walked away from the house, ignoring Rizpah Tucker and her offer. "You were right all along," she said softly. "You had every right to want revenge."

He followed Celia, barely hearing Rizpah Tucker's coarse good-bye followed by the slamming of her front door. "It doesn't matter," he began.

"Last night, when you told me that your father loved my mother, I didn't believe it," Celia said crisply. "I pretended to, because I knew you needed to believe it. The portrait in his watch didn't convince me. You didn't convince me . . . and all this time you were right." Ben grabbed Celia before she could throw herself into the saddle, as was obviously her intention.

"It doesn't matter who was right."

She turned deep brown eyes up to him. "You must hate me," she whispered.

"I could never hate you."

It was true. After all this time, after all his

plans, it didn't matter what her father had done. It didn't matter. He knew the truth, and that was what he'd needed. The truth. Something to stop the doubts and the anger that had always been in his heart.

"My father ruined your life." Celia's voice trembled. "He ruined your father's life, he lied and manipulated, and he allowed my mother to believe that the man she loved was just using her, that she was just one of his many women. She was never the same after that night."

She tried to turn her pale face away from him, but he wouldn't allow it. How could she believe that he would blame her? How could she believe that he could ever hate her?

What an idiot he was. He'd proven to her again and again that she had to pay for her father's sins.

"When you believed my father was a scoundrel who had seduced and abandoned your mother, you didn't hate me." He kept his voice low, calm. "I took everything you owned and tried to run you out of town, I set you up to suffer the same kind of humiliation my father suffered because I was stupid enough to think that somehow that would make things right, and still you didn't hate me. You claimed to, once or twice, but it was a lie."

"I tried to."

"You did a poor job of it," he answered in a whisper. His fingers gently stroked her face, studying the softness and the perfection of the woman who was his wife. "Tell me, Celia, why you couldn't hate me, even then."

He knew why. At least, he thought he did. And now he needed to hear her say it as much as he'd ever needed to hear the truth about his father. More.

She hesitated, parted her lips as if to speak, and then brought them together again.

And then she spoke quickly. "Because I love you."

He wanted to pick Celia up and crush her against his chest, shout, "It's about time you admitted it," and kiss her until the sun set. But he didn't.

He held her face in his hands and got lost in those deep brown eyes. "Let me love you back." Evidently it was the right thing to say, because color rushed back into Celia's face, and her eyes sparkled with renewed spirit.

"Do you mean it?"

"I do."

Epilogue

"Margaret still hates Ben, and I don't understand it." Faye pouted as she made this vehement statement, and Floy nodded her head in agreement.

Except for Margaret's continuing dislike of Celia's new husband, life had taken a wonderful turn.

She'd been right all along. Ben did love Celia. Since they'd returned from their wedding trip, she'd heard him tell her so several times . . . and he didn't seem to care who heard. Of course, Ben told the two of them that he loved them, too, but it was always followed by something like "brats" or "little demons." Still, she thought he meant it.

Celia was so different. Of course, Ben had insisted on this odd ceremonial bonfire, way out past the old brick house. He said it was a way to put the past to rest, but most of what he'd burned had been Celia's clothes. Then he'd bought her all new clothes, calicos mostly, in blues and yellows and pinks.

The new clothes suited her, but mostly Floy thought it was Ben who'd changed Celia the most. She smiled a lot more now.

Everything would be wonderful, if only Margaret would come around.

They were walking toward the boardinghouse when they heard Ben's familiar shout. He was all dirty and sweaty, and dressed in old work clothes. He looked wonderful.

"Have you seen Celia?" he asked as he approached. "I went home and she wasn't there."

Floy smiled widely. He actually looked worried.

"I think I saw her headed for the cemetery," Faye said. "She goes there, sometimes, to talk to Mother."

"She does?"

Faye nodded, and Floy did, too.

"Sometimes we go with her, but most of the time she goes alone," Floy added.

Ben seemed to give their comments serious consideration. Then, for some reason, he checked the time.

Celia had spent many hours here in the past several years, kneeling at her mother's grave and talking to the headstone. It was here that she'd voiced dreams and fears she didn't dare share with anyone else, and here that she'd first confessed her love for Ben aloud.

She placed a bouquet of wildflowers against the base of the marble.

"I've often felt that you were listening to me, especially in this place," she said softly. "I hope you're listening now."

A wind came up and ruffled the petals that brushed against cold marble.

"He loved you. Those other women, what they said was all lies. It was an elaborate scheme to get him away from Piggville. Ezekiel loved you, and only you." Celia plucked at the grass at her side. "Maybe you know that already. Maybe you're together right now. I hope so."

She didn't feel it was necessary to tell her mother that Ben had been trying for the better part of a week to convince her to forgive her father. It was quite an unexpected turn of events, Benjamin Wolfe defending Hamilton Pigg. He'd told Celia to remember that her father must have loved his wife, in spite of the doubts she'd expressed in her diary.

And Ben told her, quite vehemently, that he would lie, cheat, blackmail, and kill to keep her, if it ever came to that.

She didn't doubt it.

"We haven't told the girls that they and Ben have the same father, but we've decided that we will one day. When they're old enough to understand."

That was another fact in her father's favor that she couldn't ignore. He had known all these years that the twins were not his children, and still he'd loved them. He'd treated them as lovingly as he'd treated her, and had even seen to those trust funds so they'd never be left wanting. No matter how his finances had fluctuated, he'd never tried to touch those trusts.

"I just thought it was important that you know the truth, after all these years," Celia finished. "Ezekiel Wolfe did love you."

She turned her head when she heard the yapping. Lucky leaped into her lap and raised up to give her a kiss, and Celia smiled. Ben was not far behind, and he was carrying a shovel in one hand.

He'd been working hard these days, building the new house. They'd decided they needed a fresh start, a new beginning, and a new home was the first step. A big house just beyond the little brick house where they continued to live. Ben had promised the twins that they could each have their own pink room in the new house. He'd even sworn to paint the very walls pink, if that was what they wanted. Eventually they'd have cattle, and horses, and a big garden.

"The girls said you might be here," he said as he reached her. Celia stood and offered her face for a kiss. Ben obliged, wrinkling his nose as he pulled away. "You taste like Lucky."

"I find it rather frightening that you know what Lucky tastes like."

He grimaced at her again, pulled her back slightly, and placed the blade of the shovel against the ground near her mother's headstone.

"What are you doing?" she asked as he pressed

the shovel cleanly into the ground and pulled out a plug.

He didn't answer, but took his father's watch from his pocket and placed it carefully into the hole. Then he glanced up at her. "What do you think?"

"I think you're wonderful."

He carefully replaced the plug.

Lucky ran ahead of them as they walked down the hill, hand in hand.

"So," Ben said as they reached the bottom of the hill and turned toward town, "what do you want this baby to be? A boy or a girl?"

Celia shrugged her shoulders. "It really doesn't matter what I want, and besides, I don't care."

"I want one of each, I think," he said, looking down at her relatively flat stomach. "Twins run in my family, you know."

"I know."

"We've got to fill that big house I'm building."

"Not all at once," Celia said sensibly.

Ben stopped in the middle of the road, and pulled Celia into his arms.

"Shall we scandalize the entire town with a shocking display of public affection?" he asked, his breath warm and tantalizing against her lips.

"You've been doing your best to shock the entire town since you arrived. Why stop now?"

"Is that a yes?"

Celia grinned as Ben brought his lips to hers. That was most definitely a yes.

"I was thinking this morning, before you woke up," Ben said as he pulled his lips from hers. "I fulfilled my vow to my father after all."

"Oh, you did?" Celia wrapped her arm through his and started walking down the street with her husband on her arm. "I'm still here, and so are the girls."

"Yes, but you're not a Pigg anymore, you're a Wolfe, and the girls were Wolfes all along."

"If the proposal to rename the town Perfection goes through, then I'll have to say you've really succeeded." It was her idea, but John was seeing to the details. It would be his last task before relocating to Dallas.

It was just as well. Piggville—Perfection—didn't need two lawyers, and it didn't look as if Huff was going anywhere. He'd purchased the old house, the mansion that had once been her home and had for a brief time been the Piggville Gentlemen's Social Club, and he and Rosemary would be married in less than a month.

Ben had grudgingly converted Lucky's back into a staid, boring boardinghouse, a proper establishment that was being run by Margaret—since she continued to refuse to live in the same house with a Wolfe—and as the word spread the town began to return to its normal lethargy. Celia had seen the sheriff yesterday, and he hadn't been wearing a gun.

"There you are!" Faye's bright shout was unmistakable, and Ben grinned as the twins ran to join them. Their fair hair danced, and pink calico billowed around them as they approached. "Thank goodness!"

Ben's smile faded. "What's wrong?"

362

"There's this man at the boardinghouse, and he's drunk, and loud, and very big, and he's pestering Margaret something awful." Faye pressed a dramatic hand to her chest. "You must hurry."

Ben handed the shovel to Celia. "You've already been to the sheriff's office, right?"

Floy and Faye exchanged a quick glance, blue eyes fastened to blue eyes in a disconcerting way, and Celia bit her bottom lip. No good ever came of a look like that one.

"Oh, no," Floy said seriously as Ben joined them. "Margaret asked specifically for you."

Ben hesitated, glanced over his shoulder, and grinned crookedly. "Here we go again."

NO ANGEL'S GRACE

LINDA WINSTEAD

From the moment Dillon feasts his eyes on the raven-haired beauty, Grace Cavanaugh, he knows she is trouble. Sharp-tongued and stubborn, with a flawless complexion and a priceless wardrobe, Grace certainly doesn't belong on a Western ranch. But that's what Dillon calls home, and as long as the lovely orphan is his charge, that's where they'll stay.

But Grace Cavanaugh has learned the hard way that men can't be trusted. Not for all the diamonds and rubies in England will she give herself to any man. But when Dillon walks into her life he changes all the rules. Suddenly the unapproachable ice princess finds herself melting at his simplest touch, and wondering what she'll have to do to convince him that their love is the most precious gem of all.

_4223-1 $5.50 US/$6.50 CAN

Desperado's Gold
Linda Jones

Jilted at the altar and stranded in the Arizona desert by a blown gasket in her Mustang convertible, Catalina Lane hopes only for a tow truck and a lift to the nearest gas station. She certainly doesn't expect a real live desperado. But suddenly, catapulted back in time to the days of the Old West, Catalina is transported into a world of blazing six-guns and ladies of the evening.

When Jackson Cady, the infamous gunslinger known as "Kid Creede," returns to Baxter, it's to kill a man and earn a reward, not to use his gold to rescue a naive librarian from the clutches of a greedy madam. He never would have dreamed that the beauty who babbled so incoherently about the twentieth century would have such an impact on him. But the longer he spends time with her, the more he finds himself captivated by her tender touch and luscious body— and when he looks deep into her amber eyes, he knows that the passion that smolders between them is a treasure more precious than any desperado's gold.

_52140-7 $5.50 US/$6.50 CAN

Dorchester Publishing Co., Inc.
P.O. Box 6613
Edison, NJ 08818-6613

A Faerie Tale Romance

Big Bad Wolf by Linda Jones. Big and wide and strong, Wolf Trevelyan's shoulders are just right for his powerful physique—and Molly Kincaid wonders what his arms would feel like wrapped tightly around her. Molly knows she should be scared of the dark stranger. She's been warned of Wolf's questionable past. But there's something compelling in his gaze, something tantalizing in his touch—something about Wolf that leaves Molly willing to throw caution, and her grandmother's concerns, to the wind to see if love won't find the best way home.

_52179-2 $5.50 US/$6.50 CAN

The Emperor's New Clothes by Victoria Alexander. Cardsharp Ophelia Kendrake is mistaken for the Countess of Bridgewater and plans to strip Dead End, Wyoming, of its fortunes before escaping into the sunset. But the free-spirited beauty almost swallows her script when she meets Tyler Matthews, the town's virile young mayor. Tyler simply wants to settle down and enjoy the simplicity of ranching. But his aunt and uncle are set on making a silk purse out of Dead End, and Tyler is going to be the new mayor. It's a job he accepts with little relish—until he catches a glimpse of the village's newest visitor.

_52159-8 $5.50 US/$6.50 CAN

Dorchester Publishing Co., Inc.
P.O. Box 6613
Edison, NJ 08818-6613

Please add $1.75 for shipping and handling for the first book and $.50 for each book thereafter. NY, NYC, and PA residents, please add appropriate sales tax. No cash, stamps, or C.O.D.s. All orders shipped within 6 weeks via postal service book rate. Canadian orders require $2.00 extra postage and must be paid in U.S. dollars through a U.S. banking facility.

Name_____

Address_____

City_____ State_____ Zip_____

I have enclosed $_____ in payment for the checked book(s).

Payment <u>must</u> accompany all orders. ❏ Please send a free catalog.